"YOU MUST BE PUNISHED..."

A huge rock came crashing through the window. Seconds later, it was followed by another, then another, until the room was filled with stones flying in all directions. Karen was frozen, unable to move as rocks struck the walls and knocked things from her dresser. There seemed to be hundreds of them, making a deafening noise.

"Evil girl! You should be stoned for your dirty, vain ways! I have seen you paint your face and twist your hair. Only the devil's own would alter the body, a temple of God. You are wicked!"

"I'm not wicked!"

Karen's mousy tone suddenly changed, and her screams filled the air:
"NNNNOOOOO!!!!!"

She heard the door crash open.

And then complete silence...

ADDISON HOUSE

CLARE McNALLY

AVON BOOKS ◆ NEW YORK

ADDISON HOUSE is an original publication of Avon Books. This work has never before appeared in book form. This work is a novel. Any similarity to actual persons or events is purely coincidental.

AVON BOOKS
A division of
The Hearst Corporation
105 Madison Avenue
New York, New York 10016

First Avon Books Printing: December 1988

AVON TRADEMARK REG. U.S. PAT. OFF. AND IN OTHER COUNTRIES, MARCA REGISTRADA, HECHO EN U.S.A.

Printed in the U.S.A.

K-R   10   9   8   7   6   5   4   3   2   1

For my brothers and sisters:
Bill, Annie, Patrick, Sue,
Neil, Martha, Tom, and John

1

Doreen Addison walked to her office window. The anger she felt seemed to channel itself through her arms as she took hold of the frame, and the sounds of the children playing outside abruptly stopped as she slammed the window shut. She needed quiet, a few minutes to make sense of the letter she had just received.

She went to her desk, clunked herself down into the leather chair patched with packing tape, and picked up the letter again. It was addressed to "Doreen Addison, Proprietor, Addison House" and signed at the bottom by a man named Harold Carruthers. Doreen had seen the name often enough—once a month when she signed a rent check over to him, in fact. Carruthers had decided that the children's shelter Doreen operated was a prime piece of upstate New York real estate, and he wanted to sell it. He was giving Doreen six weeks to get out.

"Six weeks! How am I supposed to find a house that's big enough for six kids and two adults in just six weeks?"

She heard a knock, and looked up to see her housekeeper, Yolanda Berle, standing in the doorway. Doreen had known the elderly black woman for many years, because she had come to clean the homes of some of the different foster families where Doreen had lived as a child. When Yolanda's son and daughter-in-law had tried to put her into a retirement home, Doreen stepped in and offered Yolanda a place at Addison House. The old woman received a small allowance—all Doreen could afford on the little money the state provided—and room and board. Doreen was eternally grateful for her, and Yolanda was pleased to have escaped an old folks' home.

"I heard a crash," she said. "Are you all right?"

"That was the window closing. I was a little too rough. Yolanda, we're in trouble. Carruthers has decided to sell this building!"

"Oh, no," Yolanda mumbled. "What's wrong with that man? We've never missed paying the rent! How could he do this to these innocent children?"

Doreen shook her head. How, indeed? Maybe if Harold Carruthers met a few of her charges, Doreen thought, he'd change his mind. Doreen had opened Addison House nearly a decade earlier to help children in her hometown of Oakwood, New York. Since then she'd taken in dozens of kids, giving them all support and comfort. Carruthers couldn't take this place away from her!

Doreen searched the desk drawer for the lease for the house. She read it quickly and realized that Carruthers knew exactly what he was doing. The lease expired in thirty days, so there was no way she could legally fight him. They'd have to move. At least school was out for the year, so the kids wouldn't miss anything.

Sighing, she got up and stood next to her housekeeper, both women looking out the window. At this time there were six children in her care, and each of them had a heart-wrenching reason for being here. The baby of the group was Cindy Ardus, a sweet five-year-old whose mother was serving time in jail for robbery. Cindy was laughing now as seven-year-old Frankie pushed her on the swing. The dark-eyed, curly-haired boy couldn't hear her laughter. Severe beatings through his early life had shattered both his eardrums. But now there was a smile on his face, the expression of a child who knows he has found a safe haven at last. Doreen couldn't imagine betraying him by sending him to the state institution.

Doreen heard a shout and turned to see ten-year-old Randy Welder chasing his twin sister, Tara. With similar Dutch boy—style brown hair and dark eyes, they were as alike as fraternal twins could be. They had been with her for two years, ever since their parents were killed in a plane crash. Doreen could never understand why none of their relatives wanted to take them in. They were such nice, *normal* kids. That was the amazing thing about all her children. They were all very normal, despite their hardships. And, Doreen thought—pushing false modesty aside—she and Addison House had had a lot to do with it.

To her right, sitting on the back steps, were Karen Steiff and Harry-John Little. Harry-John was as mischievous, adventurous, and full of humor as a boy of nine should be. It didn't seem possible this was the same child who'd been found by the police wandering in a bus station after his aunt left him there. When they escorted Harry-John home, his aunt's body was discovered hanging from a pipe in the basement.

Karen, at thirteen, was the oldest of the group. She was a tall black girl, already showing signs of stunning beauty. Years of mental cruelty and physical abuse at the hands of her aunt and uncle had not quashed her natural teenage vibrance. She liked makeup, rock and roll, and boys just as much as any thirteen-year-old. And she was a hopeful child, always believing that one day her sick father would wake up from the coma that had claimed him after a stroke the previous year. Most kids would have been bitter and surly, but not Karen.

Doreen couldn't fault her for being hopeful. Orphaned herself at two, she knew the pain of losing her family, and as a child had often imagined her own parents coming back for her. Using her imagination, she had conjured up an image of perfect parents. She believed her mother had the same long, rippling, wheat-colored hair and slightly upturned nose that she had. Doreen's hazel eyes and full lips must have come from a handsome father. And they'd both been small-boned, just like she was. She told herself many times that they weren't dead, that they'd just gone away...

And when she grew up, she vowed that no child would ever suffer as she had.

Yolanda spoke, bringing her back to reality.

"How will we find a place we can afford?"

"I have no idea," Doreen said. "But the nearest shelter is two hours from here, and I can't have these children shipped so far from their own hometown. I didn't work so hard for so many years to turn my back on my kids now because of financial problems."

She opened her closet door and pulled out a jacket.

"Keep an eye on the children, will you? I've got some real estate offices to visit. Somebody must have a house we can afford!"

Pulling on her jacket, Doreen left the house and drove her station wagon into downtown Oakwood, which occupied just three square blocks, most of them taken up by the town hall and police and fire stations. There was a small grocery store, a clothing boutique, and a diner, all with white, multipaned windows. And there were four real estate offices, because although there were less than a thousand people in and around Oakwood, there was a lot of land, and its relative closeness to Buffalo made it a prime living area.

For the rest of the morning Doreen visited one realtor after another. Their answers were always the same: they'd keep her in mind just in case *something* came up, but right now there was simply nothing available. Doreen was stunned to hear how much houses cost in the Allegheny region. With each office she left she felt a little more discouraged. By one o'clock there was only one realtor left to see. What would she do if they had nothing?

"I'm not sending my kids to the state institution!" she vowed, striding toward a small white building with bay windows.

A woman with tight black curls smiled at her as she entered, and Doreen read NANCY SMITH on the nameplate in front of her. Though the woman's eyes brightened when she looked up, Doreen remained expressionless. She'd had enough of friendly, smiling brokers who could do nothing for her. Sitting in the black-corduroy-covered swivel chair at the side of the desk, she blurted, "I run the children's shelter, Addison House, but the owner of the building wants us out. I've got six kids in my care and six thousand dollars in my life's savings. Can you do *anything* for me?"

Nancy laughed.

"Catch your breath!" she cried, reaching for a fat little black book. She opened it, flipping through pages printed out in dot matrix.

Nancy continued to turn pages.

"Nothing here seems right, at least not if you have only six thousand dollars for a down payment. Maybe we could . . ."

She stopped, busily reading one of the book's small pages.

"Wait a minute," she said. "Here's a place."

She shook her head.

"Forget it," she said. "I'm sure you don't want this house."

"What house?" Doreen asked, leaning forward. "I'll look at anything with four walls and a roof."

Nancy opened the rings of her binder and took out the page. She showed Doreen a faded black-and-white picture of a brick house. Doreen counted eight windows across the top.

"It looks big."

"It's huge," Nancy replied. "But it's in terrible shape. No one's lived there for twenty years, and no one seems interested in buying the place. It's a twenty-room mansion tucked away in the mountains, and it's at least a mile from the nearest neighbor."

"Twenty years?" Doreen asked. "Why has it been empty for so long?"

"As far as I know," Nancy said, "a tragedy occurred there back in the early sixties. Something to do with a man committing suicide. I guess people are superstitious."

Doreen straightened.

"Well, I'm not," she said. "Do you think I might be able to work out a deal with the owner?"

"The owner is the Oakwood Savings and Loan," Nancy said. "The house is in foreclosure, and it's available for just twelve hundred dollars in back taxes."

Doreen gasped. "Oh, it sounds too good to be true!"

"It might be," Nancy said. "I've only shown it to a few other people in the last few years, and none of them wanted it. It's quite run-down, needs a lot of repair."

"That doesn't bother me," Doreen said. "People around here are generous, and maybe some local contractor will volunteer to help me fix the place up. I'd like to see it this afternoon, if I can."

Nancy looked at her watch.

"This afternoon is hard," she said. "I'm going to be at a closing."

"But I'd really like to see the house today," Doreen said.

"I tell you what," Nancy replied. "I'll give you directions and a key and you can have a look for yourself. If you decide you're interested, you can call me and we'll make arrangements."

Full of hope, Doreen headed out to find the house. After driving away from the town for fifteen minutes, she turned at the huge boulder Nancy had indicated as a landmark and drove down a weed-choked road to the house. As she got out of the car, she looked up with amazement at the windows across the top of the brick facade, their shutters weathered and hanging askew. Ivy curled around the cracked stone bodies of two lions that glowered at her from either side of the leaf-covered steps. Doreen walked up to an old wooden door. Though it had been battered by years of snow and rain, the key opened it easily.

She was immediately struck by the smell of must and

mildew that had been accumulating over many years. Doreen rested her hand on a small table in the hallway, only to pull it away with a feeling of disgust. There was a thick layer of dust on the table, as well as on everything in sight, like snow that had fallen and never melted.

Something scuttled across the floor, hidden in the shadows. Doreen jumped back a little, waiting for a rat to appear. But there was only silence.

It was cold in the house. The foyer, darkened by pulled shades, had not accepted the sun's warmth in years. Doreen rubbed at her arms and walked farther inside. The archway to her right was draped with cobwebs. With a grimace, Doreen ducked below them and entered what seemed to be a parlor. There were tooth marks on the mantel of the massive fieldstone fireplace, where long-ago rodents had gnawed down their ever-growing teeth. Doreen moved in for a closer look and found shredded newspaper, bits of furniture stuffing, and twigs where kindling should have been.

A rat's nest.

"Oh, God," Doreen sighed, looking back over her shoulder. She thought of the noise she'd heard out in the hall. Rats. Could she stand living in a house infested with rats?

She set her lips together hard and straightened up with determination. All she had to do was call an exterminator. Someone in Oakwood would certainly volunteer for the job. People in this town were kind, always ready to help the kids at Addison House.

Thinking of Karen and Frankie and the others, Doreen turned back to the room and surveyed it. She tried to imagine it cleaned up, painted, and furnished. In spite of the cobwebs and cracked ceilings and peeled wallpaper, it was a beautiful room. Three tall windows lined one wall, dust on the glass blocking the sunshine as it tried to pour over the dusty wood floor. The wall opposite the fireplace had been fitted with arched bookshelves, empty now except for the dust.

No, not empty. Doreen noticed that in one corner the cobwebs jutted out at an angle. Standing on tiptoe, squinting in the dim light, she was able to see the spine of a very old book. Curious, she fished through her handbag for something to push the cobwebs aside. Then, grimacing in anticipation of whatever might crawl out, she took hold of the book and pulled it off the shelf.

It was a Bible. Awed by the obvious antiquity of the book, Doreen opened its pages carefully. Long ago, someone had underlined certain passages with ink that had now faded to a light blue.

A movement in the window made her look up. She jumped back with a gasp, the Bible falling to the floor. Two eyes were peering at her from a dark silhouette.

"Who are . . . ?"

As she cried out, Doreen swung around to see if anyone had come in behind her. The doorway was empty. She looked back at the window again, but saw nothing that even resembled eyes.

A shiver passed through her, but she tried to tell herself that she was imagining things. She had the whole house to look at, and she was already letting herself be spooked by it! She walked out of the room.

The sudden scare had made her forget about the Bible. But something else had seen her drop it. Beneath the carpet of dust, the floorboards parted ever so slightly. Gnarled fingers reached upward, trembling with effort as they sought their prize. They clamped over the Bible, pulling it down into the dark abyss below the floor. The boards moved together again, as if they had never been disturbed.

In the hallway, Doreen heard a loud creak from the parlor. She turned, but saw nothing.

"Old house noises," she told herself, comforted by the sound of her voice.

She continued her investigation. The room she found through the double doors to her left had tall windows that were similar to the ones in the parlor. The chandelier had been stripped of its crystals, and it hung like a brass skeleton. Doreen could picture it as it had been years ago, with shining prisms casting rainbows over a large table where a family shared their meals. Just who had lived here? Doreen wondered. Nancy had mentioned a man who'd killed himself, but Doreen didn't care to think about him. She was more interested in the people who had first lived here, around the turn of the nineteenth century. Wouldn't it be romantic to know about their lives, the work they did, and the people they'd loved? Funny how the house was drawing her into its spell.

Doreen pushed open a Dutch door that led to an ancient kitchen. The burners on the old stove she found there had rusted so badly that they were almost nonexistent. As with the other rooms, spiders had strung webs in every available corner. The linoleum tile was cracked and loose, revealing the black glue beneath it. Instead of a refrigerator, a squat icebox stood near the doorway. Doreen's mind conjured up images of what might still be in that trapped, stale cubicle. She fought her imagination and hurried from the room.

There was another door leading from the kitchen into a triangular-shaped hallway, and here Doreen found the entrance to the cellar. When she opened the door, a cold blast of air shot out at her, chilling her. She could just make out the top few steps leading down into the darkness below, but decided she had no desire just yet to see what was under the house. She planned to hire an engineer to look the place over anyway, to see just how bad it was, actually, so she would leave the investigation of the basement to him.

When she pushed open another door, she found herself again in the long hallway, which led past several more empty rooms on its way to the front foyer. An enormous staircase stretched up toward the black void of the second floor. Many of the posts along its balustrade had been chewed, and the faded blue runner was badly frayed. Doreen started to lay her hand on the banister, and then paused, having second thoughts.

If the downstairs had made her a little uneasy, with its dilapidated rooms and dark shadows, the thought of climbing these stairs tied knots in her stomach. But there was only one way to find out if this was the right place for her kids. Doreen took a deep breath and headed up the stairs. Each step creaked below her weight, and it seemed the stairs would give way at any moment. She longed to hold on to the banister for support, but the dust was far too thick.

It was cold and dark upstairs, and the abundance of shadows did little to comfort her. Even though logic told her the house was empty (surely the real estate people had been here many times), Doreen could easily imagine someone lying in wait behind one of these closed doors. But she tried to convince herself that that was just the kid coming out in her—the child who had been thrown outdoors by a foster mother and told that ghosts were going to get her. Doreen was a grown-up now, and she knew there were no such things. Still, she was grateful more than curious when her reflexive flick of the light switch illuminated the long hallway. Among the many rooms there were two baths, both with rusting fixtures. Another bath had been added just off the master bedroom, but there was nothing luxurious about it. The tub needed work and the window over the tub, like all the windows in the house, was so filthy that sunlight could barely shine through. Doreen could scarcely make out her reflection in the tarnished mirror.

As she closed the medicine cabinet door, she heard something in the hall. She quickly hurried out, but there was no movement, no sound.

"Is anyone there?" she called.

The hall was empty.

She said out loud, "You're just hearing house noises, Doreen!"

Or rats.

Doreen shook her head hard and pushed open a door across the hall. She found a bedroom wallpapered with circus scenes. Though the red of the clowns' noses had faded to pink, and the gray elephants were almost the same color as the graying white background, Doreen found the room very charming. She imagined the child who must have lived in it long ago, happy among his playthings.

Doreen went to the window to look out at the property below, wooded acres that stretched to the base of a nearby mountain. Tall grass choked the ground around old pine trees, but Doreen saw enough space to create a play area once the lawn was cut down. Despite the house's condition, Doreen somehow felt strangely at peace. The house seemed to be luring her to move into its many rooms. With a place this big, she'd be able to take in even more children who needed her. This musty, dusty old house might be a dream come true, a way to make Addison House a real contribution to the children of the area.

Doreen made up her mind to take a chance on this place. Satisfied, she turned around and screamed in surprise to find herself face-to-face with a dark-eyed stranger.

2

In the warm June air, the dripping blood was like a hot shower on the backs of the old man's hands.

The leg of the freshly killed raccoon in Marty Laudon's grip was gnawed to a stump where the animal had tried to free itself from a steel-jaw trap. The body was still warm, and Marty licked his lips to think of that night's dinner. He stuffed his catch into a burlap bag and pulled the drawstring shut, heaving the bag over one hunched shoulder.

When he turned to walk through the copse, the gleam of sunlight on chrome made him stop. Marty leaned forward, squinting to stretch his vision toward the giant house that sat nearly a thousand feet away. He snorted, his breath forming a cloud, and lumbered toward the edge of the woods for a better view.

Marty sneered at the run-down station wagon, the grip on his sack tightening. So, someone else was looking the place over? Someone else was fool enough to be interested in that house?

"Nothin'll come of it," he growled. "Once they hear 'bout what happened, they won't want the place. No one ever does."

It had been many months since the last person came here to look at the house back in October. The house had sat forgotten through the winter and spring by everyone but

Marty, who had been unofficially hired by the bank who owned it to keep vandals away. Vandals were easy enough to handle with his shotgun, but Marty wanted no part of whatever lurked inside those brick walls. He'd never set foot inside the place.

He mumbled a short prayer, the way he always did when he saw a car parked near those stone lions. Each time someone came to see the place, though it didn't happen often, Marty expected to hear screams of terror. But each time the visitors came out unscathed.

He turned and headed down the path to his own place. It bothered him that someone might actually move into the old mansion. He was only paid a small amount for his neighborly vigilance, but those few dollars bought traps in the winter and cool wine in the summer. He'd been doing this for so many years that it was impossible for him to imagine not doing it. What would it be like to have a neighbor after all these years?

But then again, Marty thought, no sane person would ever move into a house so full of evil.

3

Doreen wrenched her shoulder from the stranger's grip.

"Who on earth are you?" she demanded. "What are you doing in here?"

He did not answer her at first, but stared at her with eyes so deep and dark they were hypnotic. A thought came to her, unbidden: *I've never seen anyone with eyes like that.*

Doreen straightened herself, startled and annoyed by her reaction to the stranger. He was a young man, perhaps not older than her thirty-four years. But there was a sternness in his expression that reminded Doreen of strict schoolteachers she'd known as a child.

But that was ridiculous. She wasn't a child; she was a grown woman, with every right to be here!

"Well?" she pressed, meeting his deep gaze. "Who are you?"

"I might ask you the same question," the man said at last, carefully enunciating the words in a rich, soft-edged British accent.

"I was sent by Nancy Smith," Doreen said. "Not that it's any of your business, but her real estate office is handling the sale of this place. She gave me the key."

The grim look faded from the stranger's face, and it seemed that his eyes lightened a few shades.

15

When he smiled, he was actually quite handsome.

"I have been waiting a long time for you," he said. "I did not know when you would come."

"I don't understand," she said. "Nancy didn't tell me there would be anyone here."

"My name is Brendan Delacorte," the man said. "I'm sorry if I frightened you. But I was walking outside, and when I saw movement in the windows, I thought I should investigate."

"And I'm Doreen Addison," Doreen replied, relaxing considerably. He was so polite!

"Please," Brendan said, "it would be best if you'll allow me to walk you downstairs again. It's dark up here."

Doreen laughed a little.

"So I noticed," she said. "I kept imagining rats in the shadows."

The stranger shook his head, a lock of black hair falling down over his tanned, rough-skinned forehead.

"No rats," he said. "I would not allow rats. I know how much they frighten you."

Doreen backed away nervously.

"How did you know I'm afraid of rats?" she asked. She wondered if he had been following her.

He waved a hand. Doreen could see that he had the rough, callused hands of a man who did manual labor.

"I didn't say that correctly," he answered. "I meant, I know how much rats frighten *people*."

"Well, I'm just glad to hear there aren't any rats in this house," Doreen said. "You see, I may be moving in with six small children, and—"

"You are a teacher?"

He seemed excited by the idea.

"Not exactly," she said. "I'm a social worker. I've got a state license, of course, but I only run a small establishment. I founded it especially for children in Oakwood who need help. The state helps me a little bit, but not enough. And now our landlord is kicking us out of our old home.

When I heard this place was for sale, I knew I had to come look."

"And do you like what you've found?"

"Very much," Doreen said. "It's certainly big enough. And if it was just cleaned up and repaired . . ."

She looked up at him.

"Are you the caretaker, Mr.—Mr.—"

"Brendan Delacorte," he reminded her. "There is no need to call me 'mister.'"

"All right," Doreen said with a smile. "Well, *are* you the caretaker?"

"No, he died many years ago," Brendan said. "I sometimes watch the house, like a good neighbor."

Doreen thought of the eyes she had seen in the parlor window. Could it have been Brendan looking in? Or could she have been seeing a reflection of the eyes of someone standing behind her . . . ?

"Is there anyone else living nearby?"

Brendan nodded. "An old hermit. I've heard people calling him Marty. He also watches the house. I'm sure you'll meet him one day. Now, if you'd like me to show you more of the house . . ."

He walked to the bedroom door, holding it open and stepping aside to let Doreen walk past him. Brendan, describing the house as it had been years ago, kept at her side as they walked.

"It was a beautiful place," he said. "I remember the luster of these wooden lintels and and the way the windows sparkled when all the wall sconces were lit."

"It's a shame it's been left to deteriorate," Doreen said. "But I'm sure a good cleaning will make a real difference. The house does look structurally sound, although I will have someone come in to look it over. Much as I'm in need of a new place, I don't need the headaches involved in rebuilding an entire house!"

"This house is solid," Brendan said as they came to the staircase.

As he went on talking about the house, Doreen studied

his face. She understood why she'd been momentarily taken by him when she first saw him. He had the looks that made some men movie idols: dark hair and rugged skin and those incredible eyes. He wore his dark brown hair medium-long, letting it curl around his ears and fall in tangled tendrils over his forehead. His rugged skin spoke of many hours outdoors, and the well-defined muscles of his arms indicated a man who worked hard. There was a faint smell of horses about him, detectable even over the mustiness of the hallway.

". . . parties were the talk of Oakwood," he was saying.

"It looks as if it must have been very beautiful at one time," Doreen said. "But tell me, why was it left empty for so many years?"

Brendan shrugged.

"There was a tragedy here," he said.

"So I heard," Doreen said grimly. "The realtor mentioned a suicide."

"Much more than that," Brendan said. He brightened suddenly. "But I don't want to spoil our meeting with morbid talk."

Doreen nodded, not eager to hear any frightening stories. She was not superstitious, but she had noticed a melancholy feeling about the house already and didn't want to think about what might have caused it.

"Do you know how old the house is?" she said, changing the subject.

"It was built in 1810," Brendan said. "Although the colonial style was chosen, as you can see."

They descended the staircase and stood in the foyer. Doreen looked at her watch, surprised to find she'd been at the house for almost two hours.

"Well, I'm pretty well sold on this old place," she said. "Maybe we'll be neighbors."

"I'd like that," Brendan said. "And if there's any way I can help you . . ."

Doreen smiled.

"I'm sure we'll talk again soon," she said. "But I really must leave now."

Brendan stood on the porch's top step, watching her walk away. Although summer had officially begun, a chilly wind suddenly blew up around him and the house seemed gray and melancholy—as if the house itself caused the weather. As Brendan watched Doreen get into her car, he whispered, "You belong here. I will make you very happy."

Six Weeks Later

Doreen hurried out the front door of the ranch house, waving a hand at the movers.

"Careful with that!" she cried, watching them struggle with an old piano.

A woman with strawberry-blond hair in an ear-length cut appeared at her side. Judy Wagner was Doreen's part-time assistant—a recent college graduate who taught high school math and volunteered at Addison House three afternoons a week. In anticipation of hard work on the hottest day so far that year, both women wore jeans and T-shirts. Judy had a figure that rounded out her clothes, unlike Doreen's thin silhouette, and though she was twenty-four she looked like a model for a teen magazine. But there was nothing childish about Judy. Doreen had hired her because of her intelligence and love for children, and she was a hard worker who never disappointed her employer. The high school was on summer vacation, so Judy worked with Doreen almost every day, especially to help with the move. This morning, for instance, Judy took full charge of the kids, leaving Doreen time to supervise the movers without a million interruptions.

"I can hardly believe this day has finally arrived," Doreen said. "From the title search to the inspection, I thought we'd never get into this house. It's been hectic!"

She stepped aside as two burly men carried the kitchen table, wrapped in green quilted padding, to the truck.

Doreen felt a tug at the leg of her jeans, and looked down into Cindy's round blue eyes.

"Did you send my mommy our 'dress?" the five-year-old asked. "I wanna be sure she knows where to find me when she comes!"

"Of course I did," Doreen reassured the child, running her finger around a tiny, seashell ear. The lie hurt. It broke her heart to think how much Cindy still loved her mother, even though Hannah Ardus had abandoned the child in a heatless apartment the previous winter while she went out on a robbery spree.

Just then Randy and Tara came running from the house, squealing with laughter.

"Hey, are we outa here or what?" Randy demanded.

"We'll be 'outa here' in a little while," Doreen said. "You just be certain you have all your things."

"We packed really careful," Tara said. "Didn't we, Randy?"

Randy grinned at his sister. "Sure did. And I want to go now!"

A tall man came over to her and asked her to sign a paper. Checking her list against the mover's, Doreen scribbled at the bottom of their packing list, then watched as the truck rumbled down a road lined with bluebells, heather, and goldenrod.

"Okay, that's it!" Doreen cried. "Everyone into the car! We're on our way!"

The children scrambled for seats, chattering among themselves. Finally, the station wagon drove up the road that led to their new home. When it came into view, Randy hung out his tongue.

"Yuck!" he cried. "What a scuzz-joint!"

"Can it," Karen snapped. "I think it's nice."

"Don't tell me to can it," Randy cried, yanking one of the short beaded braids that hung across Karen's forehead.

Doreen pulled up behind the moving van and turned off the ignition.

"Settle down, you guys!"

She really couldn't blame the kids for their distaste—it would be a long time before the house became respectable again. There were workers everywhere, most of them carrying toolboxes or paint cans or planks of wood. Doreen had gone to the local parish to ask for help in fixing up the place, and was finally able to hire a contractor by combining their donations with what was left of her own small savings. They'd been working hard for weeks, and the house looked better already. The crooked shutters had been painted and repaired, and dead bushes around the house had been pulled out. The windows were clean now, and all debris had been swept from the porch.

"Come on," she said. "Everyone grab your own suitcase, and I'll show you to your rooms."

Behind the station wagon, Judy pulled up in her Civic, and she and Yolanda got out of the small car as the children raced toward the front door. Ever efficient, Yolanda quickly went inside the big house to find the equipment she needed to get lunch started. But Judy paused for a few moments to admire the new Addison House. She had been there several times herself over the last few weeks, checking on the workers' progress for Doreen. As she stood gazing at the much-improved appearance of the mansion, she wondered if the odd feelings she'd had about this place would come again once she set foot on the old porch.

The first time she came to the house, she'd almost been overcome by an overwhelming sense of despair. It wasn't the cold emptiness of the rooms that bothered her so much, but a strong perception about the lives of the people who had once walked through them. Judy knew about the suicide years ago, but she really didn't know much about the story. Sometimes she thought she almost heard the cries of a frightened child and the screams of a terrified woman. Almost, but not quite. She always caught herself, attributing the phantom noises to her overactive imagination, replacing the screams in her mind with the concrete sounds of saws and hammers. All big old houses had stories, she told herself. And empty houses always gave people a feeling of loss.

But that couldn't possibly be the case now. Not with six active children racing through the rooms! Not with a dozen workers rejuvenating a beautiful manse that had been neglected for years.

It was time to get to work. She had volunteered for the job of putting files back into their cabinets, and she figured it would take all morning. Tucking her keys into her pocket, she went up to the house.

But the feeling *was* still there. The moment she set foot on the porch, she felt a chill rush through her. What was it about this house? She'd never had the gift of empathy, or any other paranormal talents for that matter. So why was she overcome by this foreboding?

She couldn't let herself dwell on it. The new Addison House had been all Doreen could speak about for the past few weeks, and she wasn't about to spoil this important day with illogical fears. It was going to be a great place.

As soon as she pushed open the front door, the sounds of laughing children set her at ease. Maybe the house had a melancholy history, but the future was starting right now, and they would all make it a happy place. Forcing irrational thoughts of gloom from her mind, Judy headed toward the room Doreen had picked for her office.

Doreen herself had been giving the children a tour of the house, and now she was upstairs showing them their rooms. She had chosen the room with the circus wallpaper for Frankie, somehow wanting him to have the room that had charmed her the most. Moving past her, Frankie ran over to the window to look out at the yard below, then turned to sign *big* to Doreen.

"It sure is a big yard," Doreen said, looking straight at the deaf child to let him lip-read her words. "And once you hang up your things in the closet, you can go out and play. That goes for all of you."

"Where's my room?" Randy asked. "Is it next to Tara's?"

"There's a door between them," Doreen said. "I picked those rooms especially for you two."

She opened another door and ushered Randy into a small bedchamber. There was only one small window, and most of its light was blocked by a huge tree. Unlike Frankie's room, this room had wallpaper of a drab green-and-brown stripe, almost matching the dark wood floor.

"Kinda dark," Randy said. "I can't see very good."

"Fresh paint and bright curtains will lighten it up. You kids have to give yourselves time to get used to this house, especially while it's being renovated."

Doreen went back out to the hall. Karen had found one of the bathrooms, and was standing in its doorway with her hand on the crystal knob.

"Look at that weird bathtub," she said. "It has feet on it!"

"It's very old," Doreen said. "Here's your room, Karen, right across the hall."

In their adjoining rooms, Randy and Tara began to unpack. Tara opened up a box marked FRAGILE on all sides. Nothing in it was fragile, but Tara's collection of books was very precious to her, and she hadn't wanted anything to happen to them. Before she even unpacked her clothes, she wanted to set out her books to be sure they had all safely arrived. She was delighted to find a shelf built into her wall, but dismayed that she couldn't reach it. She went to the door that led to her twin's room and called to her brother.

"You have a chair in there?" she asked. "I'm trying to put my books up on a shelf but I can't reach it."

Randy turned from the box of Space Warrior figurines he'd been unpacking and looked around the room. He found a short wooden chair by his window, and lugged it into his sister's room. Clunking it down on the floor, he let out a loud moan.

"Oof!" That thing weighs a ton!" he said. "It sure is ugly, too. Who ever heard of carving ghosts on a chair?"

"I think those are angels, Randy," Tara said, taking a closer look.

Even when she climbed up on the chair, she had to stretch to place the books along the shelf. Tara lined them up in size order, starting with a large book on fairies and working down to smaller novels about life on the prairie. When one volume wouldn't slide back toward the wall, Tara reached up and groped around. Her fingers felt the edge of something soft and torn, and she pulled out a frayed black book.

"Hey, look what I found!"

Holding the book in her hand, Tara jumped to the floor.

"Look at this old book, Randy," she said. "It's a Bible."

She opened the cover, pieces of yellowed paper falling to the floor.

"Oh!" she cried. "Listen to this! It says: 'The Winston Family, 1814.' This is really old!"

Tara sat on the chair, with Randy leaning over her shoulder.

"'Miles Winston,'" he read. "'Wed to Charity Jefferson on July 10, 1810.'"

"Turn the page, Tara," Randy urged.

Tara did so, finding a page completely filled with tiny, faded handwriting. Her lips moved as she read.

Suddenly, she threw down the book.

"I don't like it anymore," she said.

"What did it say, Tara?" Randy asked.

He opened it to the page she had been reading.

"'I have raised my daughter in the light of God's grace,'" he read, "'yet for all my efforts have had to turn her over to the depth of God's wrath. I hear her screaming, but I know I must not heed her cries for help. She must suffer, if that is what will teach her the folly of her sins. If there be pain, it is God's will!'"

Randy wrinkled his nose.

"It sounds mean," he said. "But so what? It's just something a guy wrote a long time ago."

"I know," Tara said, shrugging hesitantly. "But it scares me! I mean, I felt so cold when I read that!"

Afraid he'd make fun of her, she didn't want to tell Randy she felt as if a spider might come crawling out of the buckled spine of the book.

"Well, it is bad," Randy agreed finally. "I mean, I hate to think of bad parents, like this guy musta been. It makes me think how nice our parents were."

"Mom and Dad would never hurt us," Tara agreed.

Randy looked down at his sneakers.

"Except they went and died on us," he said. "Tara, do you sometimes wake up in the night and want to call them? And do you think they'll come running?"

"All the time," Tara said, her big brown eyes reflecting the sadness in her brother's. "It sure doesn't seem like two years since the accident."

A knock came at the door just then. The twins looked at each other, and an unspoken message crossed between them. Tara shoved the Bible into the top drawer of her dresser as Yolanda entered.

"How are you children doing?" she asked. "Tara, Cindy's having trouble unpacking. Could you help her? Then we can all have the nice lunch I've prepared."

"Sure," Tara said. "See you later, Randy."

Tara found Cindy sitting on the red-and-gray carpet in her room and holding up a doll. She had her back to the door, and didn't realize Tara was there.

"And this is my friend Mindy," she was saying. "I told her all about you, Mommy. She thinks you're very pretty."

Tara shook her head. Weird! This kid had some imagination!

"Hi, Cindy," she said. "Who're you talking to?"

"My mommy," Cindy said, in an isn't-it-obvious tone of voice.

"Sure," Tara said. "Listen, you leave your mommy alone and we'll finish unpacking your stuff."

"I don't want to!" Cindy cried. She ran to an empty corner of the room. Her arms encircled nothing, but her face was full of rapture. "My mommy came all the way from the big city to be with me, didn't you, Mommy?"

Cindy tilted her head up and made a kissing face, then backed away with a laugh.

What an actress, Tara thought.

When Cindy turned to face her, Tara let out a cry of dismay, dropping the small jewelry box she'd just taken from Cindy's suitcase.

There was a red mark on the little girl's cheek, as if someone had just kissed her.

4

Doreen was unpacking a crate of knickknacks when someone knocked on the front door. Stepping around the maze of boxes, she hurried to answer it, and was delighted to see Brendan Delacorte.

"Good morning," he said.

"Hi!" Doreen said. "Come on in!"

"I saw some of the children playing in the meadow out back," Brendan said, following her into the living room. Despite the heat, he wore black leather boots that made hollow clicking noises on the wood floor. His white shirt-sleeves were rolled up over his muscular arms, and there was the slightest shadowing of dirt on his hands. That same smell of horses that Doreen had noticed at their first meeting was still with him.

"Are there other children around here?" Doreen asked. "I never noticed any on my visits."

"There were, once," Brendan said. "But they've left."

He looked around for a place to sit. The couch was crowded with boxes, and the chairs were still covered with tarpaulins. Doreen moved quickly to uncover one, folding the cumbersome, paint-stained canvas and laying it behind the chair.

"The place is a shambles," she apologized.

"What can I do to help?" Brendan asked.

"Well, there is this box of laundry supplies that needs to go down to the basement," Doreen said.

Brendan gave her a smile, his teeth stark white in his tanned face, and stood up. Hoisting the box onto his shoulder, he said, "Perhaps you should show me exactly where you want this."

They walked to the small triangular hallway that had two heavy wooden doors, one leading to the kitchen and the other to the basement. The latter was secured with a latch, and Doreen had to stretch up to pull it back. Opening the door, she reached into the dark abyss to switch on the light.

"Please watch yourself on the stairs," she said. "They're really in bad shape."

She started down the steps first, carefully going one step at a time.

"I'll be careful," Brendan promised.

The ancient, rotting wood steps creaked beneath Doreen's weight. Pieces were broken away, and nails poked out dangerously. It seemed that cobwebs were the only things supporting a rusted strip of metal that once had been an iron handrail.

Doreen squinted in the dim light. She didn't like the basement, with its musty smells and dark shadows. It reminded her of how much she'd feared the dark as a child, and her chest tightened nervously, despite the fact that she knew nothing would happen to her.

Don't be such a scaredy-cat! Brendan is here with you, and you're not a little kid anymore!

Suddenly, something reached out of the darkness to touch Doreen's face, running over her cheek like icy fingers.

"Hussy!"

With a scream, she stumbled back, falling against the railing. It gave way under her weight, snapping like an old twig. Wide-eyed, Doreen cried out in terror as she lunged backward, arms and legs flailing wildly.

"Brendan!"

But she never fell. Brendan's arms locked around her waist. He crushed her protectively against his body, one hand on her back and the other on her thigh. The box he had been carrying crashed to the floor below. Open-mouthed, Doreen gazed into his dark eyes, so close she could see tiny flecks of green in his irises. Her heart thumped painfully. She felt an odd tingling where his rough palm touched her leg. As if he had suddenly realized this, Brendan quickly moved his hand up to her waist.

"Oh, my God," she whispered, her voice shaking.

"Are you hurt?" Brendan asked worriedly.

Breathing deeply, Doreen pulled away from him and backed down a step.

"I'm—I'm okay," she said. "Something touched my face, and it startled me. I guess I ran into a cobweb."

She combed her fingers through her hair. She hadn't really heard a voice, had she? It had simply been the creaking of the stairs! Doreen looked over the side of the stairs. Ten feet below her, blue liquid puddled its way across the cement floor.

It could have been my blood.

"I—I suppose I'll have to clean that mess up," she said, trying to calm herself by getting down to business. But her composure was short-lived, and a shudder wracked her thin frame. "Brendan, if you hadn't been there . . ."

Taking her hand, Brendan led her back up to the door.

"It's all right now," he soothed. "I'm glad you weren't hurt."

In the hallway again, Doreen pushed the cellar door shut and threw the latch. Then she turned and managed a smile for Brendan.

"Brendan, you've been so nice," she said. "This has been quite a morning for new neighbors! Would you like to stay and have lunch?"

Brendan held up two broad-palmed hands.

"No, thank you," he said. "I only came to welcome you, and I really must be going."

"It's the least I can do for you," Doreen said.

"There are things I must do," Brendan said.

He turned and left her in the hallway, his boots clicking. Doreen was a bit put off by his sudden departure. She realized now that her heart was still beating fast, but she wasn't certain if it was because of her near accident or from the feel of his arms around her.

"How ridiculous," she said, tucking in her shirt. "You just met the guy!"

"Who'd you meet?"

Karen was standing behind her, holding a tray.

"Never mind," Doreen said. "What have you got there?"

"Lemonade for the workers," Karen said.

"Isn't that nice!" Doreen said. "You're very thoughtful."

Harry-John's voice came from somewhere in the kitchen.

"She just wants an excuse to flirt with some guy she saw working on the back windows!"

"I do not!" Karen protested.

"I heard you talking to him," Harry-John said, still in the kitchen. "Just 'cause the guy's a high school senior, you think he's special or something."

One by one, the other children chimed in. Listening to their conversations, it was hard for Doreen to believe this place had been cold and severe when she first saw it. It was already beginning to feel like home.

That night, after the last of the children had been tucked into bed, the three adults of Addison House gathered in the mansion's library. The arched bookshelves had been filled that afternoon—a project shared by Cindy and Karen—and cheerful pictures had been hung on the drab gray walls.

"What a day this has been," Doreen sighed. She cradled a mug of Red Zinger tea in her hands, letting the fruity aroma relax her.

"I'm still hearing the sounds of hammers," Judy said, removing her pink-and-purple button earrings. She reached down to her stockinged feet and began to rub them. "Then again," she said, "I'll probably be so tired by the time I get home that I'll conk out tonight without dreaming."

Yolanda handed her a platter of freshly baked blueberry muffins. Judy took one and settled back with it. She realized just then that the strange feelings she'd had when she first arrived had faded considerably. As she bit into the muffin, she decided that the whole episode had been her imagination, with a dose of moving day nerves thrown in.

"It's a shame you have to travel all that distance," Yolanda said. "Especially when we have empty bedrooms right here."

"Why don't you move in with us for the summer, Judy?" Doreen asked, setting her cup down. "With so much to do, I could certainly use you. And I'm sure I could swing a small salary for you if I juggled the books a bit."

Judy hesitated.

"Well, I don't . . ."

"It would only be for the season," Doreen promised. "Once you start teaching again, we'll return to our old schedule."

"It isn't the timing," Judy said. "It's my parents. My mother has a hard time accepting the fact that I'm twenty-four, and I can just imagine how she'll react if I move out—even if it is just for a short time!"

She stood up, sliding her feet back into her shoes.

"Well, I'll think about it," she said. "I'll see you tomorrow afternoon."

Yolanda began to gather up the empty coffee mugs and muffin tray.

Doreen said good-night to them, but she really didn't feel like going upstairs. She was too wound up to fall asleep. Moving day had been quite an adventure! Brendan came to mind, and she wondered what impression she'd made on him. He probably thought she was a hysterical klutz, nearly killing herself because of a cobweb!

Well, there wouldn't be much time to think of Brendan

for a while. Not with six kids and a new house to keep her
busy! Knowing that the next day would be very active,
Doreen decided she should go upstairs and at least try to
fall asleep.

As she walked out of the library, she thought how much
nicer the place looked already. Simply cleaning up the dust
and hanging pictures on the walls made a real difference.
Doreen stopped halfway up the stairs and studied the old
wallpaper. She wondered how much work would be involved in taking it down and replacing it with something
more appealing to the children. Judy was a gifted painter,
and Doreen made a note to ask her about the possibility of
a mural.

The sound of scampering feet made her hurry up the
stairs. Looking down the darkened hallway, she caught
sight of a blond-haired boy dressed in footsie pajamas.
Thinking Harry-John had gotten up to use the bathroom,
she called out softly to him. The child stopped and looked
at her, his yellow hair like a halo around his shadowed
face. Then, strangely, instead of turning in to his own
room, he opened Doreen's door and disappeared into hers!

"Harry-John?" Doreen called.

The poor kid, she thought. *Maybe he's having trouble
sleeping, and needs reassurance on this first night in a
strange place*. Harry-John had been raised by an aunt who
deserted him in a bus station almost two years earlier. He
had wandered around for a whole day, lost and confused,
until the police picked him up. Harry-John never saw his
aunt again, because soon after her disappearance, her body
was found hanging in her cellar.

Doreen opened her bedroom door, fumbling through the
darkness to find the lamp on her dresser.

"Want to talk, HJ?" she asked, switching on the light.

The large mirror over her dresser reflected most of the
room behind her own reflection. Harry-John wasn't on her
bed; he wasn't in the rocking chair she'd set in one corner.
She turned to look for the child. There was no sign of him,
no sounds of soft crying.

"Harry-John?"

No answer.

Doreen sighed. "I'm really more tired than I realized. Now my mind is playing tricks on me!"

Still, she couldn't shake the shadowy image of that boy who had turned to look at her. Maybe Harry-John had entered another room, and she hadn't been able to clearly see which one it was from the opposite end of the hall.

"Better check on him, and for that matter, all of the children," she said.

They were all sleeping peacefully, some cuddled around stuffed animals. Doreen mouthed the words *I love you* to each one as she left his or her room, thinking how much these kids meant to her.

She found Harry-John sound asleep on top of his covers, one foot off the side of his bed. Gently, Doreen rearranged him, adjusting the twisted leg of his white karate pajamas. She kissed him good-night and went to her own room.

She was fast asleep long before the thought could rise in her mind that all the children, including Harry-John, had gone to bed in summer pajamas.

The little boy she had seen in the hall was wearing a heavy flannel sleeper.

5

The sound of settling wood woke Randy from a fitful, dream-filled sleep. The little boy rolled over, his arm brushing the sheets in a wide arc, searching for someone. Slowly, Randy opened his eyes and realized he was alone. He no longer had to share a bed with Harry-John. It felt weird, being all alone like this after sharing a room with the other boys for two years. The black stillness began to turn into a frightening world for this ten-year-old.

But Randy wouldn't let scary things into his thoughts. He brought his hand up and clutched the Space Warrior he had taken to bed with him. Holding the small plastic embodiment of good and strength made him feel just a little more secure on his first night in his new home.

In the moonlight, he noticed a black, rectangular shape near his headboard. It was that Bible. He didn't know why he had taken it from his sister's drawer, but for some reason he wanted to keep it near him. He thought of the flashlight his father had given him on his sixth birthday, now carefully tucked away in a dresser drawer with his other special belongings. Randy got out of bed to look for it. His space station, all set up on his dresser, looked strangely distorted in the moonlight shadows.

Nervously, he pulled open the drawer and fished around for the flashlight. When he found it, he felt suddenly braver. He remembered the nights he and his father explored their backyard with this flashlight, but now it almost seemed that that backyard had never existed.

Randy went back to bed and sat cross-legged with his back against the headboard. He opened the Bible and flashed the light into it. It didn't really matter that he could hardly understand the words. He just knew, somehow, that it was very important to concentrate and keep reading.

He heard a shuffling sound near his window, and looked up to see the curtains billowing softly. A dark and elongated shadow obliterated his view of the tree outside.

"Who's there?" Randy whispered, his voice high-pitched. "Tara, is that you?"

Randy put the Bible aside and climbed out of bed, aiming his flashlight toward the window. At the foot of his bed, he stopped—frozen in place.

A woman was there, pointing at the Bible on the bed. She wore a long, diaphanous black gown with flowing sleeves rippling in a wind that came from nowhere. There was a stern look on her face, and her eyes glowed in the flashlight's beam.

"Heathen child," she hissed. *"Reading the word of God in secret, as if ashamed!"*

Randy's mouth opened, but the scream he heard in his mind refused to come out. His hand began to shake and the flashlight cast wild arcs around the room. The Space Warriors figurines seemed to come to life, huge shadows reaching out to grab him . . .

He heard a noise behind him and swung around, watching the door to Tara's room open. When his sister walked in, he suddenly found his voice.

"Tara, get Doreen!"

Tara frowned at him, her nose wrinkled.

"What's wrong with you, Randy?" she asked. "Are you having a bad dream?"

Randy looked toward the window. The curtains were still, and there was no one in the room. Even so, he jumped a little when Tara touched his arm.

"Wow," she said. "You're all sweaty!"

Maybe it had been a dream, he thought. But the lady he saw seemed so real!

Feeling terribly cold, Randy wrapped his arms around himself and said in a small voice, "Stay with me, Tara?"

"Sure, Randy," Tara said. "I can't sleep anyway. Guess I got used to Cindy talking in her sleep all the time. It's so quiet now! What are you doing with that flashlight?"

They walked to his bed and sat on the edge together. Randy picked up the Bible. Holding it, Randy began to feel immediate comfort.

"I was reading," he said. "Do you want to listen?"

"I guess so," Tara said with a shrug. "But I'd rather play a game or something."

Ignoring her request, Randy opened the book and began to read out loud. Tara thought the words were strange, but she didn't stop him. She just watched his face as he read, mesmerized by the sound of his voice. It seemed so deep, so *grown-up* here in the dark.

"'I am putting before thee this day,'" he read, "'a blessing and a curse. A blessing if thou should heed the word of the Lord, a curse if thou should disobey—'"

Tara interrupted.

"Randy, that gives me the creeps," she said. "Can't we read something else?"

Ignoring her, Randy began to read again. Even though Tara thought the story he was reading was frightening, she soon found herself again mesmerized by the droning sound of his voice. After some time, Tara fell back on her brother's mattress, the makings of a dream working in her mind as his words echoed there. Sleep brought visions of her parents, standing far away from her, reaching out. Their faces were contorted with worried expressions, as if they were afraid something bad was going to happen to her.

Doreen awakened to a variety of noises from workers' tools to childish voices the next morning. As she washed and dressed in her private bathroom, a small voice called from the other side of the door. She opened the door to find Cindy standing there in a pink dotted swiss party dress that someone had donated to the children.

"Do I look pretty?" she asked.

"Beautiful," Doreen said. "But why are you so dressed up today?"

Cindy put her hands on her hips and tilted her head to one side.

"Because my mommy's coming!" she said.

Doreen knelt to Cindy's height.

"Honey," she said. "It's fun to pretend your mommy's coming to visit. But you know she really isn't, don't you?"

"She is! She is!" Cindy cried. "You just don't want her to come because you hate her!"

Doreen stood up, amazed. She'd never seen Cindy so angry.

"Cindy..."

The little girl ran out of the room, her patent leather maryjanes thumping over the hall carpet and downstairs.

Great way to start the morning, Doreen thought, as she walked down the hall toward the stairs.

Eager to start their first full day in their new home, the children had already finished breakfast by the time Doreen appeared in the kitchen. She greeted each one as they rushed by with a chorus of good-mornings except Cindy, who was ignoring her.

"Stay away from the workers!" she called.

Outside, they played tag, running bases, and Red Rover. Then Harry-John suggested they go exploring.

"I'll bet there's some neat stuff in those woods," he said.

"Lots of gross bugs," Randy said.

Tara wrinkled her nose. "I hate bugs. Don't you go bringing any into the house, Randy!"

Frankie gestured that he, too, wanted to explore.

"We better not wander all off different ways," Karen

said. "We don't know this place yet, and we could get lost."

"Tara and me'll go together," Randy said.

"Okay, then HJ and Frankie can come with me," Karen said.

They went off in opposite directions, trudging through the wildflowers and overgrown grass. Karen began to pick bluebells and heather to weave through her hair. When she found a striped beetle wiggling in the grass, she gently picked it up to show the others. HJ was tossing a rock up and down, but Frankie was nowhere in sight.

"Where'd Frankie go?" she asked.

"I don't know," Harry-John drawled. "I'm not the oldest one here, so I'm not in charge."

Karen covered her eyes against the sunshine and looked as far away as she could. She saw Randy and Tara in the distance, but there was no one else with them.

"Come on," Karen said, pulling Harry-John's arm. "Let's go look for him before he gets into trouble."

Frankie had gone into the woods and had come across a run-down metal shack. It stood in the center of a clearing, odd-smelling smoke puffing from a crooked pipe sticking out of its roof.

Frankie scanned the yard for toys, signs that he might find a new playmate. But he saw only broken pieces of wood, some chicken wire, and a few squirrel traps. Deciding there were no children here, he turned to head back to Karen and Harry-John.

Someone grabbed him from behind, and Frankie cried out. He felt himself being swung around, and was suddenly touching noses with an old man.

"What you doin' here?"

Frankie shook his head, unable to speak.

Marty peered at the child.

"Can't talk, can you?" Marty guessed. Frankie tried to run, but Marty caught hold of his T-shirt with fingers stained purple from berries. "Hold on, kid. I ain't gonna hurtja. Just wonderin' what a pipsqueak like you's doin' on my property. Ain't been no one here in years."

Frankie tried to read the old man's lips, but Marty's habit of jerking his head to look behind himself made it difficult. Even so, he sensed that the old man meant no harm, and he began to relax.

"You're one of them new kids, huh?" Marty asked. "You live with that fool woman who bought the big house?"

Frankie nodded.

"I been watchin' over that place for the past twen'y years," Marty said. "Sort of a caretaker, you might say. Glad someone else has the job now, but I think you'll be sorry."

The little boy said nothing, unable to understand.

Marty looked past Frankie's shoulder, as if he had heard something. The little boy looked around, hoping the other children were coming.

"Guess you gotta go," Marty said. "But afore you do, I got a message for that skinny lady who takes care of ya. You tell her if she's smart she'll pack up your things and get you all outa there, fast. Bad things are gonna happen if you stay. I seen it afore so I know what I'm talkin' about. Ain't been watchin' over that place for nothin'. There's gonna be blood and death and horror!"

"Frankie?"

Though Frankie couldn't hear Karen's voice, he guessed one of his friends was calling him by the way Marty looked beyond his shoulder. He turned and bolted for the meadow, unaware of what Marty was screaming.

"You hear me?" the old man called. "Blood and death! It'll come again! Blood and death!"

6

Frankie slammed head-on into Karen, knocking her to the ground. Crying out, Karen pulled herself to her feet and brushed pine needles from her T-shirt.

"What's the big idea?" she yelped.

Frankie looked back over his shoulder, gesturing madly. Now Karen's frown turned to a look of concern.

"Hey, something's wrong."

Frankie shook his head, pulling her along with him until they were out of the woods. Harry-John hurried up to them.

"What's the matter?" he asked.

"How should I know?" Karen snapped. "I can't understand him!"

She took the younger boy by the hand.

"Come on, Frankie," Karen said. "We'd better go talk to Doreen."

The children raced across the meadow, ignoring Randy and Tara's questioning yells. When they found Doreen, she immediately recognized Frankie's distress.

"Calm down, Frankie," she said. "You know I can't understand you when you sign so fast! Take a deep breath."

Frankie did as he was told. Then, in sign language, he managed to tell Doreen he had met a scary old man.

41

I'm scared, Doreen! Frankie signed, crying and throwing his arms around her.

"What happened?" Karen asked.

"It seems Frankie had a run-in with one of our neighbors," Doreen said. She pushed the deaf child gently away and spoke clearly to him. His eyes were round with fear as he lip-read her words. "I'll talk to him, Frankie. You don't need to be afraid."

She stood up and walked toward the front door. The children followed, standing on the porch as their guardian pushed past two workers carrying a ladder.

"I'll be right back," Doreen said.

Doreen took the path that cut through the woods, walking until she came upon the run-down shack. There was a pile of steel-jaw traps to one side of the dirt clearing, and thoughts of what happened to the animals caught in these cruel devices made Doreen shudder. What kind of man was she dealing with—who frightened little boys and subjected innocent animals to hideous deaths?

Refusing to be intimidated, Doreen pounded on the door. The whole shack rattled from the blows of her fist.

Moments later, an old man opened the door. His hair came down to his shoulders and was pure white, and stubble darkened his jaw. He glared at Doreen through cloudy blue eyes. He reeked of some unidentifiable smell.

"You come about that kid?"

"Frankie, you mean," Doreen said. "My name is Doreen Addison, and as you probably know I'm the new owner of the big house just outside these woods."

"Marty Laudon here," the old man said, holding out a gnarled hand.

Hesitating only a moment, Doreen took it. She had expected to meet some ranting, half-crazed mountain man. But Marty seemed polite, if in a begrudging way. She decided it was better to make friends than enemies.

"There seems to be some misunderstanding," she said, laughing a little. "Frankie was very upset when he came home. He told me you said it was dangerous for us to stay in the house. Of course, I'm certain he didn't understand. The child is hearing impaired, and—"

Marty had reached out with both hands just beyond Doreen's head. He clapped his hands together, making her jump.

"Damned skeeters," he said, wiping the dead insect off on the leg of his threadbare overalls. He looked at Doreen again. "The boy understood as well as anyone. That's exactly what I said. You have any smarts, girl, and you'll pack your things and get out. Haven't seen one good thing happen in that house in years."

"I'm not interested in the past," Doreen said.

"Then you're a damned fool," Marty sneered. "You think I'm some old man shootin' off his mouth, but I ain't. You'll see. When the evil in that place rises up again, you'll see who's crazy!"

Doreen took a deep breath.

"I have one thing more to say to you," she said, tired of being polite. "Don't ever frighten any of my children again. Now, I'll instruct them to stay off your property, but in turn I expect you to leave them alone."

"Got more right to be in that house than you," Marty said. "I've been takin' care of it these past decades. Kept the vandals and hippies away."

"You didn't do much else," Doreen said accusingly. "That house is going to take months to fix up!"

Marty snorted in reply, then turned and went back into the shack without a word. Doreen stood her ground for a few minutes, wondering what to do next. She hadn't expected to be dismissed so abruptly.

Well, she thought as she finally turned away, maybe there was no sense in wasting her time standing there any longer. As long as the children kept their distance, nothing bad would happen.

Haven't seen one good thing happen in that house in years.

But no one had lived in the house in twenty years, so it really didn't matter what Marty had said.

"You shouldn't be walking alone here."

Doreen gasped at the sound of a man's voice. It was Brendan, coming up behind her.

"You startled me!"

"I'm terribly sorry. Are you all right?"

"Of course I'm all right. It's just that I had an argument with a neighbor, and I don't really like getting off on the wrong foot that way."

She told him about Marty Laudon.

"I have seen him near the house at times," Brendan said. "But we have never spoken. If he ever threatens you, let me know. I'll see that he doesn't hurt you."

Doreen smiled. "I appreciate that, but I think I can handle things."

"You are a very strong woman," Brendan said. "I think that's why I like you. You're strong in spite of your parents."

Doreen backed away, shaking her head.

"My parents?" she asked. "What do you mean?"

"I know they hurt you," Brendan said. He reached out, brushing back a lock of hair that had fallen in her eyes. "But you don't need to worry. Nothing will hurt you again."

"I really don't understand," Doreen said. "I never mentioned my parents to you."

Brendan continued walking. "I'm sorry. Perhaps I'm invading your privacy. Of course you never mentioned your parents, and I don't blame you. I must have overheard your housekeeper talking about them."

"That could be," Doreen said, annoyed that Yolanda had been discussing her personal business. She changed the subject as they neared Addison House. "Brendan, would you like to come in for coffee?"

"Not now," Brendan said with a smile. "I have things to tend to. Besides, I'm all dirty and I smell of horses. You wouldn't want me at your table."

Doreen laughed.

"I love the smell of horses," she said. "Do you have

very many? The children would love to see them."

"I take care of half a dozen," Brendan said. "One day, I will let the children ride. But at the moment I have to be going. Good-bye!"

He gave her a quick kiss on the cheek and disappeared into the woods. Doreen ambled back to the house, smiling broadly. As much as Marty Laudon had angered her, Brendan Delacorte made her feel happy. Even giddy!

But her feeling of elation was short-lived. She suddenly remembered that he had mentioned her parents, and she wondered what he had meant when he said he didn't blame her for not wanting to talk about them. He couldn't mean her last foster parents—Nicholas and Betty Winters, who had been the kindest of all, taking her in even though she was sixteen years old and labeled unplaceable. In fact, Doreen had started Addison House with the money they left her when they passed away. And surely he couldn't have been referring to the family that had cared for her before that. Those people, the Stones, had wanted a demure little lady, and when they learned that Doreen was outspoken and somewhat tomboyish they tried strict, sometimes cruel, means to "correct" her.

"How could he know about them? I don't even like to think about them," she told herself firmly.

Still, she wondered how Brendan might have known about her past.

7

There really wasn't much time for Doreen to dwell on her strange conversation with Brendan. No sooner had she entered the house than Karen ran up to her, adjusting a dangling rhinestone earring. Her neck was swathed in colored beads, and she had a rhinestone brooch pinned to her pink T-shirt.

"Look what I found!" the teenager cried. "There was an old jewelry box in the back of my closet!"

"Good for you, Karen," Doreen said. "Who knows what other goodies you'll find in this big house."

"Maybe I could look in the attic," Karen suggested.

"Karen, I'm not sure—"

Doreen's words were cut off by a shrill scream from the direction of the kitchen. When they got there they found Cindy wailing in Yolanda's arms.

"The kitty! The kitty!"

"Cindy, what happened?" Doreen asked, looking at Yolanda with worry. "What kitty?"

Cindy picked up the hem of her blouse and wiped her nose. With a click of her tongue, Yolanda handed her a tissue.

"There's a k-kitty on the s-steps," Cindy stammered.

"What's so bad about that?" Karen asked.

Doreen stood up, taking Cindy by the hand. She expected to find some raggedy stray, maybe a cat who'd been

47

in so many fights that it was covered with ugly, frightening scars. But when she got outside and saw the animal her stomach turned, and she quickly pushed Cindy back into the house.

"What's out there?" Karen asked.

"Stay inside!" Doreen snapped. "Yolanda, come here please."

Yolanda went outside. She covered her mouth to stifle a gasp. The cat Cindy had found was hanging from the railing, a stripe of blood shining where a string cut into its oddly bent neck. Its mouth was agape, as if the cat had tried to scream in protest.

"Oh, that's horrid," Yolanda gasped. "There's . . . there's a piece of paper on its back, Doreen."

Leaning as close as she could without actually touching the cat, Doreen plucked the paper from the animal's body and read a message that had been carefully printed in black crayon.

GET OUT. DEATH IS NEAR.

She straightened up, disgust turning to anger.

"Who could have done such a thing?" Yolanda asked.

Karen started to open the kitchen door, too curious to stay inside.

"Doreen?"

"Karen, I said don't come out here," Doreen snapped. "Get me a paper bag from under the sink."

She looked at Yolanda.

"I know who did this," she said. "It must have been that crazy old man, Marty Laudon. I don't know why he wants us to leave this house, but I'll show him I won't be easily intimidated!"

The back door opened, and Karen came out with the bag.

"Oh, gross!"

"Just give me that," Doreen said, taking the bag. "And go back inside. Cindy's still crying, and she needs comforting."

Yolanda took Karen by the arm. "I'll be in with them," she said to Doreen. "You be careful."

As the housekeeper led Karen back into the house, Doreen stared at the cat for a moment, trying to decide how to get it down. In just a few moments it had gone from something horrible to something hateful, a symbol of one man's cruelty. Well, she thought as she reached carefully for the string, holding the paper bag open under the cat with her other hand, a man used to hunting and trapping would probably consider a stray cat just another type of game.

"You'll have to do better than this, Marty," she said, snapping the string. The cat fell into the bag with a thud, and Doreen quickly rolled the top closed. Then she headed across the field to the woods. She found Marty behind his shack, sitting on a small woodpile and rolling joints.

"Do you smoke a lot of that stuff?" she demanded.

Marty licked the edge of the paper and twisted the ends. "What stuff?"

"Marijuana!" Doreen said. "It might explain why you'd pull a stunt like this."

She dropped the paper bag, forcefully, at his feet. Marty nudged it with his toe but made no attempt to open it.

"This ain't pot," he said. "Just old-fashioned tobacco. Rolled my own all my life."

He stood up.

"What's that?"

"I'm sure you know," Doreen said. "You left it on my back steps. Poor little Cindy was terribly frightened! It was bad enough when you scared Frankie earlier today. But you really must be some kind of lunatic, hurting an innocent animal this way."

"I don't know what you're talkin' about," Marty said. He picked up the bag and unrolled the top. Taking a look inside, he sniffed loudly. "Just some dead cat."

"Just some dead cat!" Doreen cried. "Is that all you have to say? Mr. Laudon, I know you left this, thinking the scare would drive me out of Addison House. But it won't, and I'm here with a warning. If you ever—and I mean *ever*—try something like this again I will have you arrested!"

She was talking through her teeth, her patience completely gone, her hands clenched into fists.

"You're crazier than I am," Marty said. "I didn't kill no cat. I never kill nothin' I wouldn't cook and eat."

He leaned toward her, the burny smell of tobacco scratching at her nostrils.

"But someone else done it," he said. "Someone horrible. And there's gonna be more blood spilled if you don't leave!"

Doreen backed up a few steps.

"There *is* no one else," she insisted. "Your threats won't work—we aren't leaving our new home!"

As she turned to storm away, she didn't hear Marty mumble to himself.

"Don't have to make no threats," he said. "That house'll drive you 'way soon enough, if it don't kill you first."

When she began teaching at Oakwood High School, Judy was so dedicated to her students that she went home directly after classes to work on the next day's lessons. But in time she'd come to realize that teaching was more than grades and assignments. She started remaining after school to help those students having trouble with math. She enjoyed talking with the students and she admired their ideals about changing the world, remembering her own ambitions when she was their age. After one such discussion with a particularly civic-minded student, Judy decided to look into volunteer work. That investigation led her to Addison House.

If her parents were upset by her driving forty-five minutes twice a day to teach, they were beside themselves when she took on additional work.

"And you're not even being paid!" her mother cried.

"Mom, that's what *volunteer* means," Judy pointed out.

"But baby," her father said, in a tone he reserved for

those times when he wanted to lay a guilt trip on her, "it's such a long drive. And if you work after school hours, you'll be coming home in the dead of night. And on these mountain roads! My heart isn't good, Judy. If I have to spend each night worrying about you . . ."

Back then, it hadn't even occurred to her to suggest that she might move into an apartment in Oakwood. It wasn't just that she was still bound to her parents (being an only child—and a much pampered one—that was a rugged bond, indeed), it was mostly because her small teacher's salary made it impossible to even think about paying rent. But now, with Doreen's offer of a free room for the summer months, living close to the school seemed feasible after all. When September came, she'd merely ask to stay on at Addison House.

Her parents, however, had other ideas.

"Is there something wrong with this place?" her mother asked at breakfast that morning. "We don't stifle you, do we, dear? Because if I thought you were unhappy . . ."

"Of course she isn't unhappy," her father insisted before Judy could even speak. "How could she be? She has everything she'll ever need right here."

Except the right to be treated like an adult.

She let the thought stay unspoken, and hid her grumble by taking a long sip from her cup of coffee.

"I'm just thinking about it," she said. "It makes sense. I won't have to drive in the dark, and I won't be so exhausted from commuting."

"You wouldn't be exhausted if you gave up that extra work," her father said. "Summer is a time for teachers to vacation, like their students."

"I couldn't do that," Judy said. "You know me, Dad! Always busy, always on the go. I'd rot if I had to stay here all summer."

Poor choice of words, but before she could retract them, her mother was wailing.

"You see, Fred? She does hate it here!"

* * *

As she sped toward Oakwood, Judy flipped on the car radio to drive away the last echoes of her mother's voice. It would take some doing, but she knew she had to break away sometime. She wondered who the severance would be harder for—herself or her parents. She loved them dearly and would never hurt them. But it was time to move on, and as Doreen had pointed out the night before, she would need all the help she could get with the big new house. Judy could just imagine her mother's reaction if she knew that Judy had actually felt afraid on her first day there.

When she arrived at Addison House, she pulled up beside a battered a pickup truck. She had to walk sideways to avoid tripping over a pile of lumber waiting to be turned into new columns for the front porch. Since that was being worked on today, she walked around the back of the house to enter through the kitchen. And as she turned the corner of the house, Doreen came storming from the woods toward the house herself, her hands clenched at her sides. Judy held the door open for her.

"What happened?" she asked, following Doreen inside.

"We have a maniac for a neighbor!"

Cindy tugged at Doreen's pants leg.

"Did you take the kitty away?"

"I gave it to its rightful owner," Doreen grumbled.

"Will someone tell me what happened?" Judy demanded.

"I found a dead kitty," Cindy said.

"It was in a paper bag," said Karen. "All bloody."

Judy grimaced.

"Do we have to talk about it?" Tara groaned. "It's making my tummy hurt."

"Then I'll change the subject," Judy said, glancing at Doreen to indicate she wanted more information, later. "I've got some good news. I'm going to be moving in for a few weeks, to help out."

The children's cries of approval indicated that the cat incident was all but forgotten.

"It'll be fun having you with us all the time," Tara said.

Doreen and Karen sat down, helping themselves to sandwiches and iced tea.

"It'll make things easier for me, having another hand twenty-four hours a day," Doreen said. "If it wasn't for Yolanda, I don't know what I'd do."

"We need a man's help," Yolanda said. "Some kind of caretaker."

"Actually," Doreen said in a singsong tone," "I *have* had an offer of help from one of our neighbors. His name is Brendan Delacorte, and he's awfully nice. I can't wait for you to meet him."

Karen leaned forward, her eyes bright with interest.

"Is he young? Is he cute?"

"He's gorgeous," Doreen said.

"What does he do?" Judy asked.

Doreen shrugged, reaching for her glass. "That's all I know about him, Judy. Oh, he did tell me he has six horses."

"What does he look like?" Judy pressed. "This is so romantic!"

"He's got dark, wavy hair," Doreen said, grinning. "And incredible, deep brown eyes."

"Sounds dreamy," Judy said. She winked at Yolanda. "Maybe something's brewing?"

"Oh, wait a minute!" Doreen cried. "Don't be playing matchmaker just yet! The guy may be great-looking, but I don't know him well enough for that."

"Not all guys are like that fellow you went with last year," Judy said. "Give yourself a chance, Doreen."

Doreen didn't answer. She jiggled the ice in her glass, thinking about Brendan and wondering if he could possibly be different from the other men she'd known.

"Can we go outside now?" Tara asked.

"Sure, if you're done," Doreen said. "Just don't bother the crew."

"We know!" Harry-John moaned.

The children took off in various directions.

Cindy went out the back door, carrying a doll in her arms. She wondered where her mommy was today. Yesterday she had been in Cindy's bedroom. It was funny, but she didn't look very much like the mommy Cindy remembered from the apartment where she used to live. That mommy never smiled and had messy hair. But this mommy was very pretty, with beautiful curls. Cindy didn't mind that this mommy was different, because this mommy loved her. Pretty soon, she thought, she would go home again and be happy. Smiling now, she held her doll out at arm's length, her dress swirling around as she danced along the path that cut into the woods.

"Mommy's takin' me home! Mommy's takin' me home!" she sang.

A woman appeared behind her. The woman's black gown rustled softly in the breeze. Cindy stopped dancing, looking up with wide eyes that saw, not a mysterious stranger, but the woman she truly wanted her mother to be: beautiful, clean, smiling warmly. Without a word, she accepted the woman's hand and began to walk with her. She felt droplets of rain, but didn't pay attention to them. They crossed the field together, unseen. Even the workers up on the roof were not aware of the small child and the tall woman moving across the flowery grass.

"*I have a place to show you,*" the woman said. "*A place where you will be safe.*"

"Is something bad gonna happen?" Cindy asked.

"*Evil is always imminent,*" the woman said. "*Only prayer and sacrifice protect us. Come, and do not speak.*"

The land sloped upward just a bit. Cindy had to walk faster to keep up with the woman. On its downside, the hill was choked with barren vines, all twisted and cracked and smelling of dead things long buried beneath the tangle. Cindy struggled over the network of sticks, but the woman moved so gracefully it seemed her feet didn't even touch the ground. The rain had begun to fall steadily, but it was a summer shower, warm and gentle. The woman stopped suddenly at a spot where the vines still had life. They had climbed an ancient oak, growing so long over the past years that they created a curtain. Slowly, the woman parted them. Droplets of rain ran down her sleeve.

"Go inside," she said.

Cindy leaned forward, gazing into blackness.

"It's too dark," she protested. "I'm scared."

"There is nothing to fear," the woman said, *"if your heart is with the Lord. Only those who have sinned will find pain within the darkness."*

Cindy backed up a step.

"I don't really want to. Mommy, why are you scaring me? You're supposed to be my nice mommy, not the mean one from the 'partment!"

"I will be with you, child," the woman said. *"Follow me."*

She got down on her knees, the black gown billowing around her. She crawled forward until her black dress was camouflaged by the darkness and only the bottoms of her shoes were visible.

"Mommy, wait!" Cindy cried. "Don't leave me!"

She got down herself, but before she was even near the vines something grabbed her ankle. Cindy flipped onto her back and looked up at Marty Laudon.

"You let me go!" she cried.

"Not to that place I won't!" Marty shouted.

Cindy gasped with realization.

"You're the bad man who killed that kitty!"

"I never hurt no—"

"Mommy!"

"Hush up, you!" Marty ordered, so sternly that Cindy's mouth clamped shut. He let go of her ankle. "What're you doin', crawlin' into a dangerous cave like that?"

"My mommy's in there," Cindy said.

Marty looked over her shoulder, his already fair skin going a shade whiter.

"She told you that?"

Cindy nodded.

"Well, she's lyin'!" Marty cried. "You keep away from her, you hear! You keep away!"

The little girl jumped to her feet and started running back to the house as fast as she could. The rain began to fall harder, sending workers onto the front porch for shelter and the other children inside.

"Cindy, you're soaked!" Doreen cried when Cindy found her.

The little girl was trembling all over. Doreen embraced her.

"What happened, sweetheart?"

Cindy told her about the cave, and how the old man had prevented her from going inside.

"Well, I can't be angry at him for that," Doreen said. "Cindy, caves are very dangerous places!"

"But he scared me!"

"He should have been more gentle," Doreen said. "But you might have been hurt!"

Cindy shook her head, droplets of water spraying from her hair.

"My mommy wouldn't let me get hurt."

"Your mommy isn't here, Cindy," Doreen said firmly.

"Yes she is!" Cindy cried.

"Cindy, I'm not going to discuss this," Doreen said. "Listen, why don't you pick out a book from the shelf? I'll read you a story to get your mind off what happened."

"Okay," Cindy said halfheartedly.

She climbed from Doreen's lap and ran to find a picture book. As Doreen read, the little girl fidgeted with the gold horse charm on Doreen's necklace. By the time Doreen reached the final pages of the story, Cindy's eyes had closed and she was fast asleep.

Outside, the rain had increased to a rumbling thunder-shower. Fat drops pelted hard against the windows, the sound steady and soothing. As she rocked Cindy, Doreen began to grow tired herself, and soon she, too, was asleep.

She began to dream, seeing a dark-haired girl sitting by a roaring fire. She wore a long dress, and her back was ramrod straight as she turned the pages of the book in her lap. She turned and smiled as someone entered the room. In her dream, Doreen could not see the face of the man as he bent over the girl. He kissed her . . .

. . . and suddenly he was kissing Doreen.

She sighed, reaching out with her arms to encircle his neck, smelling a mixture of pine, horses, and sweat on him. His lips pressed harder against hers, his hands unfastening the buttons that ran down her back. His embrace was strong, and she pressed herself against him, wanting to gather in his warmth, wanting to be one with him. No one would hurt her when he was by her side. He would care for her, love her . . .

"*Love me*," he breathed. "*Love me, my gentle butterfly.*"

"*Yes*," Doreen moaned, her voice sounding so real in her dream. "*Yes, I want to love you. Hold me . . .*"

He tightened his grip around her, his mouth exploring hers once again. His embrace grew more and more urgent, almost as if he wanted to crush her.

"*You're hurt—*"

"*—ing me!*"

Doreen sat up abruptly, startled awake by the loudness of her own voice. Cindy jumped from her lap, rubbing her eyes in confusion.

"Oh, dear," Doreen said, leaning back with a sigh. "I guess I fell asleep and had a dream."

Some dream, she thought. *I can still feel pressure on my lips!*

"I didn't know big people slept in the daytime," Cindy said.

"The rain put me to sleep," Doreen told her. She stood

up. "Come on, Cynthia Margaret. The rain's stopped, and the sun's too nice for us to be indoors sleeping. Do you want to go to the store with me?"

"Sure!"

Doreen turned to leave the room, but stopped when she heard Cindy's giggles.

"What's so funny?"

Cindy pointed.

"Your dress," the little girl said, indicating the V back of Doreen's shift. "It's all unbuttoned! And what are those funny red marks?"

Doreen hurried to the full-length mirror in the hall. Indeed, all her buttons had come undone. Doreen shivered, remembering that the mysterious figure had unbuttoned her dress in the dream.

"I—I don't know," Doreen said, moving quickly to button them. "Maybe they came loose when I was rocking you."

But the red marks on her back looked like fingerprints from the embrace of an impassioned lover.

8

Following Doreen's orders, work began on the basement staircase the very next morning. Trevor Crane had been the first man to volunteer for the job because the wildflowers made his allergies almost unbearable. Although he was only forty-five, he was still one of the older men on the crew, and therefore got to pick the best work. At his side, hacking away at the staircase with an ax, stood his twenty-year-old nephew, Hector.

"You know, Uncle Trev," Hector said, swinging the ax, "this staircase doesn't really fit with the rest of this place."

"How so?"

"Well, most of the work we've been doing has been cosmetic," Hector said. "The house itself is structurally sound—like someone built it to last for years. But these stairs—they're a piece of junk."

Trevor hoisted a heavy piece of rotted wood onto his shoulder and carried it to a junk pile he'd started at the back of the cellar. The light was dim, even with the windows open. Suddenly he thought he saw something large and long running through the shadows. He guessed it was a rat, and turned away.

"Maybe the builder got lazy at this point," Trevor said. "Or maybe these aren't the original stairs. Somebody could have replaced them somewhere along the line."

"Yeah, that could be," Hector agreed. "The rest of the

house is real fancy, but these things are plain-Jane."

"We won't be doing anything ritzy ourselves," Trevor said, "but you can bet our staircase will last a long time. Here, help me clear out some of this stuff before you do any more."

Together, the two men carried debris to the pile at the back of the cellar.

"It stinks back here," Hector complained.

"What do you want from a basement that's been closed up for all these years?"

"But how come it only smells bad in this one area?" Hector asked. "It's like something up and died."

Trevor thought of the rat he'd just seen, and he wondered what kinds of vermin had lived out their lives in this dark place. He sniffed deeply, but couldn't detect much.

"With these sinuses," he said, "I could climb into a coffin and not smell the stiff."

Hector laughed and went back to his ax. The job he shared with his uncle today was to tear down the existing staircase. They'd use a ladder to get out, and tomorrow more of the crew would join them to build a new one. Hector and Trevor alternated between axing the wood and carrying debris. Each time he went back to the shadowed pile, Hector found the smell a little stronger.

"Lemme borrow your flashlight, Unc," he said, holding out his hand. "I'm gonna figure this out."

He aimed the light at the pile of old wood, but found nothing unusual there. Just a few cobwebs and some broken pieces of glass. But as the light climbed up the wall, his question was answered.

"Gross," he said.

"What is it?" Trevor asked, coming up behind him.

"Look at that green fuzz all over everything," Hector said. "Stuff growing here must be three inches thick."

Trevor leaned over his nephew's shoulder. Indeed, thick patches of shiny moss covered much of the wall at this end of the room.

"How come it's only here?" Hector asked. "The other walls are clean!"

"Don't ask me," Trevor said, reaching into his tool belt for a screwdriver. He leaned forward and started scraping at the growth. "We'd better warn Miss Addison that she might have a water leak somewhere down here. That'd be the only thing I could think of to explain this."

The end of the screwdriver made a loud scraping noise.

"This wall isn't smooth under here," Trevor said. "I'd guess it's wood, although I don't know why they'd put up a wood wall when the other three are stone. Maybe there were shelves up here at one time. But we'd better clean it up in the next few days."

Throughout the morning, the two men continued working on the stairs, exchanging small talk and stopping on occasion to rest. When the work was finally through, Hector helped his uncle to carry the ladder to the doorway over their heads. It had been kept closed and locked from the inside for safety reasons. Trevor rested the ladder against its base, then began to climb to the top.

"Glad that work is over," he said.

"I'm sweating like a pig," Hector agreed. "Man, I thought working under the sun was hard!"

"I'm not sure pigs sweat," Trevor said. "That's why they wallow in the mud all the time."

"So, find me some mud and I'll wallow in it," Hector answered, holding fast to the base of the ladder.

Trevor reached for the lock and unhooked it, then backed down a few rungs to make room for the door's swing. He opened it carefully, just in case one of the kids might be running around. Bright light from the hallway shone down on him, turning the image Hector saw from down below into a silhouette. Unused to the brilliance after several hours in dim light, Hector shaded his eyes with one hand.

But Trevor could do no such thing. His gaze was fixed on the face of a woman who glared down at him with the stern expression of a headmistress. She held up one of her arms, and Trevor saw that she was about to strike him with a cane! He opened his mouth, ready to ask who she was, but no sound came out.

"Intruder! How dare you deface my property? How dare you destroy that which I built according to God's plan?"

"Uncle Trev?" Hector called from down below. "What's the matter?"

Hector could not see the woman, nor could he see the cane swinging through the air, smashing hard against his uncle's forehead. All he saw was the birdlike movements of Trevor's arms as the older man lost his balance, struggling frantically to regain it as he fell back off the ladder.

"Uncle Trev!"

Hector jumped back as his uncle crashed to the floor, landing in a broken heap at his feet. Strangely, the noise was almost like the clap of wood against cement they had been hearing all day as they threw broken pieces of the steps into the debris pile. Hector sunk to his knees, his mouth hanging open, and gently touched his uncle's shoulder.

"Uncle Trev, what happened?" he asked, his voice like a child's. Blood began to trickle out from beneath his uncle's body, soaking through the knees of the younger man's jeans. "Uncle Trev, can you answer me?"

He wouldn't let himself think that Trevor couldn't answer him. He had to get help for his uncle! He had to act fast!

"I'll be back! Right back!"

Hector scrambled up the ladder, leaving the cellar door wide open as he raced down the hall for help. Randy, who had been looking through the refrigerator for a snack, heard his cries and went to investigate. The cellar below was like a bottomless pit, dark and foreboding. But the light over Randy's head shone directly down on Trevor's twisted shape, and the blood surrounding him gleamed red.

Slowly, Randy sat down, staring at the construction worker. The child's feet dangled over the edge of the doorway. Thoughts raced through his head, thoughts that were unnatural for a boy of ten. Passages on destruction and damnation from the Bible he'd found came to mind, and Randy tried to use them to make sense of the gruesome sight fifteen feet below him.

"It was the Lord's will," Randy whispered. "You brought this devastation upon yourself with your wicked ways."

Randy did not ask himself what the man could have done to deserve such punishment from God, or what his wicked ways might have been. There was no time for such questions, because he was suddenly being yanked up to his feet.

"Randy Welder, what are you doing here?" Doreen cried.

Randy turned around to look at her, blinking a few times.

"I—I don't know," he mumbled, unable to remember entering the hallway.

Doreen was surrounded by several of the workers and their foreman, who hurried down the ladder to Trevor's side.

"My God, if you had fallen down there, too . . ."

It was too horrible to consider, so Doreen just pulled Randy close and hugged him. She glared at Hector.

"You left the door open!"

"I—I'm sorry," Hector stammered. "But my uncle . . ."

The foreman yelled from down below.

"Get an ambulance!"

"I'm sorry," Doreen said to Hector. "I shouldn't have jumped on you. Your poor uncle!"

Ignoring her, Hector looked down into the cellar.

"Is he okay, Sam?"

"He's alive," Sam called. "But just barely! We've got to get him to the hospital."

One of the other workers, a young woman, had already hurried to the kitchen phone to call for help. Hector climbed down the ladder himself, praying that his uncle would be all right. Hushed whispers ran through the small group in the hallway. Doreen heard Randy mumbling something, and she leaned closer to hear.

"The Lord is my shepherd," he was saying. "I shall not want. He leadeth . . ."

To her surprise, the child recited the entire Twenty-third Psalm. Doreen was about to ask him where he'd learned it when shouts heralded the arrival of the ambulance. Two burly men raced down the hall and into the cellar, working quickly to save Trevor Crane's life. Some of the other children appeared, watching the whole scene with wide-eyed curiosity. Frankie inched closer to Doreen. Marty's crazed words came to his mind.

Bad things' ll happen in that place!

But the little boy had no way of telling Doreen this.

"Okay, move aside up there!" someone yelled.

The paramedics had strapped Trevor to a hard plastic stretcher, and with the help of several others were slowly pulling him to the floor above. Trevor's eyes were closed, and blood splotched his face. Karen turned away with a groan, feeling sickened by the sight of the man's bloodied skull.

"I don't know how it happened," Hector was saying. "He was climbing up the ladder, and then he just fell back, like he lost his balance."

The paramedics hurried through the house with Trevor, as Hector followed close behind.

"Don't make any sense to me," the young woman who'd called for the ambulance said.

"What's that, Claudia?"

"I don't see Trevor losing his balance," she said. "Hell, he used to work on high rises in Manhattan, and on some bridges, too! How does a guy with twenty-five years experience lose his balance?"

Some of the workers shook their heads in wonder.

"I'll pray for him," Randy said.

"We'll all pray for him," Judy put in. She began to gather the children. "Come on, it's dangerous here."

As Judy led the children out of the tiny hallway, Doreen pushed the basement door shut and locked it. While part of her hoped to God the worker would be okay, another part worried about possible lawsuits that might arise from this accident. Would she be held responsible? Would her insurance cover all the costs of being sued? What if they tried to take Addison House away from her?

"What would happen to the children?" she asked out loud.

Without another thought, she hurried to her office and rummaged through her desk drawers for the name of the lawyer who had helped her close the deal on this house. Maybe he could give her advice. She dialed his number and heard his voice come over the line. It took a moment for Doreen to realize she had a recording. Disappointed, she left a message, telling him it was important that she talk to him as soon as possible.

When she hung up, Doreen's worries grew stronger. The worst thing that could happen to her was to lose Addison House and the children she had grown to love!

Doreen folded her arms across her stomach and hung her head, fighting tears.

Suddenly she felt two warm hands on her shoulders. With a cry, she turned around to find Brendan behind her.

"Did I startle you?" he said. "The front door was open, and no one heard me call. I hope you don't mind that I just walked in."

Doreen smiled a little.

"There you go again," she said, "always here when I need someone."

Brendan leaned against her desk, then reached down to lay a finger gently on Doreen's cheekbone.

"You have tears in your eyes," he said, concern in his expression. "Has someone hurt you? Was it that old man, the one named Marty?"

Doreen shook her head.

"I'm just worried," she said.

She told him what had happened that afternoon, and

how she was terrified that she'd lose Addison House.

"But that can't happen!" she cried. "I've worked too hard for this, and I can't lose my children!"

Unable to control her emotions any longer, Doreen burst into tears. She did not protest when Brendan eased her out of the chair and into his strong arms. It felt good to be held so lovingly. For a long time after her tears subsided, she simply rested her head against his chest. Then she pulled away, rubbing her eyes.

"Oh, look at me," she said. "After all that's happened in my life, I didn't think anything could make me cry again. But here I am, sobbing like a baby!"

"You have every right," Brendan said, stroking her cheek. "But don't worry, he'll be all right and you won't lose this place. You were meant to be here, to care for children as you do. I promise you, nothing will hurt you."

"I wish I could be sure," Doreen said. "But until I hear what happens to Trevor Crane, I'm going to do a lot of praying."

Brendan pulled away from her suddenly.

"Yes, pray," he said. "That is what's expected of you. But I can see that now you need to be away from this house for a while. Why don't you come for a walk with me? I'd like to show you the lake near my house."

"I'd like that very much," Doreen said. "Let me tell Yolanda I'm leaving, and—"

"No," Brendan said. "We won't be gone that long. And if the children know where you are we'll be interrupted."

"But what if something else happens?"

"Nothing will happen," Brendan promised. "You have others to watch the little ones. Please, don't you deserve some time alone?"

Doreen nodded. "I do need time alone, whether or not I can afford it. Come on, Brendan. Let's go see that lake."

Arm in arm, they walked from the house together. Doreen didn't know that a strange woman was watching her, wanting desperately to pull her away from Brendan's side. But the stranger kept her distance, standing in the midst of the workers, who couldn't see her. There would be time to end that romance, time to have Brendan for herself. She would make the pretty young woman sorry she ever came here.

9

"I didn't even know there was a lake here," Doreen said. "I'm sure the kids will love it."

As she walked with Brendan across the field, they looked down at the grass and wildflowers.

"It's very beautiful," Brendan said. "More like a pond. It was dug quite a few years ago by a family who used to live here. I find it's perfect when I need to rest."

"I need to relax myself," Doreen said. "This accident has me so upset I can't even think straight."

They started out on a wide path that cut through the forest, the same path that led to Marty's shack. Doreen's senses were quickly confronted by a strange smell, and she wondered what game Marty had stewing in his kitchen.

"Has the old man bothered you again?" Brendan asked.

"Sometimes I think you can read my mind," Doreen said. "No, I haven't heard a word from him."

She thought of how Marty had frightened Cindy, and she felt a bit guilty that she hadn't yet confronted him about it. But she wouldn't let herself worry now. She was on this walk to put herself at ease, and she just wasn't going to think about any other problems she might have.

"Just for a few minutes," she said, "I don't want to talk about anything bad. Then, maybe, I'll be able to handle things a little better when I get back to the house. I really—"

She stopped short, her words cut off by the scene that suddenly came into view. Before her, a small sapphire-colored lake hugged the base of a hill so thick with evergreens it seemed carpeted. Weeping cherry tree branches drooped toward the water, casting finger-length leaves onto the surface to mix with windblown flower petals.

"Oh, look at the swans!" Doreen cried, pointing toward a pair of regal white birds. She sighed. "Brendan, this is beautiful. How could I think of any problems while I'm here?"

"That's why I brought you," Brendan said. "Come with me, and I'll show you the place where I like to sit and think."

Taking her hand, he led her through the bluebells, thistle, and buttercups that trimmed the water's edge, stopping at a low, flat rock. As they sat down together, Doreen realized that he hadn't let go of her hand, and it made her feel a little giddy.

Steady, Doreen! You've put yourself in a helluva situation, and you know how easily you fall in love! Don't let him take advantage!

Suddenly, Brendan released her hand. He crossed his own hands over his lap and leaned forward. When he spoke, his dark eyes seemed to be fixed on a lily pad floating just a short distance from the rock.

"I never thought we'd be together," he said.

"Brendan?"

Doreen wasn't certain she had heard him right.

"There are so many things to keep us apart," Brendan said. "So many people who wouldn't want this. I suppose —I suppose you'll have a lot of explaining to do when you get back."

"Of course I won't," Doreen said. "I don't understand what you mean. Who wouldn't want what?"

Now Brendan looked at her.

"The people you live with," he said. "I know they disapprove of me."

"Nonsense," Doreen said. "They haven't even met you."

"But we're alone together," Brendan said. "Won't they disapprove?"

"Who?" Doreen asked. "Six little kids? My house-keeper? I can tell you, my friend Judy would think this was very nice."

A twinge of worry shot through her. He was talking so strangely, as if they were lovers meeting in secret! But Doreen quickly pushed the thought aside. He was just being polite, worrying about her reputation, for heaven's sake! It was nice to meet a guy who cared like that. Maybe his genteel but antiquated manners came from a secluded upbringing in the mountains, far from modern city life.

"Still, I don't think we should stay," Brendan said. "I don't want to cause any trouble."

"I'm in no hurry to get back," Doreen said. She stretched backward, resting her palms on the rock behind her. "We just got here. And it's so beautiful here I just can't believe it. Like something an artist would paint to show the perfect summer day."

Brendan was silent as Doreen watched the swans circling the lake. After a few moments, she realized that he was staring at her. She turned to him.

"You're very beautiful," he said. "More beautiful than I remembered."

"Oh, thanks," Doreen said.

Now, that sounded dumb! Oh, thanks! Stop acting like a thirteen-year-old, Doreen. Even Karen could do better!

"You—you're really nice to say that," Doreen said. She felt awkward, having an idea where this strange conversation was leading and afraid to go there.

She stood up quickly.

"You know, maybe I *should* go back," she said. "The kids are probably wondering about me."

"We'll come back again, won't we?" Brendan asked, standing himself. His eyes were so hopeful that for a moment he reminded Doreen of one of the children.

"Of course we will," Doreen said. "It's just that I have a lot to do. Would you walk me back to the house?"

Brendan nodded. They walked in silence until they were out of the woods.

"I hope I didn't offend you," Brendan said.

"What do you mean?"

"Well, I was a little forward," Brendan said, "back there by the lake. It was just that you were so beautiful, and I was so moved. . . ."

"The lake got to me, too," Doreen said. She decided it was as good a time as any to talk about her own feelings. "I like you too, Brendan. I think about you a lot. But I'm afraid, also."

"Of course you are," Brendan said.

Doreen frowned at him.

"I don't think you understand," she said. "I'm afraid of starting any new relationship. The last man I went out with turned out to be a real bastard."

Brendan straightened up, breathing in sharply.

"I would rather not hear words like that," he said. "Not from a woman."

Doreen glared at him.

"Oh, really?" she snapped. "Well, you have no idea what my life was like with that man! He was a crazy person!"

"I'm sorry," Brendan said. "But why did you stay with a crazy person?"

Doreen shrugged, starting to walk again.

"He was handsome and, in the beginning, very devoted," she said. "But one day, with no provocation, he hauled off and gave me a black eye."

Brendan touched her cheek, as if to feel a phantom wound.

"I would kill him," he said.

"He's long gone from my life," Doreen said. "But he taught me that you just can't know what a person might be hiding."

"I'd never hide anything from you," Brendan said.

"Maybe not," Doreen told him. "But I don't want to be rushed into finding out. I'd like to get to know you better slowly, Brendan. Please don't expect things to happen too quickly. I just couldn't handle it."

They reached the back of the house.

"Just remember this," Brendan said. "I've waited a long time for you. And nothing is going to keep us from being together."

Taking her face in his hands, he bent down to kiss her softly on the lips. It was a quick kiss, actually chaste, but it left Doreen's heart pounding. She stood on the back steps, watching his retreating figure through what seemed to be a mist. Brendan disappeared into the woods before she opened the kitchen door. As she did so, a gust of icy wind wrapped around her.

"Hussy!"

Doreen looked behind herself, but there was no one there. Funny, she had imagined that same breathless word the day she nearly fell off the cellar steps. Thoughts of that day brought back Trevor Crane's accident, and the brief respite from reality that she'd enjoyed at that lake was lost. She hurried into the house, deciding she'd call the hospital to find out the man's condition.

More malevolent words were whispered at her back, but Doreen was completely unaware of the being that watched her.

Conversation at dinner that night centered on the accident, though Doreen was careful not to let the children know she was worried. The hospital refused to give her detailed information because she wasn't family, but she understood that Trevor was at least still alive. The children soon dropped the subject and chattered on about their own interests. By the time bedtime arrived for the younger ones, it seemed they had completely forgotten about the accident.

* * *

"So, what do you think of our house so far?" Doreen said as she signed the question to Frankie while she tucked him in.

Frankie shook his head, looking toward his window. In sign language, he reminded Doreen that Marty had warned them that bad things would happen.

And the man fell today, he signed.

"That was just an accident," Doreen said. "When people are doing dangerous work, like fixing staircases, things like that are bound to happen."

But Marty said—

"You never mind what Marty said," Doreen interrupted. "He's a nutty old man and he won't be bothering you again."

She leaned down to kiss him.

"Good-night, Frankie," she said. "See you in the morning."

Just before closing the door and clicking off his light, she whispered, "Love you!"

Frankie signed *I love you* back, then closed his eyes. His dreams came quickly, visions of Marty chasing him. His screams sounded muffled, like something heard from underwater, and Marty's shouts were like the distant rumble of train engines. Then the dreams changed, and instead of being part of them Frankie was an observer. He watched another little boy being chased, a blond-haired boy in pajamas. There was a man running after him, but it wasn't Marty. The man grabbed the little boy, tucking him under one arm. As the dream child screamed and kicked, Frankie thrashed under his covers. In his mind, he watched as the man threw the boy onto a bed and raised a belt into the air...

Frankie flipped from his back to his stomach, burying his head under his pillow as he came awake. He curled his legs up underneath himself, his heart thumping. Memories of the abuse he'd received as a toddler came flooding back to him. He could see his parents towering over him, his mother pointing an accusing finger, his father pulling his belt off through the loops of his pants.

But the man in the dream wasn't his father, and the little boy was a child he didn't know. It was just a nightmare!

Doreen had told him no one would ever hurt him again. He'd been with her longer than any of the other children, and she was the one who had been teaching him sign language. He wished Doreen could adopt him, or that maybe one of the nice people who sometimes came to visit would take him home, the way they'd taken other children home over the years. But his parents refused to give him up, even though they were forbidden to have contact with him. There was always the fear they'd come back for him, and sometimes that fear gave him nightmares.

Frankie felt something rub against his arm, and as he pulled it quickly under the covers he turned to see who had come into his room. He felt his heart jump in his throat.

It was the little boy from his dream.

Go 'way, Frankie signed, thinking he was still dreaming.

The child shook his head, then started to back away. Frankie sat upright, watching him as he tucked himself into a dark corner of the room. The other boy's eyes were wide, and tears streamed down his round cheeks. He held out his arms to Frankie as if asking for help.

Somehow, Frankie understood. He knew the little boy had been hurt the same way he'd been hurt. Unafraid now, he climbed out of bed and went to comfort the small stranger.

But when he tried to put his arms around the child, his hands shot through thin air, striking the wall in front of him. Frankie backed away, looking all around. The child was gone. Maybe he'd been dreaming again, but it was so *real*. Was he awake? Was he still sleeping?

He only knew he didn't want to be alone. Groping through the darkness, he opened the door and headed toward Doreen's room. But when he saw a light underneath Randy's door, he knocked on it instead. A moment later, Randy opened it.

"I said 'Come in,'" Randy said, annoyed. "Oh, it's you, Frankie. What's up?"

Frankie understood the questioning look in his friend's eyes. He moved past Randy, his head bowed.

Bad dream, he signed.

"Oh, yeah?" Randy said. "You can climb into bed with me."

He gestured the younger boy toward his bed, folding back the covers. Frankie climbed in gratefully.

"You have too many bad dreams," Randy said. "But if you let the Lord into your heart, you'll be free of them."

Frankie shook his head, unable to understand. He watched as Randy opened up a black book, studied Randy's lips as he began to read from the Bible. Frankie couldn't make out a lot of the words, which were far beyond a second-grader's abilities. But just being with his friend comforted him, and soon he settled back onto Randy's pillow to fall asleep. Oblivious to the smaller child's snoring, Randy went on with his reading.

Down the hall, Doreen waited in her own bed for one of the children to enter her room. She'd heard a door open, and small footsteps on the hall rug. When no one showed up she rolled over and went to sleep herself.

Some time later, she was awakened by the feel of warm pajamas against her back. Doreen turned and took a small body into her arms. In the dark, she couldn't tell which child had climbed into bed.

"Frankie? Cindy?"

There was a sniffle, and then: *"Daddy's after me."*

Realizing that one of the children must have had a nightmare, Doreen reached out to turn on her light.

She was alone in her bed.

There was nothing there but a pillow she'd tossed to her side while sleeping.

10

Anxious to know what was happening with Trevor, Doreen made another call to the hospital. She waited impatiently as she was connected from one desk to another. Finally a woman came on and asked, "Are you a member of the family?"

"No, Mr. Crane was hurt here at my house. I just wanted to find out how he is."

"He's in Intensive Care," the woman replied. "That's all I can tell you."

"What does that mean?" Doreen asked. "Is he going to be all right?"

"I'm sorry," the woman said a little more abruptly. "But unless you're a member of the family, and come here in person, I can't give out any more information."

"All right," Doreen said with a sigh. "Thank you for your time."

Frustration made her muscles tense as she hung up the phone, no more informed now than she'd been before her walk to the lake with Brendan yesterday.

I know what I'll do, she thought. She picked up her purse and her car keys and walked down the hall to the kitchen.

"Yolanda, I'm taking a trip to the hospital. Can you handle the kids for a while?"

"You know I can. Are you going to look in on that poor workman?"

"Yes," Doreen said. "I can't get a straight answer when I call. But it helps to have a friend over there. I'm going to see what Larry Harlan can find out for me."

As Doreen walked across the yard to the station wagon, Randy and Tara came running up to her.

"Where are you going?"

"To the hospital," Doreen said. "I'll be back a little later."

"Can I come for the ride?" Tara asked.

"Me, too!" Randy cried. "If Tara's going, I'm going, too!"

"Neither one of you is going," Doreen said, laughing. "I've got some business to attend to, and hospitals are no place for you two. Go on back with the others and play."

Disappointed, Randy and Tara turned and walked hand in hand to the backyard. Doreen was relieved to see that Randy wasn't acting strangely, as he had been when he saw Trevor's broken body. She decided that Randy's mumbling of the Twenty-third Psalm was the result of shock. The image of Trevor lying at the bottom of that ladder, in his own blood, must have been horrible to a ten-year-old!

As she drove down the road that led to the main highway, Doreen thought about Trevor. For the most part, she'd been worried about Addison House, and now that she was on her way to the hospital to inquire about him, she felt a little guilty. Poor Trevor! She wondered what damage the fall had done to him, and hoped he'd be okay.

About a half mile from her house, Doreen noticed someone walking along the edge of the road. It was a woman, dressed in a long brown dress that swept up clouds of dirt. Her dark hair fell all the way to her hips. As Doreen came closer, the woman turned, and Doreen gasped when she saw her face.

There were bruises under her deep-set brown eyes and a trickle of blood at the edge of her swollen lip. Her dress was torn and filthy, and she walked hunched over as if she was in terrible pain.

That poor thing! Doreen thought. She looked for a place that was wide enough for her to pull over. At last, she managed to park on an overgrown patch of grass and gold-enrod. She turned off the engine and got out of the car, intending to walk back to where she'd seen the woman.

But as far as her eyes could see in either direction there was no one in sight.

That's strange. Where on earth could she have gone?

There were woods on either side of the road—ever-greens, oaks, and maples growing clear to the edge of the blacktop in most places. Could the young woman have turned into the trees? Doreen walked back down the road for a few yards.

"Hello?" she called, hoping the woman was near enough to answer her.

But there was only the chattering of a raven.

When Doreen finally arrived at the parking lot of Oak-wood General, she checked her watch and realized that Larry was probably on a break.

The lobby was crowded, and no one paid much atten-tion to Doreen as she passed the front desk. As she rode the elevator up to Pediatrics, she wondered if her friend Larry would be able to help her.

Dr. Larry Harlan had been assigned by the state to be the children's pediatrician. They liked him for his good humor and his patience, and especially for the fact that he always remembered birthdays. He was a year older than Doreen, and through the years he had become one of her best friends.

She heard his loud, hearty laughter as she stepped off the elevator, and she looked down the hall to see him just coming out of a room. His eyebrows went up when he saw her, and he opened his arms. Larry was a short man with muscular arms that spoke of years of weight lifting. He had blond hair and sky-blue eyes that seemed to dance when he smiled.

"Doreen! What brings you here? I haven't seen you in a long time."

"I've been so busy with the new house," Doreen said.

Larry took her arm and started to lead her to his office.

"When are you going to invite me over?"

"You know you're always welcome," Doreen said.

When they reached his office, Doreen explained what had happened to Trevor Crane.

"I really need to know how he's doing," Doreen said. "I'm so worried his family is going to sue, Larry. I know that sounds insensitive, considering what that poor man is going through, but I really do have to think about my kids. I can't afford a lawsuit!"

"I doubt they'll sue," Larry reassured her. "What could they take from you?"

"That house must be worth something . . ."

"Doreen, I'm not the right person to talk to," Larry said. "Why don't you call your lawyer?"

"I did," Doreen said. "He's no help. Larry, for my own peace of mind I just need to know how Trevor Crane is doing. Is there any way you can keep me posted?"

Larry nodded. "Probably. One of the doctors in the Intensive Care unit used to be a classmate of mine. He still owes me money on a bet, so I'm sure I can collect payment in this way, instead."

"You don't know what this means to me," Doreen said. "Just to know the man's status will really help. Thanks, Larry."

She stood up.

"I'm sure you've got kids to see," she said. "And my own kids are probably wondering where I am."

"I'll be by soon to visit," Larry said. "Tell them all I said hi."

He walked Doreen to the elevators.

"Listen," he said, looking down at the tiled floor, "I'm off this weekend. Want to do something?"

"Oh, I can't," Doreen said, regret in her voice. "There's just too much work to be done at the house. Maybe in a few weeks . . ."

"Sure," Larry said. "In a few weeks."

The elevator door opened, and Doreen walked in. She waved good-bye to Larry until the door shut, feeling a little guilty. Larry was always offering to take her on a date, but there had never been a chance to accept. Well, she had to admit to herself that she was afraid to accept. She was afraid of ruining a good friendship by allowing herself to get involved with the doctor.

When Doreen arrived home, there was a message waiting from Larry—Trevor Crane had suffered a badly broken elbow and two broken ribs as well as some serious lacerations and bruises on his head. But worse than that, he hadn't regained consciousness yet. And although Larry tried to sound confident that the man would come around, Doreen knew the news was not good.

11

Karen leaned over the bathroom sink, staring into the mirror as she carefully penciled liner under her dark lashes. Harry-John came in, stopping abruptly in the doorway.

"That figures," he said. "I told Doreen you'd be hogging up the bathroom all the time."

"It's mine just as much as yours."

"And I've got to go," Harry-John said. "So get lost."

"I will not! Use the bathroom down the hall."

"It's too cold."

He reached for a small cut glass bottle that sat on the edge of the sink. Holding it up to the light, he twirled it to make rainbows on the pink-and-white tiled walls.

"Give that back!" Karen cried. "That was my mother's and I don't want you to break it."

Harry-John handed her the bottle.

"Yolanda's already called us to lunch," he said. "You'd better hurry."

"I've got to make myself look nice," Karen said. "I'm thirteen years old and I'm almost a woman. I can't look like a sloppy kid!"

"You just want the workers to notice you," Harry-John said.

Karen groaned. "You're impossible, HJ!"

With that, she turned and stormed from the bathroom.

In her own room, she carefully placed the glass perfume vial on her dresser. She had seven such bottles, all from her mother's collection. Karen enjoyed taking the bottles down and looking them over, then placing them back in precise order on the eyelet runner that topped her dresser.

She got so caught up in what she was doing that she lost track of the time. When she finally went downstairs, Doreen, who had just gotten back from the hospital, and Yolanda were the only ones left in the kitchen.

"This isn't a restaurant, Miss Steiff," Yolanda said. "With six children to feed, I serve lunch only once. If you want to waste your time putting on makeup and . . ."

Doreen reached across the table, tapping the back of Yolanda's hand to silence her. She understood what looking nice meant to Karen, a girl who had been told many times throughout her childhood that she was ugly and worthless.

"It's all right. Karen, sit down and eat. And when you're finished, please take off some of that jewelry. It's pretty, but you look like you're dressed for a party, and I don't think you'd want to lose any of it when you go outside."

"Okay," Karen mumbled, picking up her spoon. "But I still think I should look nice."

"You *do* look nice," Doreen said. "You're very pretty, even without a speck of makeup. I only wish you'd believe me."

"My aunt and uncle said—"

"We've discussed your aunt and uncle before, Karen. They were wrong. You aren't ugly, and that's that."

Doreen and Yolanda went into the living room while Karen finished her lunch by herself. She was trying to forget the unkind words of her aunt and uncle, when Tara came in looking for her.

"Judy was getting some stuff out of the attic," Tara said. "And she left the ladder down. I'll bet there's some neat things up there. You want to look?"

The two girls carefully climbed the ladder to the dark

attic above. The warm air from the house had risen up and
had become trapped under the eaves of the roof. With no
open window to cool it, the attic was steaming hot and
musty. Fuzzy mold grew everywhere, and as they walked
across the floorboards the girls did their best to avoid it.

"Yecch," Karen said. "It smells disgusting up here!"

"Look at all these boxes!" Tara cried. "Maybe there's
toys!"

"Or neat old clothes or jewelry," Karen said.

Looking around, she spotted a string of pearls dangling
from a partially open jewelry box. It was a child's box,
made of cardboard and covered with white vinyl that had
buckled and shriveled in the heat. She could barely make
out the picture of a ballerina on the top. She opened the
box all the way and pulled out the beads. The clasp was
broken, and a few of the fake pearls had cracked in half.
But Karen thought she could fix the necklace and have a
new piece of jewelry to add to her wardrobe.

"That's pretty," Tara said, looking into the box herself
as Karen hung the beads around her neck. "Oh, look! Isn't
this dog pin cute? Look at the pink diamonds in his eyes!"

"Here, I'll pin it on for you," Karen said.

She turned for another look, squinting to see through the
light that came through the small, grimy window.

"Let's see what's in that trunk over there."

They pulled out old clothes, giggling as they dressed in
oversized circle skirts, padded sweaters, and embroidered
cumberbunds.

"I could make a *great* wardrobe out of all this, "Karen
said. "This old stuff is what you see in all the magazines."

She crossed the attic to a tall, broken mirror that sat near
the window. Giving a model's twirl in front of it, she admired herself as the beads swung out from her neck. Suddenly, something caught hold of them, yanking them.
Karen was too startled to cry out, and for a second she
didn't fight back as the beads tightened around her neck.
The outer edges of her vision darkened, and the small tunnel she was looking through filled with tiny stars. She

could see Tara across the room, her back to what was happening. Karen hung out her tongue, gasping for air, reaching up to loosen the strand. The more she fought, the worse it became.

"Brazen child. Decorating thy flesh!"

"What'd you say, Karen?" Tara asked, turning now.

At that same instant, the beads snapped, scattering in all directions. Karen thumped to the floor and lay there, gasping for breath. The dusty wood floor was cold against her cheek.

"Karen, what happened?"

"Someone—someone tried to choke me."

Tara looked around. "What're you talking about? There's no one up here but us."

Karen looked over her shoulder as Tara helped her to her feet. The younger girl was right—they were all alone. But she was sure she'd heard a voice!

"I heard someone talking!" she insisted.

"I only heard you," Tara said. "I think you said something about flesh, but I'm not sure. Anyway, are you okay now? How'd your beads get all broken?"

Karen shook her head. "I—I don't know."

It was just her imagination, of course. No one had been there at all! She looked at the mirror's intricately carved frame and began to realize what must have happened. When she swirled around, the beads had gotten caught. And when she tried to get away, they just kept twisting tighter and tighter. She couldn't explain the voice she'd heard, but maybe it was someone shouting downstairs.

Everything was okay now. The attic was a place of wonder again, not a place of fear. It had been just an accident.

"You aren't going downstairs, are you?" Tara asked. "I'm still having fun."

"Okay, I'll stay," Karen said.

Tara bent over a box of clothes and began to rummage through it. The two girls spent the next half hour exploring and trying on old clothes and jewelry.

Someone stood nearby, hating the sound of their laughter. She did not need the darkness of the shadows to hide in, for the girls could never have seen her. She watched, remembering the laughter of children who had lived here so long ago, children who had interfered with her plans for happiness. And now they had returned, and her chance to regain what she had lost was once again taken from her.

But soon enough they'd be sorry they ever came back to this house.

12

Cindy sat with her feet dangling over the side of the back steps, her head resting against the railing. A woman stood on the ground, hands folded in front of her, watching as Cindy cried softly.

"It was so mean, Mommy," Cindy said. "How come somebody did such a mean thing to a kitty-cat?"

The woman shrugged.

"I'm glad you're here, Mommy," the little girl said, reaching out with one hand. The woman made no attempt to take it, but nodded in silence. "I'm so scared without you. When are you going to take me home?"

A voice came from behind the little girl.

"Who're you talking to, Cindy?" Doreen asked.

"My mommy," Cindy said, turning to look up at her guardian.

Doreen sat down next to the child, pulling her away from the railing.

"Don't lean against that," she said. "Not until I wash it—there might be cat hairs."

"My mommy doesn't mind," Cindy said.

"Doreen sighed. "Cindy. . ."

"Tell her, Mommy! Tell her it's okay!"

Cindy looked where the woman had been standing, but to her disappointment found that she was gone. The child stood up, hurrying down the stairs and around the side of the house.

"Mommy?"

She could see workers busy with their jobs, but there was no sign of the woman. Doreen came up to her, pulling her away.

"You know it isn't safe for you to be near the workers," she said.

"But my mommy left without saying good-bye," Cindy said with a pout. "Why? Why does she always go away?"

Doreen was in no mood to argue with a five-year-old about her overactive imagination. She sensed that the little girl had made up the imaginary "mommy" just to deal with the move to a new house, and decided she'd play along if it made her happy. Cindy would forget her soon enough, Doreen was sure.

"I don't really know," she said. "I guess she was in a hurry. I'm sure you'll be hearing from her."

Fat chance of that. Hannah Ardus hasn't written this child once since she's been in prison!

"Come on, let's go inside," she said aloud. "I'll get something down from the special toy closet to help you forget about what happened."

The special toy closet contained toys that were either too messy or too expensive to be left lying around. The toys people sometimes donated were also there, kept apart from the children's other playthings until special occasions. Hand in hand, Doreen and Cindy went back into the house to Doreen's office.

"Can I have the sewing kit?" Cindy asked, her blue eyes bright.

"You sure can," said Doreen.

Doreen opened a metal cabinet at the back of the room and took down a child's sewing kit that consisted of hole-punched pictures, giant buttons, and fat plastic needles. Cindy settled into the big chair near Doreen's desk to sew as Doreen took out her things-to-do list. Just then a shrill scream sounded from somewhere upstairs.

"Doreen! Dorrreeeeen!"

"Oh, what now?" Doreen asked out loud, annoyed. Cindy looked up, but she didn't get off the chair as Doreen raced upstairs.

"Help me! Helllllp!"

Coming around the landing, Doreen first spotted Tara, and then she saw a hand jutting out from behind the hall closet door. She ran to it and found Karen lying on the floor, moaning loudly.

"My leg! My leg!"

"Run and get Judy," Doreen told Tara. "Tell her to call Dr. Harlan."

Tara stood her ground, paralyzed with fear.

"Tara, move!"

With a cry, Tara bolted away.

"Karen, what happened?" Doreen asked, kneeling down. She could tell by the old clothes and jewelry the child was wearing that she had been playing in the attic.

"I fell off the ladder and through the trapdoor," Karen said through clenched teeth. "My leg hurts!"

Gingerly, Doreen rested her fingers on different parts of the child's leg. When she touched the ankle, Karen let out a scream and began to cry.

"It's all right, Karen," Doreen said. "The doctor will be here soon."

"I don't want to go to the hospital!"

"I'll stay with you no matter what," Doreen said. "Don't worry!"

She knew Karen's fear of hospitals went beyond a child's natural wariness. Karen had been taken to the emergency room of St. Aloysius in Buffalo several times after being severely beaten by her guardians. To the teenager, hospitals meant cold, uncaring hands and strangers who didn't believe her stories of abuse.

"She's been hurt enough," Doreen whispered. "No more, please!"

Doreen felt a hand on her shoulder, and looked up to see that Karen's screams had brought Randy and Frankie.

Randy looked solemn. He said, "Seek comfort from the Lord thy God."

Doreen frowned at him, but before she could say anything Judy was hurrying up to her.

"Dr. Harlan's on his way," Judy said. "What happened?"

"I think she's sprained her ankle," Doreen said. She shook her head at Judy. "What else is going to happen? We've only been here a few days and already there's been more trouble than we had in the last five years at the old house!"

Doreen's voice had risen in frustration, and Judy wished she knew what to say to comfort her. She made an attempt.

"We've just moved in," she said. "Things are hectic, and no one's settled into a routine yet. Once we've been here a while . . ."

"I can't take much more," Doreen said. "I'm determined to make our lives happy here, but how can I when these things keep happening? Two people fall off ladders in just a few days, some crazy old man murders a cat . . ."

She rubbed her eyes wearily, shaking her head.

"Doreen, make it stop hurting," Karen whined.

"The doctor'll be here in a little while," Doreen said. "Try to stay calm, okay?"

She realized that the only way she could get Karen to relax was to get control of herself. She took a deep breath.

It seemed as if an eternity passed before the doctor arrived.

"Looks like you had a little accident," Larry Harlan said, kneeling at Karen's side. The teenager gazed at him with wide, fearful eyes. "Don't be afraid, Karen. I'm just going to have a look."

"What's the difference between a piano and a fish?" he asked, looking at Karen's pain-stricken face as his fingers carefully explored her swelling leg.

"What?"

"You can tune a piano, but you can't tuna fish."

Karen giggled just a little, but the sound ended in a loud moan.

"Your ankle is sprained, all right," he said sadly. "And judging from the height of this ladder, you're lucky that's all that happened. Doreen, why don't you come with me in my car, and we'll drive to the hospital together?"

"No hospital!" Karen yelled angrily.

"Just to take X rays and make a cast," Larry said. He also knew about Karen's fear of hospitals.

"I don't want to," Karen mumbled.

"No choice in the matter," Larry said. "I'm going downstairs for the stretcher."

"I'm not leaving you, I promise," Doreen added.

A few moments later Larry came back upstairs. The stretcher dangled between him and one of the workers. They lifted Karen onto the stretcher and carried her downstairs.

"Is the little girl going to be okay?" the foreman called out as they crossed the yard to Larry's Bronco.

"I'm sure," Doreen said, climbing into the back.

Sam was wondering if the accident had been his fault. He had sent Bill Alexander up a ladder to work on replacing the attic window frame. According to Bill, Karen had stumbled into the open trapdoor just when he smashed a hole through the window with his hammer. Both Bill and Sam wondered if the sound of shattering glass had somehow startled the child. But they wouldn't say anything, not after Trevor Crane's accident. There was just one problem. There was someone who might tell Doreen what had happened. Bill had seen a woman standing near Karen in the attic just before the child fell.

Just after supper, Larry returned with Doreen pushing Karen in a wheelchair. The other children ran up to greet her.

"Wow! Can I sign your cast?" Randy asked.

Frankie signed, *How are you?*

"I'm okay," Karen said. "It just tingles a little."

Larry patted her shoulder. She was a great patient, he said.

"We have to get Karen up into bed," Doreen said. "She has to rest so that ankle heals faster."

"And the medicine should be making you sleepy," Larry said.

Carefully, he lifted the little girl out of the wheelchair and carried her up the stairs. Doreen followed close behind, accompanied by the other children. They all gathered around Karen's bed as Doreen made her comfortable with pillows.

"If your leg hurts," Larry said, "Doreen can give you another dose of this medicine. It should help you to sleep through the night."

"How long is she gonna wear that cast?" Harry-John asked.

"A few weeks," Larry said. "It's a bad sprain, but luckily nothing was broken. Doreen, I'd suggest declaring the attic off-limits."

"You can bet on that," Doreen said. "There have been enough accidents here. Now come on, everybody. Let Karen get some rest."

Karen took hold of Doreen's hand.

"I don't want to be alone until I fall asleep," she said. "Can Tara stay with me awhile?"

"All right," Doreen said. "For a little while."

She bent down to kiss the teenager's forehead.

"I'll look in on you later."

After everyone left, Tara sat on the edge of Karen's bed.

"Does it hurt bad?"

"Not now," Karen said. "But it was horrible when I fell. Tara, I have to ask you something."

"Sure . . ."

"You—you weren't standing near me when I fell, were you?"

Tara shook her head. "Oh, no. Don't you remember? I was looking in that big trunk full of shoes. How come?"

"Well, it's weird." Karen looked up at the ceiling, trying

to remember the events that led to her fall. "I'm not sure, but it felt like somebody pushed me really hard."

"How? We were the only ones up there. I think you just tripped in the dark."

Karen thought about the beads that had tightened around her neck as if someone had been trying to strangle her. Had someone else been up there, hiding in the shadows? Someone Tara didn't see?

She was so tired, and her thoughts were becoming jumbled. They had to have been alone, but she was certain she'd felt someone push her. It was too crazy...

"I'm tired now, Tara," she said, closing her eyes.

"Okay," Tara said softly, standing up. "Want me to stay a little longer?"

Karen did not answer her, so Tara left the room, shutting the door behind her.

But a voice began to lure Karen from her drug-induced slumber.

"Wake up, girl!"

Karen moaned in her sleep. She began to dream, seeing a woman in a long black gown holding her arms open. She couldn't make out the woman's face, but something made her dream-self hold her ground.

"Wake up, girl! Wake up!"

Slowly her eyes opened, but they did not focus on anything.

"Come to the window!"

"Can't walk..."

Suddenly, the covers were ripped from her bed, and Karen found herself lying unprotected. Her leg was propped up on a pillow, and this shot out from under her as if by its own power.

"Stand near the window!"

"I don't want to," Karen said groggily. "Go 'way! I want to sleep!"

Something grabbed her by the arm, tightening around her. Karen saw the indentation in her skin, saw the red marks of fingers. But there was no hand.

"Who . . . who . . . ?"

She couldn't speak. She felt herself being yanked from the bed, sparks of pain shooting up her leg as the cast thumped onto the floor. Drugged, confused, Karen could not fight back as an unseen hand pulled her toward the window. She was dreaming, and she wanted to wake up. Maybe if she called out, maybe if she could just call Doreen's name . . .

As she felt herself being dragged across the rug, she opened her mouth, but could not make even a tiny sound escape. Someone was going to kill her! This wasn't a dream at all, and she was going to die! She was going to be thrown out the window!

In her mind, she screamed.

A huge rock came crashing through the window. It sailed just past her ear, hit the headboard of her bed, and ricocheted across the room. Seconds later, it was followed by another, then another, until the room was filled with stones flying in all directions. Karen was frozen, unable to move as rocks struck the walls and knocked things from her dresser. There seemed to be hundreds of them, making a deafening noise.

"Evil girl! You should be stoned for your dirty, vain ways!"

Karen felt a stone hit the bottom of her cast, sending burning pain up her leg.

"I have seen you paint your face and twist your hair. Only the devil's own would alter the body, a temple of God. You are dirty and you are wicked!"

Karen found her voice, though it sounded tiny and distant amid the sounds of the flying stones.

"I'm not wicked!"

"Dirty and wicked!"

"No . . . no . . ."

Karen's mousy tone suddenly changed, and her screams filled the air.

"Nnnnnnoooooo!"

She heard the door crash open.

And then complete silence.

"Oh, my God!" Doreen yelled, running across the room. "Karen, what happened? What are you doing out of bed?"

Karen began to sob. "S-someone tried to kill me. She threw rocks at me! Look, they're everywhere!"

"Karen, I think you were dreaming," Doreen said, holding the child close. "There aren't any rocks in here."

"She threw them through the window!" Karen wailed.

"Karen, look around," Doreen said firmly. "There is nothing in here! No one tried to kill you!"

Slowly, Karen opened her eyes. Doreen was right—the floor was completely bare. There were no marks in the walls; nothing had fallen from her dresser.

"But . . ."

"It was a bad dream, honey. The medicine must have brought it on. Come on, I'll help you back to bed."

Karen let herself be helped up. Leaning on Doreen, she limped back to bed, where she was tucked into her covers again. She grabbed Doreen's hand and held it tightly.

"My leg still hurts."

"It'll be sore for a while. That's what Dr. Harlan told you."

"No, I mean it hurts where the rock hit my cast," Karen insisted. "It hit me hard on the bottom of my foot."

"Karen, there was no rock . . ."

"I'm scared, Doreen."

Doreen hugged her. "It was just a dream. I'll stay with you until you fall asleep to make sure you're okay. Now, close your eyes."

Karen did as she was told, and to Doreen's relief she was soon fast asleep again. Whatever the medicine had done to give her nightmares, she seemed to be resting now. Slowly, Doreen got up and started to leave the room. But she stopped short when she noticed a strange shadow on the heel of Karen's cast. It was a small indentation.

Like someone had thrown a rock at it.

13

Larry Harlan swung his Bronco onto the patch of sand and gravel at the side of Addison House, easing it between a van and a flatbed truck. He turned off the motor and jumped to the ground with a large red-and-white paper bag in his hand. Greeting the workers he passed, he bounded up the newly fixed porch steps and knocked at the front door. Cindy answered, squealing with delight as the doctor lifted her up.

"That smells like chicken," Cindy said, pointing to the bag as Larry balanced her on his hip. "Is it?"

"Don't tell anyone," Larry said in a conspiratorial whisper. "That's dinosaur. Roasted brontosaurus."

Cindy giggled. "There aren't any dinosaurs."

"Well, how about that?" Larry said. "I can't fool a big girl like you, can I? Say, you look very pretty. What's with the dress, Cindy? I'm used to seeing you in overalls."

Cindy took him by the hand and led him toward Doreen's office.

"My mommy comes to visit," Cindy said, "and she said she likes me to wear a dress. Nice little girls wear dresses, she says."

"You'd be nice no matter what you were wearing. Here, you take this to Yolanda and tell her lunch is on me."

"Oh, boy!" Cindy cried, racing toward the kitchen.

Larry found Doreen stamping envelopes, piling them neatly into a small shoe box.

"Hi, Larry," she said. "I'm just finishing up some correspondence. It's amazing how many people you have to contact when you move—especially when you move with foster children!"

Larry took a seat beside her desk.

"Cindy tells me her mother's been visiting," he said. "What's that all about?"

Doreen sighed. "That poor little thing really believes her mother's going to come back for her."

"I don't get it," Larry said. "She made it sound as if her mother's been here and she's actually spoken to her."

"That's a five-year-old's overactive imagination. I used to do it myself, make up a mother and father, or siblings. Make-believe was a lot better than some of the homes I put up with when I was a kid."

She put a lid marked TO MAIL on the shoe box and set it aside.

"Larry, I really appreciate your coming here," she said. "I know it's your day off, and . . ."

Larry held up both hands.

"And I'm your friend," he said. "We'll say this is a social call, so you don't have to feel guilty. How's Karen?"

"She slept soundly, and she's resting quietly today. She seems rather distant, hasn't had much to say."

"It's the medication," Larry said. "She'll be her cheerful self in a day or two."

"Something else happened. Last night she had a dream that rocks were flying around her room. When I went into her room, it took me a while to calm her down, but she kept insisting what she saw was real."

Larry folded his fingers together, bringing his hands to his mouth.

"That's interesting," he said. "I haven't known this medication to cause hallucinations. But kids do have nightmares, and the fall was a traumatic experience. So long as it doesn't happen again, I wouldn't worry about it."

"What if it does?"

"You call me. And I'll talk to Karen myself. But as far as bad dreams are concerned, sometimes it's best not to make such a big deal of them. If a kid thinks you're upset, she'll be upset, too."

Doreen nodded. "You're right. I'm sure it was a one-time incident. Karen's pretty well adjusted for a kid who's had a terrible childhood. She's entitled to an occasional bad dream."

Doreen stood up.

"Come on to the kitchen," she said. "We can have lunch with the kids."

"I brought take-out chicken," Larry said, following her into the hall.

"You're kidding," Doreen said. "That's a treat. We usually can't afford take-out food."

"Well, it sounded like you needed cheering up," Larry said. "And since ours isn't a flowers-and-candy-type relationship, I figured food was the next best thing."

Doreen laughed. When they entered the kitchen, all of the children except Karen were gathered around the table, enjoying chicken and French fries.

"Randy, you pig," Cindy said. "That's your third piece!"

"I'm hungry!" Randy cried.

"Let him eat," Doreen said. "He's a growing boy."

And a good appetite means he's thinking of something other than religion.

"I brought plenty," Larry said.

Doreen looked toward Yolanda.

"Has anyone brought a plate up to Karen?"

"I'm getting one ready right now," Yolanda said. "She must be ravenous—she hardly touched her breakfast."

Food was the furthest thing from Karen's mind. Upstairs in her room, she was struggling to pull herself from the armchair that Doreen and Yolanda had helped her to that morning. The bell she'd been given to ring for help sat unused on her nightstand. Karen knew Doreen would never allow her to do what she wanted to do.

Slowly, she rolled herself sideways, balancing her weight between her good foot and her two arms, which pushed against the side of the chair. She raised herself up, grabbing for her bureau. Perfume bottles fell to the floor, but Karen wasn't upset to see the scents she'd prized so dearly spilling over her carpet. She thought only of the bathroom down the hall and of the hot water that would cleanse her.

She had heard her aunt's voice that morning, reminding her how dirty and stupid and useless she was. All her clothes, all her jewelry and makeup couldn't hide the truth! That was why the stones came, to punish her for being so stuck-up on herself.

Leaning heavily against the walls and furniture, she made it to her door. She could hear the sound of a drill from somewhere outside, and a faint song on a radio. But she only paid attention to the voice in her head that commanded her to move toward the bathroom, step by painful step.

"You must wash yourself, girl. You must wash your sins away, scrub yourself until you are pure in the eyes of God."

"Scrub myself," Karen said, stumbling across the hall. Leaning against the wall for support, she could smell old wallpaper and plaster. Her injured ankle throbbed with dull pain.

At last she reached the bathroom, grateful that it was just diagonally across the hall from her own room. She stopped to catch her breath after she entered and turned on the light, resting against the old pedestal sink. Cindy had left her toothbrush on the side of the basin rather than putting it into its holder, and this annoyed Karen. She picked up the pink brush and shoved it into the porcelain tray on the wall. Cindy knew everything had its proper place!

"Wash yourself, filthy girl!"

The voice led her to the claw-footed bathtub. Karen

reached for the hot water faucet and turned it on full-blast, watching steam rise as the tub filled with scalding hot water. She sat on the toilet and waited.

Downstairs, Yolanda at last finished Karen's tray, adding a bud vase with a rose in it as a special touch. Excusing herself from the kitchen, she carried the tray out to the hall and up the stairs. She heard the sound of running water, and wondered if one of the children had left the tub on earlier. She gave her head a shake and set Karen's tray down on a hall table, passing the teenager's room on her way to turn off the faucet.

The water stopped just as she was opening the bathroom door.

"Who's in here?" she demanded.

She gasped to see Karen leaning against the wall by the tub, naked, the leg with the cast on it raised over the steaming hot water.

"Karen, what are you doing?" Yolanda cried out, rushing forward to catch the girl.

"Let go of me!" Karen screamed.

"Child, that water will burn the skin off of you!" Yolanda shouted, her big arms pinning the girl against her, pulling her from the tub. Karen went on screaming. "What were you thinking of? What are you doing out of your room?"

"I have to wash!" Karen cried, tears spilling freely as she struggled in Yolanda's strong arms. "I have to cleanse myself! I'm dirty! Filthy!"

"Nonsense!" Yolanda said. "You've had an accident, and you can't get that cast wet."

"Let me go!" Karen yelled. "Please!"

By that time the screams had brought Doreen and the others running upstairs. Larry came to Yolanda's aid, helping her force Karen out of the bathroom.

"What's with her?" Harry-John asked. "How come she's got no clothes on?"

"Karen, don't scream," Tara begged. "Don't be afraid!"

Doreen and Judy went to the tub, Harry-John between them.

"Oh, my Lord," Judy said. "That water is so hot I can feel it from up here."

"What was nutty Karen trying to do?" Harry-John asked. "Cook herself?"

Doreen started to reach into the tub to pull out the stopper, but found it impossible to get her hand near the water. She looked around, found a plumber's helper. Poking the stick under the water, catching the chain, she uncorked the drain. With a gurgling noise, the water began to go down.

"Stay away from that," she said, leaving the room.

Frankie stopped in front of her. *What's wrong?* he signed.

"I don't know," Doreen said. "But it has nothing to do with you. You kids go on downstairs. Everything is going to be all right!"

How often had she said those words in the few days since they had arrived at the new Addison House? But things weren't all right, and the home she'd dreamed of opening was turning into a nightmare.

Larry and Yolanda had managed to wrestle Karen into her bed, and as Doreen entered the room Judy and Yolanda pinned down the child while Larry gave her a shot.

"More medicine?" Doreen asked. "Hasn't that stuff made her crazy enough?"

"It wasn't the medication that made her walk across that hall and fill that tub," Larry said, watching Karen's movements slow down. Her head began to nod, her eyes slowly closed, as she was drawn into the drug's spell.

Yolanda carefully pulled a nightgown over Karen's head, the child's body limp in her arms. Doreen pulled the covers up over her and leaned down to kiss her.

"Karen kept saying she was sinful," Judy said. "What's this religious fixation that she and Randy seem to have?"

"I don't know, but I'm going to talk to the foreman," Doreen said. "He'll know if one of his workers is a religious nut."

"I'll keep a closer watch on the kids," Judy offered. "We've been so busy these past days that they've been left on their own too often."

The four adults left the room, only to find all the children waiting out in the hall with expressions of curiosity.

"Hey, didn't I tell you to go and play?"

"But we want to know about Karen!" Cindy cried.

Larry picked her up.

"Karen's just fine," he said. "She just—well, she just had a bad dream that made her walk in her sleep."

"Randy used to walk in his sleep," Tara said.

"Did not!"

Doreen put an arm around Randy's shoulders and pushed him gently toward the stairs.

"Let's go back to the kitchen," she said. "We haven't finished lunch yet."

"I'm not hungry," Cindy protested.

"I am," said Harry-John.

Though food sounded repulsive to Doreen, she didn't want to spoil everyone else's appetite by saying how worried she was about Karen. She was glad to see the kids were still interested in eating, that they accepted Larry's simple explanation and were not overly upset by what Karen had done. Harry-John was the first to reach the kitchen, and he let out a cry of dismay as he opened the door.

"Hey, who took our food?" he demanded.

"The chicken's gone!" cried Cindy.

"What are you talking about?" Doreen asked. She stopped at the end of the table. All the plates were there—and the glasses, and the silverware—just where they had been left. But there was no sign of the chicken. Not one piece of meat, not one bone, remained on the table. In the short time they'd been upstairs, someone had come in and completely cleaned the table of food.

14

After Larry went home, Judy went into Doreen's office and handed her a list.

"Just some ideas I've been getting over the past days," she said. "Ways to save time and money."

"You know I'm always interested in doing that," Doreen said, looking over the list. "Oh, I like this idea—closing off some of the rooms. When winter comes, that will save us some heating costs. Heaven knows what it will cost to keep this huge house warm!"

"I got the idea when I found some old keys in a drawer upstairs. There are a few rooms at the back of the house that we don't use. If you want, I'll go up and see if the keys I found lock them. That way, the kids won't be exploring and making messes for us to clean."

She left Doreen to her own work and went upstairs. Karen's door had been left slightly ajar so that she could be heard if she needed help, and Judy stopped to peek in at her. The teenager was sleeping quietly again, her cast propped up on a pillow. Judy wondered what had made the child drag herself out of bed and across the hall to the bathroom to try to take a bath with a cast on. These kids were acting so strangely ever since they'd moved into this house! Something was making it happen, and Judy decided she would keep her eyes and ears open. If someone was putting ideas in the children's heads, or playing tricks on

Doreen to drive her away from their new home, Judy would put a stop to it!

The hallway upstairs was L-shaped, and the residents of Addison House had taken over the rooms along only the longest arm. The shorter hallway provided some storage space, but three of the rooms were completely empty. Judy went into each one to be sure nothing had been left behind. As she left, she locked each door behind her.

"Now, I think these are the only keys," she said, "so I'm going to put them in a safe place."

She went to the guest bedroom, the one she planned to use when she finally moved into the house, and opened the top drawer of the dresser. As she was putting the keys inside, she heard three loud bangs. Judy hurried from the room to find the doors she had just locked standing wide open.

"Who did that?" she cried.

The rooms were all empty, with no signs of the mischievous children who must have played a trick on her.

But how had they done it? she wondered. So far as she knew, the keys she still held in her hand were the only ones in existence. And even if the kids had managed to find other keys, there hadn't been time for them to sneak back here and unlock the doors, then run away without being caught!

"Okay," Judy said to herself, locking the doors again, "this is an old house, and the locks probably don't work. I just didn't shut the doors right."

But how could all three doors have opened at the same time?

She started back to the guest room again, but then stopped short. Maybe some of the kids really were playing tricks on her, and were hiding in the storage room! She decided she'd wait a moment to see if anyone came out. Entering her room, she hid behind the door and watched the hall through the small opening between the hinges. Wouldn't it be just like Randy or Harry-John to pull something like this?

Then, one-two-three, the doors banged open again. Judy ran out into the hall, around the corner. No sign of the kids.

"Okay, guys!" she cried. "Very funny! Come on out now."

No one answered her.

"Randy? HJ?"

She heard the far-off sound of a chain saw, but nothing else.

"Okay, this is it," she said, reaching out to open the door to the storage room.

Then she heard a series of soft, high-pitched gulps. Smiling, she headed toward the sound, expecting to find one of the boys laughing behind his hand. But as she reached the middle of the room she realized that she couldn't tell where the sound was coming from. She turned a complete circle, looking at the stacks of file boxes.

"Harry-John?"

There was a shuddery kind of sigh, and a sound like shoes scuffling over the wood floor. Judy headed toward it.

There was a small boy, curled up in a ball, behind one of the boxes. He looked up at Judy with tear-stained cheeks, then cowered back away from her. He seemed to be about six years old, and for some strange reason was dressed in flannel pajamas.

"Who are you?" Judy asked, reaching toward him. "What're you doing up here?"

He moaned loudly, then jumped to his feet and ran from the room.

"Wait!" Judy cried.

She raced after him, just a few feet behind, but when she turned the corner he was gone. Judy hurried down the hall, looking into each room, but the child had vanished.

"How could he do that?" she asked herself. "He couldn't have reached the stairs before I turned the corner!"

She bounded downstairs after returning the keys to her dresser. "Yolanda," she said, "did you see a little boy run through here? Not one of ours—I found this kid hiding in the storage room upstairs."

"No, I didn't see anyone. But maybe the kids have a new friend."

"I'll ask them," Judy said. "I really don't think it's safe for children we don't know to be wandering around. Doreen has enough to worry about without some kid getting hurt and his parents trying to sue us!"

"I saw a few of them out back a little while ago," Yolanda offered.

Judy went outside to question the children. Even as she was doing so, Frankie sat in the schoolroom, a coloring book open in front of him and crayons strewn all about. He felt a cold wind behind him, and turned to see a little blond-haired boy. It was the same child he'd seen on his first night in the house.

Hi, Frankie signed. *Who're you?*

The smaller boy simply shook his head, his blue eyes wide. He pointed to the crayons on the floor. Frankie picked one up and handed it to the child, indicating he could color, too, if he wanted. The other boy backed away, his head shaking more vigorously now. He kept looking back over his shoulder as if expecting someone to enter the room.

Frankie wished he could ask the boy what was the matter, and also wished that he could understand him when he answered. If he answered! Frankie realized suddenly that the boy never said a word. Could he be deaf, too? Hopefully, Frankie signed *What's wrong?* to him, but the child only frowned and kept shaking his head.

He dropped to his knees and began to gather up the fallen crayons. Frankie tried to indicate to him it wasn't necessary, but the strange boy was persistent. He dropped the handful of crayons into Frankie's cigar box, then finally stopped shaking his head.

Once more he looked over his shoulder. His mouth dropped open, but if he screamed Frankie couldn't hear him. He threw his arms over his head.

And then he vanished.

Gasping, Frankie jumped from his chair. For a few minutes, he looked all around the room in search of the child. Then he ran from the room to find Doreen. She could tell him how the boy did that trick. People didn't really disappear like that! He found Doreen in front of the house. Frantically, he signed what had just happened.

"Frankie, you aren't making any sense. Slow your hands down."

Frankie repeated the story.

Frankie, your imagination is incredible, Doreen signed. *You know as well as I do that no one can disappear. You probably fell asleep and had a nightmare.*

Frankie could see that she wouldn't believe him, so he walked back into the house with a pout. If only he could talk! If only he could make the grown-ups understand how much this place scared him—and how much he wanted to leave.

15

From her bedroom window, Doreen could see out to the road, where the mailbox sat encircled by tall wildflowers. The mailman had raised its red flag, brightly visible even from this distance. Tying the neckline of her peasant blouse, she left her room and went down to get the mail.

Harry-John was sitting on the ground in front of the house, creating a building out of scraps of wood. Doreen stopped, admiring his work.

"That's great," she said. "You've got a new fort for your soldiers."

"The Eagle Raiders are going to hide out here," Harry-John said, pointing to the structure. "So when the evil forces of Slimo show up they'll be ready for an ambush."

Doreen laughed. "Glad to hear the Eagle Raiders are here to protect us."

She started to the mailbox again, thinking about the things that had happened here. She only wished there really was a team of good guys to help her out.

"Good morning, my love!"

She heard Brendan's voice halfway down the path, and turned with a smile.

"I was just thinking how nice it would be to have a hero," she said. "I'm really glad to see you."

"Has something happened?" Brendan asked.

113

"Well, things are crazy," Doreen said. "Nothing to worry about though. Will you walk me to the road?"

"Of course," Brendan said, taking her hand.

It was such a sweet gesture, like something a teenage boy would do, that Doreen smiled a little bit and looked down at her feet.

"You have such nice manners," she said. "Most guys are so pushy they make me nervous. But you—you come at me nice and slow. You don't threaten me."

"I'd never do that," Brendan assured her. "I love you."

They had reached the mailbox.

"Oh, good," Doreen said. "Here's the school supplies catalog I sent for."

"You like being a teacher, don't you?" Brendan asked.

"I'm not really a teacher," Doreen said. "I'm trained as a social worker, specializing in children's welfare."

"You like it here, don't you?" he asked. "You're going to stay?"

"I intend to stay here forever, if possible," Doreen said. "Despite some problems we've had, it's a pleasure to have room to breathe."

"Don't let anyone discourage you," Brendan said. "Don't let anyone make you want to leave."

Doreen stopped and looked into Brendan's eyes. She could see sunlight reflected in their darkness, but Brendan didn't squint despite the brilliance.

"I think someone *is* trying to make us leave," she said. "Do you know anything about that?"

Brendan shook his head.

"If you have any clues that might help," Doreen urged, "please tell me. I really need to know so that I can fight this person. Is it Marty? That old guy is really strange, and I think he's been saying things to frighten the children."

Brendan gripped her shoulders firmly. They had almost reached the spot where Harry-John sat playing, but the little boy seemed oblivious to them.

"Don't let anyone or anything frighten you," Brendan

said. "I don't want you to go away. I want you to stay here. I love you."

"I love you, too," Doreen said, feeling suddenly as if her body was not making contact with the air around it. She couldn't feel the ground. "I don't know how it happened so fast, but I do love you."

The grip on her shoulders relaxed, and Brendan's hands slid around behind her. He pulled her close and they began to kiss, oblivious to the children and workers milling around. Doreen felt hot and cold at the same time, ice in her joints evaporating in the heat of passion.

Brendan's arms were so strong, his embrace so warm, that she completely blocked out everything around her. It wasn't until she heard a scream that she broke away from him. What came next happened so quickly, like something out of a dream, that at first Doreen did not react. She saw one of the workers pointing up, and then another diving toward Harry-John. Something dark shot through the air, and seconds later the man who had pushed Harry-John away from his fort was lying on the ground with the arrow of a weather vane through his back.

And then there were screams and people running, and Harry-John gazing at the dead man with wide eyes.

"Oh, dear God, Brendan," Doreen whispered.

She broke away from her lover's arms and ran toward Harry-John, taking him in her arms. He began to cry, heavy sobs racking his body.

"Somebody get an ambulance!" she heard a voice shout.

Several of the workers dropped to their knees around their colleague's body, carefully touching him, calling out his name. As Doreen watched, holding fast to Harry-John, the man let out one gasp that sent a gush of blood geysering upward. Then his eyes rolled back into his head and he became very quiet and still.

"Jesus help me, Freddie!" a man yelled, jumping from the bottom of a ladder and running toward the dead man. "I don't know how it happened! I just don't know!"

Sam the foreman pushed his way through the gathered crowd.

"Oh, hell," he whispered. "Somebody get a tarp."

Yes, cover it up! Doreen thought. *Cover it up so the kids can't see!*

"What happened, Dan?" Sam asked the man who'd climbed down the ladder.

"I—I was just on the roof fixing one of the chimneys," he said, his voice shaking. He stared down at Freddie the whole time. "I had that weather vane in my hands. And then—I know it sounds strange, but I swear it really happened—it felt as if someone was trying to yank the thing out of my grip. I don't know, maybe it caught on something. But the next thing I knew it was falling off the roof."

Two of the workers laid a paint-stained tarpaulin over their friend's body. Doreen stood up slowly, her legs feeling like rubber, and looked around for Brendan. To her dismay, he was nowhere in sight.

"Freddie Ackerly saved the kid's life," someone said in a low voice.

"That thing was heading right for him," another person agreed.

Doreen turned to them.

"HJ might have been killed," she said, her voice shaking.

"But Freddie took it for him," Sam said. He sighed. "Look, there've been two terrible accidents on this job. I don't know what it is about this place, but I'm calling my people off."

"You can't . . ."

"I can't risk any more accidents, Miss Addison!" Sam cried. "There's something wrong here, and I don't want to be part of it!"

"The place is jinxed," someone said.

"Too many odd things happening for my tastes," a woman added. "What about that paint can that almost fell on Jim's head, or the way the nail gun shot off by itself a few times the other day?"

Doreen looked from one person to the next. So, they had experienced strange happenings, too?

"Have you—have you seen anyone around who doesn't belong here?" she asked hopefully. No one answered. "Somebody must have seen something! A stranger lurking around..."

Dan hesitated, looking from Sam to his feet then back at Sam again.

"I saw an old guy watching from the woods the day Trev got hurt," he volunteered.

"Marty," Doreen whispered.

There were a few moments without conversation, quiet except for Harry-John's sobs. Doreen kept her arms around him. Then she jumped at the sound of Sam's hands clapping together.

"Okay, people!" he shouted. "Get your things together. This job is over for us!"

"Please don't leave!" Doreen cried. "There's so much to be done! I can understand taking a few days off, after what happened, but..."

"Then hire someone else," Sam said.

Ambulance sirens filled the air, and moments later the rescue truck pulled into the front yard. The other children gathered around, beckoned by its flashing lights.

"What's wrong, Harry-John?" Cindy asked.

"What's that thing?" Randy asked, pointing to the blood-stained tarp.

Doreen grabbed his arm even as he was reaching toward it.

"Don't touch it!" she cried out. "There's been a terrible accident. You go on back into the house, and take HJ with you!"

"But Doreen..."

"Just do as you're told!"

Frightened by the angry tone of her voice, the children hurried into the house. A police car pulled up behind the rescue truck, and the officer began to ask Doreen questions. She hardly heard him, wishing all the while that Brendan was there. Why did he leave her?

When at last she was able to get away, she hurried into the house and to her office. Once there, she locked her door and sank into her desk chair. She buried her head in her arms, trying to drive away the memory of that weather vane sticking out of the man's body. Another accident, only this time a man was dead. They were going to take Addison House away from her. They were going to declare it unsafe, and she was going to lose what she'd worked so hard to gain.

Doreen felt a small hand on her elbow, and a child's head resting on her back. She didn't move to see which of the children was embracing her, too upset to react at the moment.

"Don't cry," a voice said in a whisper.

Slowly, the embrace subsided, and Doreen turned to see who was with her.

She was the only one in the room.

Cindy stood at her window, her back against the beautiful woman she had come to call Mommy. The woman caressed her, drawing her hair away from her face and letting it fall softly through her fingers. Cindy smiled, liking the gentle touch and wondering why her mother never touched her this way before.

"Look at them, child," the woman said. *"Look at them running away. They know the danger here!"*

"I want to go, too," Cindy said.

"Don't be afraid. I will protect you. I will protect you even as the woman named Doreen allows you to be hurt. She is not your friend, little one. I am your only friend."

Cindy turned and embraced the woman. She smelled something strange in her dark robes, and it took her a few moments to recognize the smell of candles burning in a church.

"You're my mommy," she sighed. "I love you."

The woman pulled away, taking Cindy's hand.

"You must come with me," she said. *"I will show you a place where you will be safe, where the evil will never touch you."*

Cindy looked up at the woman with trusting eyes and followed her without question out of her room, down the stairs, and through the front hallway. She saw Doreen's closed office door, and wanted to run in to her. She wanted to show Doreen that her mommy really was there, and that she wasn't making it up!

But the woman was pulling her, and there was no chance to call out. The cellar door opened by itself, and they walked down the dark staircase together. Cindy wasn't afraid, certain her mommy would never let her be hurt.

She wrinkled her nose in disgust when the woman placed her back against the wet, moss-covered wall at the back of the cellar.

"My hair's gonna smell awful!" she protested.

"Be silent," the woman commanded. She raised her arms in the air, like the wings of a bird, and enveloped the child in the folds of her sleeves. Everything went black. Cindy squirmed for just a moment, unable to breathe and suddenly growing panicky. She felt as if she were in a big bowl of pudding, all squishy and cold. The more she tried to struggle, the deeper she sank into the muddy darkness.

"Mommy, why are you hurting me?"

There was a sudden blast of cold air, and Cindy was able to gasp for breath. She knelt on what seemed to be a dirt floor, her blond tresses hanging down around her face. Slowly, fearfully, she looked up and saw only blackness.

"Mommy?"

No one answered her. She couldn't make out anything in the darkness, neither sight nor sound.

"Mommy, where are you? Turn on the light, okay?"

Still there was no answer.

Frightened now, her trust betrayed, Cindy began to cry. Her mommy couldn't have left her alone! She wasn't like the old mommy at the apartment, who went away for days and days! She was nice, and good, and kind! She wouldn't hurt her little girl!

Cindy's cries turned to great, whooping sobs.

"M-M-Mommmmmyyyy!"

But only the rats, mercifully hidden in the darkness, heard her cries.

16

At dinner time, Judy carried Karen's tray up to her. The young girl was lying in her bed, staring toward the opened window. Judy helped her sit up, then arranged the tray over her legs.

"Do you want some company while you eat?" she asked.

"I'm fine alone," Karen said, picking up a fork and poking at the crisply steamed broccoli on her plate. "Go on downstairs with the others."

"Well, if you're sure you're okay," Judy said, hesitantly.

Karen smiled. "I'm fine. I feel so much better now, and I'm really hungry."

"That's good," Judy said. "Enjoy!"

As she turned, she saw Karen's dresser and how clean it was without her perfume bottles. Then Judy noticed the white edge of the dresser scarf poking up from the trash can filled with little bottles of perfume.

"What's the matter?" Karen asked.

"Nothing!" Judy insisted. "I'll be up later to collect your tray."

She lifted the trash can and carried it out with her, meeting Doreen in the hallway downstairs.

"Look at this! All the perfume bottles she loved so much, the ones that used to belong to her mother, and the

121

makeup she saved her allowance to buy. Why would she throw them out?"

Doreen picked up the glass stopper of an old bottle.

"I have no idea."

Neither woman stating the obvious: that this was just one more incident in a series of too-strange happenings.

When they reached the kitchen, Yolanda said, "Isn't Cindy with you, Doreen?"

"No, I haven't seen her."

"Well, she knows she's expected to be on time for dinner," Yolanda said. "She'll just have to eat her food cold."

"I can't let it go at that," Doreen said. "She's only five years old, and so much has happened that I don't want her wandering around unsupervised. I'm going to look for her."

"Can I help?" Harry-John offered.

"Me, too?" Tara put in.

Doreen shook her head. "Finish your supper. I'm sure Cindy's just playing."

Judy took a longing look at the meal Yolanda had prepared; she felt real hunger after such a busy day. But she turned away from the table and followed Doreen. Thinking of what had happened to Karen, of the terrible accident that had killed a man and sent his co-workers away from their job, she prayed Cindy was all right.

"I'll go upstairs," she said. "Maybe she's in her room."

"And I'll check the yard," Doreen said. "There are nails and pieces of splintery wood lying around everywhere. I just hope she doesn't find any of them!"

Judy went upstairs to Cindy's room. It was empty, the child's favorite doll perched expectantly on her bed. Cindy had taped crayon drawings around her room, pictures of one tall figure and one tiny one. Judy's heart tightened, knowing these were portraits of Cindy and her mother. She wondered if Hannah Ardus kept pictures of her little girl in her prison cell.

She left the room, thinking Cindy might be visiting with Karen. But when she looked into the teenager's room, she saw that Karen was finishing her supper all alone. She went to the bathroom next, but it was empty.

One by one she checked the rooms, but found no sign of the little girl. She was just at the top of the stairs when she heard a small cry from somewhere down the hall.

"Help me," a tiny voice cried out.

"Where are you?" Judy called.

"Please, help me!" the voice repeated.

Judy realized that it was coming from one of the rooms in the short hallway. She hurried toward the sound and stopped in front of one of the doors she'd just locked that afternoon.

"Don't worry, Cindy," she said, realizing as she tried the doorknob that the child had somehow locked herself in. "I'll get the keys."

She went to the guest room, but the keys were not in their hiding place.

"Idiot," she said to herself. "Cindy used them to get in."

She returned to the locked door. From behind it came loud sobs, and though she tried to get Cindy to open the door from the inside, the child refused to acknowledge her.

"Damn, we'll have to break the door down," Judy said. "If only the workers were still here!"

Judy hurried to the bathroom, grabbed a bobby pin that had been left on the sink. The hallway was silent now. Judy went back to the room, unbending the pin as she walked. When she called through the door to Cindy the little girl did not answer.

Doreen appeared at that moment.

"She's not outside."

"I hear her in here," Judy said. "She's locked herself in."

Doreen shook her head, wondering what else was going to go wrong that day.

Judy knelt down and began to work the lock with the bobby pin. Because it was old, she expected it to give up easily, but she found herself working hard to unlatch it.

"This house is built like a fortress," she said. "I'm not sure this is going to do the trick."

"We might have to call a locksmith," Doreen said, sighing. "One more expense!"

"I don't know how she got hold of my keys," Judy said. "I thought they were pretty well hidden."

They heard the sound of a door slamming downstairs but neither one said anything. Judy continued working at the lock, biting her lip in the effort. Then Yolanda's voice floated up the stairs.

"Doreen? Judy? We've found her!"

The two women looked at each other in confusion. Doreen spoke first. "I'll go downstairs, but please get that door open anyway," she said.

She left Judy with her work and went downstairs to find Yolanda holding Cindy by the hand.

"She was sitting at the top of the cellar stairs sounding just like a little mouse with her crying."

The little girl was covered with smudges of dirt, and her sleeve was torn. Tears streamed down her face as she looked at Doreen.

"What on earth were you doing in the cellar?" Doreen asked. "And what happened to your clothes?"

"M-my mommy wanted to show me something. She took me down into the basement. Then it got all dark. And then my mommy went ... my mommy went away ... and ... and ..."

She burst out crying. Doreen picked her up, doing her best to hush the child.

"Cindy, you didn't go down to the cellar with your mommy," she said firmly. "You mommy is not here."

"Yes she is!"

"Cindy, why did you go downstairs?" Doreen asked. "You know it's dangerous!"

"My mommy wanted to show me something!" Cindy cried. "Why did she go away, Doreen? I was so scared!"

"Cindy, I know you wish—"

"You don't believe me!"

Cindy struggled from Doreen's grip, crying loudly as she ran upstairs to her room. Doreen followed close behind, her head full of questions. Cindy's protests were too strong. Could there be another woman pretending to be Cindy's mother? Did it go beyond a little girl's hopeful imagination?

Before Doreen reached Cindy's room, Judy appeared at the end of the hallway.

"I got the door open," she said. Her eyes were very round. "Cindy's not in there."

"We found her," Doreen said. "She was in the cellar. When I think how dangerous it is down there, with debris left over from the new stairs . . ."

"You have to come here, Doreen," Judy said. "You have to see something."

Sighing, thinking it was more urgent to tend to Cindy, Doreen went reluctantly with Judy. They entered the empty room together, and Judy pointed to a wall across the room. There, on a small hook, hung the keys.

"There was no one in this room after all," she said, her voice shaking. "But I know I heard a voice. How did those keys get in here, Doreen?"

Doreen shook her head, unable to answer. Then an offensive smell struck her senses, and she made a face.

"What's that?" she asked.

Judy sniffed. "Smells like something dead."

The two women looked around the room. With a cry of disgust, Judy beckoned Doreen to the closet.

Doreen felt her stomach flip as she looked down at a pile of maggot-covered chicken on the closet floor. A red-and-white bag lay next to it ripped to shreds.

Judy bent to the floor, picking up a small white piece of paper.

"It's got today's date on it," she said.

Doreen turned quickly, wanting to get out of the room as quickly as she could.

"What's going on around here?" Judy said, her voice quavering. "Someone's got it in for us. I'm really getting scared, Doreen. I think this house is haunted."

"Calm down, Judy. We're letting ourselves get spooked by a few pranks, and some unfortunate accidents. If we've got a ghost, he goes by the name of Marty. Somehow, that old man is causing all the trouble here. I just know it."

"Marty couldn't have carried those keys through a locked door," Judy pointed out. "And he wasn't on the roof when that weather vane fell. I'm sure he was nowhere near Trevor Crane."

"We don't know who was near Trevor," Doreen said. "Marty could have pushed him from the ladder, then run from the house. He could have shot something up at the roof to make that man drop the weather vane. He did something to that food, too!"

Judy looked around the empty room.

"But how did he get in here?"

"I really don't know," Doreen said. "Maybe he climbed through the window."

"He's an old man!"

"Well, maybe there's a secret passageway!" Doreen cried. "I couldn't tell you! But I'm sick and tired of all the things that are happening here too, and I can't handle crazy ideas about ghosts!"

"I'll clean up this mess, Doreen. Why don't you go and try to relax?"

Doreen left the room, still complaining. Judy walked out herself after a few moments, wondering how Doreen could be so closed-minded. No one could ever know everything, so how could anyone definitely say what existed and what didn't? There very well could be ghosts, and it would surely explain a lot of unexplainable happenings. Like keys showing up in locked rooms.

She looked down the empty hallway toward the staircase that Doreen had just descended.

"Maybe I'm wrong," she said, "but I'm going to find

out for certain. If something is in this house, I'm going to have it driven away before our lives are ruined!"

She continued on down the hall, unable to hear the wicked laughter of a woman who watched her.

"You think you can fight me? What a fool! You'll die before you drive me away from my home!"

17

Deciding she wanted to play a game that evening, Tara went into the back of her closet and dragged out the heavy wooden chair. She tried not to look at the carvings of angels, not liking their serious, almost mean expressions. She climbed up onto the chair and pulled out one of her boxes, then jumped down and went to the door that connected her room with Randy's. She could hear his voice rising and falling, as if he was reading aloud.

"Come on in!" Randy called, answering her knock.

He was sitting cross-legged on his bed, the Bible open on his lap.

"You want to play a game?"

"I'm reading now, Tara."

"Oh, you're always reading! We haven't played any games together since we moved in! Please, Randy?"

"Well, okay," he drawled, putting the Bible aside. "But this is more important. There's a whole lot of neat stuff in there about a family that lived here once."

"I don't care about them," Tara said, climbing onto the bed. "They died a long time ago."

She opened the box and began to set up the game.

"Just because people're dead," Randy said, "doesn't mean they aren't around. Didn't you ever hear of ghosts?"

"Randy Welder, don't you be talking about ghosts!"

Tara cried. "It's too scary! I'll get nightmares."

"Those who give their hearts to the Lord sleep peacefully," Randy said.

"You're getting bizarre, Randy," she said. She handed him the dice. "Here, you go first."

For a few moments, they played in silence, and then Randy said, "Tara, I made a new friend."

"A little boy?" Tara asked. "Judy said there was a little boy in the house before but he ran away."

"No, this is a lady," Randy told her. "She's really beautiful, and really nice. She tells me secrets!"

"What lady?" Tara asked. "And what secrets?"

"I can't tell you," Randy said. "But it's important stuff. She's a grown-up, but she talks to me like I'm grown-up, too."

Tara looked up from the game.

"Randy, grown-ups don't tell important secrets to little kids," she said. "You're just making that up."

"Am not!"

"You are, too," Tara said. "Just like you made up that story last year about meeting Bruce Springsteen."

"I did meet him!" Randy insisted. He paused, looking down. "Lying is a sin, isn't it? I mean—I saw Bruce driving by. It was the day he had a concert at the Rock Atrium Theater. But I really did see him!"

Tara sighed. "Oh, I guess I believe you. But who is this lady? Where does she live?"

"I don't know where she lives," Randy said. "But she comes up here sometimes—"

"Up here to your room?"

"Sure," Randy said. "What's wrong with that?"

"You can't have strangers up here without telling Doreen!"

Randy's eyes darkened.

"It's none of her business," he said. "My new friend told me that Doreen did some really bad things, so I don't have to listen to her anymore."

"That's dumb. Doreen never did any bad things!"

Randy leaned closer to his sister, his voice lowering.

"She let men touch her," he whispered.

"You stop talking like that! Doreen is the best friend we have, and you can't say mean things about her! I won't let you!"

Randy picked up the board and began to fold it.

"What're you doing?"

"I don't want to play anymore," Randy said. "Leave me alone, Tara. I've got some reading to do."

Tara stared at her twin for a moment, unable to believe he was rejecting her. He'd never done such a thing before! Tears began to form in her eyes, spilling over onto her cheeks, and she jumped from the bed and grabbed her game.

"Oh, read your dumb Bible, Randy!" she cried. "If you like it better than your own sister, then you can go jump in a lake!"

Randy did not even look up at her as she ran from the room. He simply opened the book and began to read aloud again, following the carefully penned words on its front pages.

"'My wife tells me of the terrible things Vanessa has done, and the children confirm it. She must be taught a lesson, and if cruel treatment is needed to cleanse her, then so be it!'"

Randy stared at the words. His new friend told him that Doreen had done terrible things, but he didn't want her treated cruelly. Maybe she was bad, but like Tara said, she had been nice to them. He really didn't want her hurt . . .

"We'll do what's necessary."

Randy smiled at the woman, who appeared suddenly at the foot of his bed. He didn't question her presence—or her ability to read his mind.

"The woman you call Doreen is wicked," his friend said. *"And we must do what we can for her salvation. I will tell you more things about her, child, and then you will know that it will take harsh punishment to save her."*

Randy nodded, moving aside as the woman sat on the edge of his bed.

"Listen to me, boy," she said. *"Listen to what I have to say..."*

Doreen walked Judy to the front door when it was time for the younger woman to go home. They stopped on the porch, looking over the front yard, where the moonlight created strange shadows out of the debris left over from the repair crew's work.

"Poor Fred Ackerly," Judy said. "I wonder what his family is doing now?"

"I sent a sympathy card," Doreen said. "I didn't know him, but I thought it was the least I could do. I'm already worried about Trevor Crane's family suing us, and now I have to wonder about the Ackerlys. I know thinking about money's a little crass, considering what happened to those two men, but with six children in my care I can't afford to be sued."

"Not only that," Judy said, "but how are you ever going to finish the repairs on this house?"

"I'll call the rectory in the morning," Doreen answered. "When Father Mason hears what happened, he'll make an announcement at Sunday's mass and maybe we'll get some help."

Judy looked over toward her car.

"Doreen, I'm sorry I said those things about ghosts before," she said. "I could see it really upset you."

"And I'm sorry I had such a fit," Doreen said. She tried to explain her feelings. "There was this family I lived with a long time ago, the Stones, and they used to lock me outside in the dark and tell me the ghosts were going to get me."

Judy gasped. "How awful! They must have been very cruel."

"I really don't like to talk about them," Doreen said. "The last family I lived with, the ones who left me the money I used to start Addison House, are the only ones I consider my true family. The ones before them were just strangers."

Judy nodded, wishing Doreen would say more about her childhood, but knowing she wouldn't.

"Well, it's getting late," she said. "And I've got a long drive home."

"I can't wait until you move in to stay," Doreen said.

"Well, tomorrow's my day off," Judy replied, "and I'm going to spend it getting my things together. Good-night, Doreen."

Doreen watched the younger woman as she headed toward her car, squinting in the beam of the headlights as Judy swung around and out of the yard. When the lights had disappeared Doreen turned to enter the house.

A shuffling noise in the bushes made her look behind her.

"Who is that?" she demanded.

Brendan came into the light, walking up the porch steps. At first, Doreen smiled, but then her lips turned down.

"You aren't happy to see me?" Brendan asked.

"Why should I be?" Doreen said. "You left me this afternoon, when I needed you!"

Brendan held out a hand to her, but Doreen backed away.

"Oh, no," Brendan said. "I didn't desert you. I'd never do that! I simply went to get help, but found someone else was already doing so. When I returned, you were busy with the little boy, and I didn't think you needed my help."

"Well, I did," Doreen said. "But I forgive you. Come on inside, Brendan. We can have some iced tea in the parlor."

"I'm not thirsty," Brendan said. "I'd rather spend all my time with you. There's so little of it."

He and Doreen went into the house, where they sat on the couch in the parlor, holding hands as they talked.

"Why is there so little time?" Doreen asked. "You always seem to be in such a rush."

"There are those who don't want us together. I must be very careful of them."

Doreen looked up at him. "Why wouldn't anyone want us together?" she asked. "We're adults, Brendan. I spent my whole life being afraid of adults, but now that I am one I'm not going to let anyone tell me what to do. I love you, Brendan, and nothing is going to change that."

Brendan put his arms around her, brought her closer to kiss her.

"I'm so glad to hear you say that," he whispered. "You mean the world to me, and now that we're together I won't let you go."

They kissed warmly, unaware that Randy was staring at them from the doorway.

"See how she gives herself without shame," his friend whispered to him. *"She is wicked and dirty!"*

"Wicked and dirty," Randy whispered, watching Doreen and Brendan.

Then in a loud voice he cried out, "Ye shall be stoned to death!"

Startled, Doreen jumped from the couch. She gaped at Randy, who stood alone in the doorway.

"Randy Welder, what are you doing there?"

Randy pointed an accusing finger.

"Harlot! Giving thyself to a man you called stranger but a few days ago!"

"What are you saying?" Doreen cried. "Who taught you to speak that way?"

"You're a sinner," Randy snarled.

"And you're in big trouble," Doreen said. "You apologize at once to Mr. Delacorte, then you can go to your room."

"Sinners!"

The word vibrated all the way up the stairs. Doreen shook her head, completely bewildered.

"I'm so sorry, Brendan," she said. "I don't know where he gets that from."

"He's only a boy," Brendan said. "He doesn't understand his words."

Randy glowered at Brendan, then ran upstairs.

"Well, I'm going to have a long talk with him," Doreen
said.

Now she could hear Tara calling her from the top of the
stairs.

"Looks like I'm the one to say good-bye first this time,"
Doreen apologized. "One of these days, we'll go out together, and we'll have a few hours without interruption."

"I'd like that," Brendan said.

"Doreen! Come on up here!"

Doreen laughed. "Guess I have to go. Please come see
me tomorrow?"

"I'll do that," Brendan promised.

They parted company in the hallway, Brendan heading
toward the front door and Doreen going up the stairs. At
the top, Tara grabbed her hand and pulled her along.

"You've gotta see what Karen is doing," the ten-year-
old said. "She's acting crazy again!"

The sound of shattering glass punctuated the child's
words. Doreen pulled her hand away and ran to Karen's
room. The teenager was out of bed, balancing herself
against her dresser with one hand as she smashed her mirror with a lamp held in the other hand. Pieces of glass
scattered everywhere, landing on the rubble of torn-up
fashion magazines, jumbled clothes, and broken bits of
jewelry.

"Karen!"

Startled by Doreen's voice, Karen dropped the lamp and
turned abruptly. The action caused her to lose her balance,
and she threw her hands out to cushion her fall. A shard of
glass sliced through her palm as she fell to the floor. With a
shaky cry, she held her bleeding hand up to Doreen, her
eyes wide with bewilderment.

"Tara, get the first-aid kit from the hall closet," Doreen
commanded. "And call Yolanda up here!"

She helped Karen to her feet, supporting her around the

waist and holding her injured hand up. Carefully, she led the crying teenager to the hall bathroom, where she began to wash the cut.

"What happened to you, Karen?" she asked, watching blood swirl down the drain.

"She—she said I was vain," Karen blubbered. "She told m-me I was g-g-going to hell because I have too many nice things! I had to get rid of them! I d-don't want to burn forever!"

Doreen unraveled a bandage and began to wrap Karen's hand.

"Karen, you haven't thought about the things your aunt said in ages," Doreen said. "What made you think of her now?"

It wasn't my aunt who told me.

Karen kept the thought to herself, biting her lip as she watched the bandage roll around her hand.

"I don't know," she said softly.

"My God," Doreen said. "You tore up your favorite magazines and messed up all the clothes you like so much. Why are you trying to hurt yourself, Karen? You seemed so happy until . . ."

. . . until we moved into this house.

Doreen stopped short of saying those words. It was true —the strange things the children were doing never happened before they lived in the big mansion! Firmly, Doreen took Karen by the shoulders and looked directly into her eyes.

"Karen, I want you to be honest," she said. "Has someone been telling you these things? Has someone been frightening you?"

Karen shook her head vigorously.

"I'm dirty," she whispered. "It's true."

"It's not true! You're a beautiful young girl, and you're very sweet! I don't know how you could think otherwise!"

Karen frowned at her.

"My aunt said my father had lots of women," she said.

"We've talked about your aunt's lies many times,

Karen," Doreen said. "She hated your father."

"People who have lots of lovers are bad," Karen said. "You had lots of men, didn't you?"

"Karen, what a thing to say!" Doreen cried.

Just then, Yolanda came into the bathroom.

"Oh, dear," she said. "What's happened now?"

"Karen had an accident," Doreen said. "Yolanda, could you bring her back to bed and stay with her until she falls asleep?"

"Sure," Yolanda said, putting her arm around Karen's shoulders.

Between her limp and the hunch of her shoulders, Karen walked like a little old lady. Her eyes were glazed and her skin ashen. The sparkle that had always lit up her expression had faded away.

"Something *is* happening here," Doreen whispered, standing in the bathroom door long after Yolanda and Karen had disappeared into the child's room. "But I'm going to deal with it. I have to deal with it! Nobody's going to take this place away from my kids!"

She went downstairs to her office and called the hospital in search of Larry. The nurse told her he was busy with a patient but would call back as soon as possible.

"Where are my friends when I need them?" Doreen sighed, resting her head on her arms. She felt someone touch her and looked up to see Frankie, dressed in his pajamas, standing at her side. Silently, she opened her arms and pulled him onto her lap. The quiet room was soon filled with the squeaking sound of her chair swiveling back and forth.

Scared, Frankie signed.

"Me, too," Doreen said, only because he wasn't looking at her and couldn't read her lips. She kept rocking him, staring at the phone and begging it to ring.

Frankie pulled back a little and signed a *K* for Karen.

Karen's fine, Doreen signed back. *Don't worry.*

The little boy leaned close to her again, his expression telling her that he was very worried. It upset Doreen to think that even a seven-year-old could see that something was wrong here. God help whoever was responsible! No one could get away with frightening her kids this way!

If she could only find out who it was . . .

She realized that Frankie was sound asleep. Carefully, she lifted him and carried him up to his room. Moonlight streaked elongated triangles across the walls, accenting the faded circus wallpaper. It was an innocent room, and yet Doreen suddenly felt very uneasy in here, very cold. Though it was a warm summer night, she closed Frankie's window and pulled his covers up to his chin. Then she bent down and kissed him.

Afraid, Frankie signed.

"It's okay," Doreen said, spelling *o* and *k* in his hand.

Frankie's breathing steadied again.

Moments after Doreen left his room, he began to dream. He was lying in bed, face up, staring wide-eyed at a big, blond-haired man. The man's hands were curled, reaching toward him, wrapping around his neck . . .

Frankie woke up with a start, a small cry escaping his lips. He looked around the room in a panic, searching for the man in his dream.

18

The sound of crying pulled Doreen out of a nightmare, and in the few seconds when sleep was still commanding her mind she thought she saw a child standing at her bedside. But when she opened her arms to offer an embrace, the shadow blended into the darkness. Breathing deeply, Doreen buried her head in her pillow and willed herself back to sleep again.

But the crying sound returned, this time very close to her bed. Fully awake, she pulled herself toward the lamp on her nightstand and flicked it on. The crying stopped.

"Is anyone in here?" she called.

Silence answered her. Feeling tense in every muscle, she dragged herself out of bed and shuffled toward her bathroom. A soft beep made her turn toward her clock, which marked five A.M. Doreen went into her bathroom, turned on the water, and filled the sink. Warm water on her face would help her relax, and then she could get the sleep she needed.

Leaning over the sink, she cupped her hands together and brought up palmfuls of water. It felt good to her, and she could feel the stiffness leaving her shoulders.

Then, suddenly, the water felt strange to the touch. A littler warmer, thicker . . .

Doreen splashed it on her face again, then opened her eyes.

Streaks of red ran down her cheeks. She gasped, covering her mouth and backing into the shower stall. The sink was full of a dark red liquid.

"Blood," Doreen whispered.

From inside the shower stall, someone took hold of her arm. Doreen turned with a cry to see an eerily familiar face.

"M—Mrs. Stone?"

It couldn't be! Mrs. Stone was dead!

I'm dreaming. I must be dreaming. Wake up!

The woman spoke, and her voice seemed to come from somewhere far away.

"You shouldn't be up so late," Mrs. Stone said. *"I'll have to lock you outside, lock you in the dark, lock you where the ghosts wait to grab bad little girls . . ."*

Doreen stood frozen, staring at the woman who had once been her foster mother, who had treated her so cruelly. Mrs. Stone reached out to touch her, and the horror of it sent such a chill through Doreen that she crumpled to the floor, unconscious.

The next thing she knew, someone was shaking her. Slowly, she opened her eyes and realized that the morning sun was shining through the small window over the bathtub. She looked up at Cindy, who stared at her with solemn eyes.

"My mommy says you're bad."

The child's words didn't register right away, and with a moan Doreen pulled herself to her feet. She grabbed the sink for support. It was full of water—not blood, water. She had had a terrible nightmare, one that conjured up the hated image of Mrs. Stone.

Doreen limped into her bedroom and took her robe off its hook. Sliding her arms into the sleeves, she caught Cindy's reflection in her mirror. The child was staring at her with an angry expression, her face unusually pale.

"Honey, are you feeling okay?" Doreen asked, coming fully awake now as her concern for the child replaced leftover fears from her nightmare.

"You're bad," Cindy whispered.

"What kind of thing is that to say?" Doreen said sternly. "Who told you that?"

"My mommy."

"Cindy, your mommy isn't here," Doreen said, exasperated. Hurting all over, still disoriented from the nightmare, she didn't feel much like humoring a five-year-old.

Cindy took Doreen's hand and gazed up at her.

"Was it very scary to see Mrs. Stone?"

"How did you know that?" Doreen asked, her heart leaping.

But Cindy pulled her hand away and ran from the room. She disappeared down the stairs before Doreen could catch her. For a few minutes, Doreen held fast to the banister, trying to understand what had just happened.

She had to talk to someone, even if it was early in the morning. She was just too shaken to let this go by! Brendan had been so kind to her, so loving. Maybe he could help. She needed him to come here.

Doreen went downstairs, planning to call Brendan. When she got to her office, she realized that Brendan had never given her his phone number. Undaunted, she pulled out a directory and thumbed through it for the name Delacorte.

"That figures," she said, slamming the book closed. "It's unlisted!"

She had to talk to someone! Larry's name came to mind, but Doreen didn't want to disturb him again. She finally picked up the receiver and dialed Judy's number.

After hearing Doreen's story, Judy said, "Doreen, I've been doing some research. You're going to think I'm crazy, like you did the other day, but I'm becoming more and more convinced there's something unnatural going on in that house."

"Please don't start talking about ghosts again!"

"It's the only thing that makes sense, Doreen," Judy insisted. "When you hear the history of that place, you might agree with me!"

"What history?"

"It's really too strange to go into over the phone," Judy said. "But I'll be at work early tomorrow, and we'll discuss it then. Meantime, hang in there. We can fight this thing, whatever it is!"

"I have to know what it is to fight it!" Doreen cried.

There was a pause.

"Uh, look, Doreen?" Judy said. "I'm sorry, but my mother's signaling me. I promised I'd take her shopping this morning."

"I really need you here, Judy," Doreen said, surprised at the pleading tone in her voice.

"And I'll be moving in soon enough," Judy said. "Good-bye, Doreen. I'll tell you everything I found out about the house tomorrow."

Doreen hung up the phone, dejected. She really needed a friend now.

"Well, if Brendan can't come to me," she said, standing, "I'll go to him. I may not know where he lives, but I can find out!"

With that, she left the house, hurrying toward the road in the hope it would lead her to Brendan's home. If he had six horses, as he told her, then it had to be a pretty large spread. She was surprised to find herself smiling a little at the thought that she would soon be in Brendan's arms.

But there was someone watching her who was not smiling. A dark-haired woman had an arm around Karen's shoulders as she stood with the young girl at her bedroom window.

"Look how she hurries from the house, from the children who need her! Don't you see now that she's wicked?"

"Wicked," Karen said, her voice dull.

"She's looking for a man," the woman said. "Her lust means more to her than the children she professes to love!"

She gave Karen a small hug.

"But we'll take care of her," she said. "She'll pay for her wickedness, and then we'll be rid of her evil forever."

Karen said nothing, staring at Doreen's retreating figure.

When she reached the end of her driveway, Doreen turned and followed the road away from town. Once she found Brendan, she decided, she'd ask him to come back to the house with her. Maybe he could figure out a way to deal with the problems she was having, a way to keep her children safe and stop whoever it was who was trying to drive them from the house.

She wondered now what Judy had meant. Her young assistant had really sounded convinced that there was something evil going on in the house. Doreen agreed there was a problem, but she strongly doubted that it was a supernatural one. She had learned early on in life that people did a good enough job hurting each other without interference from "beyond."

"Wherever that may be," Doreen said out loud, her words sending a squirrel shimmering up a tree.

She realized suddenly that she had been walking for a while and should have reached Brendan's property by then. But there was nothing to see except trees and wildflowers and streams of water scratched into the mountainside.

"It can't be too much farther," she said. "Considering that Brendan is always walking when he shows up at the house!"

She heard a soft moan, something beneath the rush of the wind. Doreen stopped and listened, and the moan became a plaintive cry.

"Please, don't!"

It seemed to be coming from the woods. Doreen looked toward the sound, trying to make out its exact location.

"Please, don't hurt me!"

A cold twist formed in Doreen's stomach—the cry was so very like that of the little girl she'd been long ago, cowering away from some foster parent's upraised, angry hand.

"Who's there?" Doreen cried. "What's going on?"

She heard a soft scream. Doreen looked around for a weapon picking up a branch that had fallen from an oak tree. The voice came again, this time a series of sobs. Common sense told Doreen that she should run away, that she might be walking into a dangerous situation that was none of her business.

But someone needs my help. And didn't I wish there had been someone to help me when I was being hurt?

"Where are you?"

No one answered her, but the cries went on. They were loud sobs now, almost childlike in their intensity. As Doreen pushed her way between two thorn bushes, she saw the young woman who was making them—the same young woman she'd seen on her way to the hospital the day before.

She knelt on the floor of the woods, her long skirt spread around her legs, her head buried in the folds of fabric at her knees. Back and forth she rocked, moaning and crying.

But there was no one else with her.

"What's wrong?" Doreen asked, stopping a short distance away, unsure about intruding into the woman's misery. She seemed oblivious to Doreen, lost in a waking nightmare.

And then something occurred to Doreen. This woman was acting crazy—could she be the same person who had been at the house, pretending to be Cindy's mother?

"Who are you?" Doreen demanded.

Without looking at her, the woman stood up, her eyes focused on the ground. Her long dress was torn, and her hair was woven through with twigs and bits of pinecone. Doreen was surprised to see she was young—perhaps no older than twenty.

"Please, who are you?" she asked, gently this time.

Instead of answering, the younger woman turned and began to run. Doreen hurried after her, begging her to stop, but within a few moments she had lost the trail.

"Damn!"

Sighing, Doreen turned and walked back to the roadway. She thought it would make more sense to go home and tell the police about the strange woman than to find Brendan today. Once they caught her, the police could handle the situation.

"I only hope she's the one I've been looking for," Doreen said.

Judy rose early the next morning, eager to get to work with the information she had for Doreen. She'd done some research on the house, and had found out some surprising things. Once Doreen heard them, she'd be convinced that they needed some kind of outside help.

For all her college education, Judy had never lost the superstitions she'd had as a child. She believed in ghosts, and in demons and dark forces that sometimes gained the upper hand if you weren't careful. Her reasoning was that no one knew everything about everything, and that there were enough unexplained phenomena in the world to allow for the macabre. The things that were happening at Addison House were unexplained, and from what Judy had learned, similar things had happened to previous owners of the mansion.

It was hot, and she had the car's air-conditioning turned up, the noise of the fans making it almost impossible to hear the radio. But interference from the Alleghenies caused static anyway, and Judy finally switched off the station. Instead, she mentally reviewed the things she had read in the library the other day. Though she had approached the subject with an open mind, and though she knew the incidents had happened long ago, little bumps of fear began to crawl over her flesh again as she recalled the words she'd found in a twenty-year-old newspaper:

"The suspect, currently under psychiatric observation, was led from the house screaming: 'They got inside me! They got inside me!'"

Who, Judy wondered, had gotten inside the man? And were they now trying to "get inside" the children?

"Not if I can help it," she said, swerving the car a little to the left to avoid a backhoe.

There was a lot of construction being done on the roads these days, and heavy machinery was a common sight along their rims. Judy hardly paid any attention to the backhoe, having passed similar equipment day after day for months. The only machine she took note of was a huge rock crusher parked just before the overpass that would turn her in the direction of Oakwood. As she drove, she kept her eyes alert for signs of movement of the giant machine.

"I'm almost there, Doreen," she whispered to her friend, wishing Doreen could hear her and be reassured. "We'll talk about the house, and you'll believe what I have to say, and we'll deal with this problem. We'll stop what's going on, and Addison House will be safe for us and the kids!"

The rock crusher was colored a brilliant orange, and was visible from a long distance. Judy saw the flash of its broad sides, and began to slow up in anticipation of her turn to go around it. As she did so, she thought she heard someone calling out, the sound muffled by the roar of the air-conditioner. But when she turned it down, she heard only silence.

And then she felt a horrible pain at the back of her head as something grabbed her hair and began to rip at it. Her head jerked back, and Judy screamed, holding the steering wheel with one hand as she reached behind herself with the other. She thought that her hair had somehow twisted up in the headrest, blown into it by the air-conditioner. But she quickly lost that notion when her hand encountered something cold and gelatinous.

"You think you can stop me? You think you can help her win again?"

"What is this?" Judy screamed. Her foot slammed hard on the brakes and her hand came back around to grab the steering wheel. It was covered with a dripping slime that carried a nauseating, rancid smell.

"You won't tell her about me! You'll die first! You'll die!"

Though her foot pressed the brake pedal clear to the floor, the car kept moving, gaining speed on the sloping roadway. Judy pumped the brake in desperation, crying in dismay, her stomach churning as the cold slime oozed down the back of her neck. What was back there? What was behind her? How did it know her thoughts?

And then one last, horrifying question as the car hurtled toward the rock crusher—a bright orange monster.

"Why am I going to die?"

19

At noontime, Yolanda knocked on the door of Doreen's office, carrying a tray she'd made up for Karen.

"Could you bring this to her?" she asked. "Judy's not here yet, and I've got something on the stove."

Karen was sitting up in bed when Doreen entered her room, the jewelry kit Doreen had bought her open on her lap. Doreen felt a sense of relief to see the teenager stringing beads. Maybe it was the first sign that Karen was recovering.

"Brought your lunch," she said, walking toward the bed.

"Thanks," Karen replied. She held up the necklace she was working on. "Look, Doreen. What do you think?"

"It's very pretty," Doreen said, waiting as Karen moved the box to make room for the lunch tray. "Once you're up and about you'll look very pretty wearing it."

"I'm not going to wear it," Karen said. "It's a gift."

"For who?" Doreen asked. "Yolanda?"

Karen shook her head.

"Judy, then?"

"Judy's not coming back," Karen said. She returned the necklace to the box, coiling it over itself like a snake. Then she picked up her sandwich and began to eat.

"What do you mean?" Doreen asked. "Of course she's

149

coming back. In fact, she'll be living with us soon."

Karen went on eating, wolfing down the sandwich as if she was ravenous. It seemed she hadn't heard Doreen's question. Before Doreen could ask it again, the bedroom door opened, and Harry-John walked in to say that Dr. Harlan was on the phone.

"He says it's real important, Doreen," Harry-John told her.

Doreen took one last look at Karen, who seemed to be concentrating completely on her lunch. She decided she must have misunderstood what the girl had said.

What could Larry want, she wondered? Was it something to do with Trevor Crane?

She picked up the receiver in her office and greeted the doctor.

"It's nice to hear from a friend. Things have been just horrid around here."

"I'm afraid I'm going to make it worse," Larry said. "Doreen, sit down, okay?"

Doreen sat, feeling unnerved by the sober tone of Larry's voice.

"What's wrong?" she asked.

"Doreen, Judy Wagner was brought in here a short while ago," Larry said. "I was checking out one of my kids in the emergency room when they wheeled her through the doors."

"Oh, God . . ."

There was a pause, as if Larry was trying to find a gentle way to tell Doreen what had happened.

"She—she was a mess, Doreen," he went on, softly. "I heard one of the paramedics saying a witness reported she hit a piece of heavy construction machinery. They said her car had to have been doing ninety."

"That's impossible!" Doreen cried. "Judy's the best driver I've ever known! She wouldn't be so reckless!"

She opened her drawer and fumbled around for a pencil and paper.

"Is she in a room yet?" she asked. "Give me her

number—I'm going to come visit her tonight."

"Doreen . . ."

"She'll explain everything, Larry," Doreen said, not hearing him. "Something went wrong with her car, and—"

"Doreen, she came in D.O.A.," Larry interrupted.

There was silence.

"Did you hear me?" Larry asked carefully.

"I heard you."

There was no emotion in Doreen's response, just the flat tone of shock.

"Doreen, do you want me to come out there tonight?" Larry asked.

"I—I don't . . ."

Doreen's lower lip began to tremble as the reality of what Larry had said began to reach her. She rubbed it with a shaking hand.

"Larry, there must be some mistake?" she asked plaintively.

"I'm afraid not," Larry said. "There's no way she could have survived, Doreen. From what I heard, she'd be a vegetable if she did. It's better this way—"

"How can you say that?" Doreen screamed. "How can it be better for a twenty-four-year-old to be dead?"

Larry didn't say anything. Doreen sobbed uncontrollably for a few minutes, then drew the backs of her hands across her eyes.

"Has anyone contacted her parents?"

"The police did," Larry said. "There's going to be an investigation, so don't be surprised if someone calls you."

"Larry, I have to go now," Doreen said. "I—I have to tell the children and Yolanda. And I have to make a call to Judy's parents. There's a lot—a lot to do."

"Do you want me to come out there tonight?"

"I'm okay, Larry," Doreen mumbled.

She tried to lay the receiver in its cradle, missed, and finally was able to hang up the phone on the third try. The room felt cold suddenly, and the sky outside seemed grayer than it had a few minutes ago. For a moment, Doreen simply stared out the window, her tears drying on her cheeks.

It was just too unbelievable. Just yesterday Judy had been talking on the phone with her about a blind date. And about something more. Doreen remembered now that Judy had found some information on the mansion's history that she'd seemed to believe would clear up the mystery of what was happening there.

"We can fight this thing, whatever it is," Judy had told her.

But what was it?

Doreen pounded her fist on the desk top.

"It isn't a what," she whispered through clenched teeth. "It's a who! Somebody's doing this to us!"

Was it possible that somebody caused Judy's accident?

The possibility was too horrible to consider. Doreen felt the muscles at the back of her neck tightening as stress threatened to bring on a headache. How was she going to handle this? She stood up, hurrying from the room and out of the house. She needed Brendan now, needed to feel his strong, comforting arms. This time, she didn't go to the road, but headed toward the woods. If she went to the lake, maybe she'd be able to find a path that would lead to his house.

Her thoughts seemed to come from every direction.

Judy's dead. Judy's dead. Hit a piece of heavy machinery.

Three accidents in a few days.

Judy's not coming back, Doreen.

Had to be doing ninety.

Judy's not coming back, Doreen. Not coming back. Not coming back.

"Nnnnooooooo!"

Doreen's scream ripped through the trees, sending small animals scattering in fear. She fell to her knees, her arms thrown up over her head.

"No! No! Nnnnoooo!"

Strong arms wrapped around her, and as she wailed

Doreen let herself be turned around and embraced. She could smell the familiar scent of horses and leather that was Brendan. He held her tightly.

"My love, what's wrong?" he asked, stroking her hair. "I heard screams, and ran as fast as I could. What's happened?"

"J-J-Judy was k-killed," she managed to choke out. "Oh, God, Brendan. What is it about this place? Why do so many horrible things happen here?"

"What do you mean, Judy was killed?" Brendan demanded.

Doreen sniffled, running the heels of her palms across her wet cheeks.

"Larry Harlan called a few minutes ago. Judy's car ran into some construction machinery. He said she—said she was D.O.A."

She began to cry again.

"D.O.A.?"

"Dead on arrival," Doreen explained. "He said she was a mess. Brendan, it doesn't make any sense! Why would Judy drive so recklessly? Larry said she was doing ninety!"

"I don't know," Brendan said, helping her to her feet. "But you shouldn't be out here, darling. Let me take you back home again."

Leaning heavily against Brendan, Doreen walked to the house with him.

"I came out looking for you. I need you so much, Brendan. I don't want to be alone."

"I'll stay with you as long as you need me," Brendan promised.

He helped her up the front steps, steering her around an empty paint can that had been left when the workers abandoned their job.

"Maybe we shouldn't stay. There's no one here to fix the place up, and with Judy gone . . ."

A shudder racked her body, but she bit her lip hard to stop a new flow of tears.

"I've got to tell the kids," she said. "They don't need to see me hysterical—it'll be hard enough for them."

But when she saw the pencil sketches Judy had drawn in the front hall in preparation for the mural, she began to cry again.

"Come inside the parlor and sit down," Brendan said. "Should I call the housekeeper? I could have her fix some tea . . ."

"I don't want tea," Doreen said.

She let Brendan lower her onto the couch. He adjusted the pillows behind her, then gently pulled back a lock of wheat-colored hair that had glued itself to her tear-stained face. In her grief, Doreen felt very small, like the child who had been bounced from one foster home to another. Memories of wanting protection against the nameless things that frightened her came tumbling out of her subconscious, and she could almost hear herself, aged six or seven, crying out in the darkened room: *"Mommy? I want my mommy! I need a hug!"*

And a cold voice answering: *"Your mommy's dead. Go back to sleep and stop crying!"*

"Oh, Brendan . . ."

"Hush," Brendan whispered, sitting beside her.

He took her face in his hands and began to stroke her temples, running his fingers back through her hair. Though callused, his big hands were warm and gentle, and soon Doreen's eyes grew heavy. Sighing, she closed her eyes and let him massage away the tension she felt. While nothing could lessen her shock or grief, Brendan's touch helped strengthen her for her next big ordeal—telling six children the young woman they adored would never be back again.

Her lips curled, and she made a slight whimpering sound.

"Shh," said Brendan. "Don't cry, my love. I'm here, and I'll stay here. I'm with you, forever."

His voice had a near-hypnotic quality. Doreen's arms and legs began to feel heavy, and her body sank deeper into the couch. Within minutes she was heavily asleep and dreaming.

One of the children was screaming. Doreen rose from the couch, following the sound to the second floor.

She opened her mouth to say she was coming, but no sound came out. The screams went on, and then something unfamiliar—a man's gruff-voiced shout.

There was someone in the hallway just outside Frankie's room. A blond-haired man, dressed in striped pajamas.

"You don't live here," Doreen said.

The man did not respond.

The child screamed again, and the man kicked open Frankie's door. Doreen ran.

"Frankie? Frankie!"

More screams.

But it wasn't Frankie in the bed when she entered the room. It was a little blond-haired boy in a red flannel sleeper. There were different toys in the room.

And the circus print wallpaper was not faded.

"Who are you?"

The child turned to stare at her, arms opened wide.

"Mommy, help!"

And then the man came out from behind a curtain, hunched forward like the monsters of Doreen's childhood nightmares.

"Heathen devils! Your evil must be stopped!"

And then he began to run toward the bed, toward the child, who had thrown his covers over his head, screaming, screaming...

"Oh, God!"

Doreen bolted upright, knocking a bolster to the floor. She clutched at her chest, her mouth open, her eyes wide as she gasped for air.

"You·were dreaming!" Brendan said. "I thought about waking you, but..."

"Brendan, it was horrible," Doreen said hoarsely. "Hold me? Please?"

Brendan took her into his arms. Doreen closed her eyes and clung to him, wishing she could take some of his strength for her own, because she was no longer certain that she could fight the terror that was growing all around her.

20

Frankie bent toward the ground, picking a bunch of violets to add to the bouquet he was making for Doreen. He pulled them with more force than necessary, taking out his anger on the delicate flowers. In his mind, he could still see the blotches of red that tears had marked on Doreen's face. She had gathered all the children in the library to tell them the terrible news. Though Frankie couldn't read her lips very well, he knew even before she signed a translation to him that something very bad had happened to Judy.

Doreen told them that Judy had been killed in a car accident. She assured them that it had happened so fast that Judy probably didn't suffer, and offered her arms for comfort as Cindy and Tara began to cry. Randy raced from the library shouting something Frankie couldn't hear, and Harry-John began to kick things. With tears of disbelief rising in his own eyes, Frankie hurried from the house. He had sat in the middle of the field for half an hour before he began to gather flowers. It was the only thing he could do, wanting desperately to make Doreen feel better.

Why do nice people die? Why do the bad people, the ones who hurt you, get to live?

He grabbed for a sprig of Queen Anne's lace, trying unsuccessfully to cut off his thoughts. His parents were alive, even though they were mean. Judy was nice to him all the time, and she was dead!

Tears began to spill from the little boy's brown eyes. He thought how someday he might be back with his mother and father, after they completed something called therapy and the judge said they were fit to be his parents. But he didn't want to go back with them, not ever! He wanted to stay here with Yolanda, and Doreen and Ju——

But Judy wouldn't be here any longer.

Frankie moaned angrily, throwing the flowers to the ground. Suddenly he felt a gentle touch on his arm, and turned to see the strange, blond-haired boy who had been in the classroom the other day. The child's blue eyes were wide in a face that was pale as the cloud-filled sky. Wind tousled his curls and played at the collar of the one-piece pajamas he wore.

Frankie arced his upturned palms through the air, indicating that he didn't know what the child wanted. He thought it was strange that the other little boy always wore pajamas, but had no way of asking him why. The blond child shook his head vigorously, pointing at the house.

Then, suddenly, he turned to look at one of the upstairs windows. Frankie looked, too, but saw nothing.

The other child grabbed at his throat, his mouth dropping open. Frankie couldn't hear the strange gasping noises that escaped the child's mouth. Suddenly, the boy's eyes rolled back, until only the whites showed, and his skin began to turn sickly blue.

Frankie began to scream, grabbing at the other boy. He felt a great rush of icy air that lifted him up off his feet, and he landed hard on his face.

With a moan, Frankie looked up. Then he scrambled to his feet, turning in a quick circle. There was no sign of the child, just acres of grass that stretched from the house to the woods. But how could the boy have gone away again?

Why do you disappear like that? Frankie wondered. *Are you magic?*

Only the wind, which he felt against his cheeks rather than heard, answered him.

Someone took hold of Frankie's shoulder. Expecting to see the mysterious little boy, Frankie turned around, and backed up with a start when he saw Marty standing close to him. The old man was speaking, and Frankie strained hard to read his lips.

"You know what's smart," Marty said, "you'll keep away from that boy. I know what he is, and why he's here. He's tryin' to tell you something."

Frankie shook his head, confused.

"He picked you 'cause you're just his size," Marty went on. "And 'cause you can understand what others can't, even if you are deef."

Instead of "deaf," Marty had said "deef," and it took a moment for Frankie to figure out what the word meant. Lip-reading was difficult because so many words looked alike on a person's lips. The best anyone could do, especially a child, was to put all the words together and try to make sense of the result. Frankie could tell that Marty didn't like the strange little boy.

Marty knelt down and took Frankie by the shoulders. He smelled funny, like a newly opened package of meat Yolanda might bring home from the butcher, but Frankie didn't pull away.

"That boy's tellin' you there's danger here," Marty said. "You listen to him, and you get away while you can. 'Cause if you don't, the evil's gonna getcha. Gonna get each and every one of you!"

Frightened now, Frankie wrenched himself from the old man's grip and turned to run back to the house. He had clearly understood Marty's last words. Someone was after all of them! Someone was going to get them!

And Judy was the first . . .

When Frankie entered the house, he found Doreen sitting in the parlor, talking to two police officers. The other children were nowhere in sight, and Frankie wasn't certain he'd be welcome among the adults. But when she saw him,

Doreen opened her arms. He ran to her and scrambled up on the couch, tucking his body close to hers.

"Should he be here?" asked one of the cops, a woman with a tight cap of curls. Frankie read the name Haines on her uniform pocket.

"Frankie can't hear you," Doreen said. "Go ahead and ask your questions."

The male officer leaned forward. His name, Frankie read, was Shaver.

"There have been an unusual number of accidents here since you moved in," he said. "The man who fell from the ladder and that poor guy who was killed by that weather vane. Not to mention the little girl who was hurt—"

"You knew about that?" Doreen asked.

"Things get around in this town," Officer Haines said. "And now everyone's talking about Judy Wagner's death."

Doreen straightened herself.

"That didn't happen on this property," she said. "Judy was five miles away."

"We know that," the policewoman replied. "But the fact that she worked for you is significant. Now, it just looks like a series of tragic accidents. But to have so many associated with one establishment—"

"Do you have any enemies?" Officer Shaver asked. "Anyone who might be trying to hurt you?"

That's what I've been trying to figure out for myself, Doreen thought. Aloud, she said: "I run an organization to help the children of this area. How could anyone object to that?"

"What about your assistant?" Officer Haines asked. "Was she in any kind of trouble? Did she have any enemies?"

Doreen felt a chill wash over her skin, and Judy's last words came back to her as clearly as if the young woman were sitting next to her.

"We can fight this thing, whatever it is."

"You don't think someone sabotaged her car, do you?" Doreen asked.

"It's been impounded," Officer Shaver said. "Not that there's much left of it. But you didn't answer my question."

Doreen shook her head. "No, Judy didn't have any enemies."

For a moment, she considered telling the two police officers what Judy had said on the phone the other day. But she held back, sensing that they'd find Judy's talk of the mansion's history completely irrelevant. After all, these were people who dealt with the reality of crime and malevolent human beings. How seriously could they possibly take Judy's beliefs that the house was haunted?

"She was a nice person who never hurt anyone," Doreen added, finally. "I don't know how this could have happened to her."

"It may not have been directed at her personally," Officer Shaver said. "She may have become a victim simply by her association with this place."

The policeman looked around, taking in the rich decor of the parlor.

"I understand this house was on the market as a foreclosure?"

"That's right," Doreen said. "That's the only reason we were able to afford it. We only had to pay the back taxes."

"Well, someone had to owe those taxes," Shaver said. "Could that person be trying to cause trouble?"

Doreen's eyes widened.

"I hadn't thought of that," she said. "But it's your job to protect us from people like that."

Officer Haines gave her partner a tap.

"Don't you remember, Stan?" she asked. "The owner of this house killed himself years ago!"

She rubbed her lip with the knuckle of her forefinger, eyeing Doreen.

"Maybe I shouldn't have said that," she said. "You aren't superstitious, are you?"

"I already knew there was a suicide here," Doreen said.

"That happened years ago, and it has nothing to do with me."

But Judy thought the history of the house was significant enough, she thought.

"My assistant," she said, "was looking up some information about that. But I don't think she could have found anything that would upset anyone. I mean, most of that's old history by now, isn't it? Who would hurt her over something that happened so long ago?"

Doreen shook her head, bringing her hands to her eyes to keep them from filling again.

"Please find the person who did this to her," she begged. "Please find out who's trying to hurt us and make them stop!"

Yolanda had taken the children into the kitchen to comfort them as best she could while Doreen spoke to the police. But Randy soon grew impatient with the housekeeper's inability to answer their questions. Without a word he slipped away from the table and went out into the hall, hoping he could hear what Doreen and the cops were saying to each other. Pressing his back against the wall just outside the archway, he slid down to the floor and wrapped his arms around his knees. What was all this talk, he wondered, about someone being their enemy? Judy was so nice—who'd want to hurt her? And how could anyone not like a neat person like Doreen?

"Love one another," Randy whispered.

He glanced toward the staircase, which looked monstrous and dark from his crouched-down position. His room was up there, with the Bible. And the Bible would answer his questions . . .

Randy hurried upstairs. He kept the Bible hidden under the Space Warriors space station he had set up on his bureau. Pulling aside the cavernous plastic model, he took out the book. Small gray-and-blue figurines fell to the rug as his hand knocked against them, but Randy made no move to pick them up.

He walked to his bed and climbed in, reaching behind himself to prop his pillow against the headboard. Then he opened the book and began to read. The pages felt soft to his fingers, edges flaking away as he turned each leaf. Randy liked the musty smell of this old book, which reminded him of so many of the volumes his father had kept in his den. But his father's books weren't about the Lord. They were about strange creatures from other galaxies and weird alien societies. His father had known about so many things . . .

The words in front of him became spots of black on the cream-colored pages. Randy blinked, rubbing his tear-filled eyes with his wrists. He couldn't focus on the words of the Scriptures, no matter how hard he tried.

"Dumb book!" he cried suddenly. He flung it across the room with all his might. "You're just a bunch of stupid words! You can't tell me why people have to go and die!"

He brought his knees up to his chest and buried his head in them, starting to sob. A painful feeling began to swell within him, something he hadn't felt since after his parents were killed.

"I want my d-d-daddy," he whined. "I want my mom!"

The bed shook just a little bit, the mattress sinking as if someone was climbing in with the boy. Randy felt arms going around him, and a hand patting him on the back. And then the Bible was thrust back into his hands.

"Read, boy," a familiar voice said. *"Read your Holy Book and you will know how the Lord deals with hussies like your guardian. You will know the reason for the horrors you have witnessed in this house."*

Randy sniffled, picking up his head slowly. The woman was there, sitting on the edge of his bed. The last gasp of his tears made his body shudder.

"How'd you get in here?" he asked softly.

"You do not question me," the woman said. *"You do as I tell you."*

Randy looked down at the Bible with stinging eyes. Slowly, he opened it again. This time, he didn't want to read. He just wanted to be alone for a little while. But he was afraid to defy the woman.

"Do you—do you know why Judy was k-killed?"

The woman did not reply.

"Why—why is someone trying to hurt Doreen?"

"She is wicked," the woman said. *"She lusts after a man who is not hers for loving. Until she leaves this place, the Lord will continue to punish her by destroying those around her."*

"But this is our home!"

"It is my home!"

The woman stood up now, black sleeves flowing from her outstretched arms. As Randy watched in horror, she began to grow, her body stretching toward the ceiling. Her screams of rage filled the room, making the curtains wave and the furniture rattle.

Randy threw his arms over his head. He tried to close his eyes, but something made him watch her elongated body as it wavered back and forth. She was huge, her wild hair brushing against the ceiling.

"My hoooommmmmme!"

Then the cloudlike apparition began to curl up, swirling until it formed a ball of light. As Randy watched from his bed, his body stiff with fear, the ball shot around the room. It knocked his Space Warriors figures from the dresser and pulled down the clothes hung on the back of his door.

Then, somehow, it squeezed itself through the keyhole and disappeared.

For a long time, Randy just sat where he was, too horrified to move. He stared at the figurines that were scattered over the floor, trying to understand what had happened to them. They were black now, twisted globs of melted plastic.

Slowly, the little boy climbed from the bed and went to retrieve his toys. They were ruined, all the figurines his father had given him over the years. Randy gathered them close to his chest and began to cry.

He wanted his daddy back again. He wanted this nightmare to end.

21

As she stood in the front doorway watching the police car pull away, Doreen was relieved to see Larry Harlan's Bronco driving up. The slam of Larry's truck door echoed loudly in the empty yard, reminding Doreen how noisy it had been just a few days ago when the workers were still here.

"I left my rounds to a colleague, and got here as fast as I could."

Doreen and Larry embraced.

She sighed. "You saw the police leave. We've been talking for the past hour. They wonder if there's a connection between the two accidents that happened here and Judy's accident."

"What do you think?"

"Judy's car crashed five miles from here," Doreen said.

"But you said she wasn't a reckless driver," Larry pointed out. "If there's one thing that connects the three incidents, it's that none of them make sense. According to his co-workers, Trevor Crane was a crackerjack worker with years of experience. And didn't you tell me the guy up on the roof has no idea how the weather vane slipped from his hands?"

Doreen rested her head in the palm of her hand, weaving her fingers through her hair. She laughed, but there was no mirth in her voice.

"Funny," she said, "I'm thinking of something Judy told me a few days ago. I balked at the time, but now it's beginning to make more sense than anything I've heard."

She looked up, directly into Larry's eyes.

"She suggested this house might be haunted."

"Oh, really," he said. "I thought you had more common sense than that, Doreen."

"Damn it, Larry! Did I say I agreed with her?"

She waved a hand at him. "I'm sorry. I just don't know how to deal with this. Part of me says we should get the hell out, before whatever's happening turns on the kids. But more of me says we're going to fight it out and stay."

"I think the 'more of me' part is going to win," Larry said. "I never knew you to give up, Doreen."

"But if there's going to be a fight, I've got to find out what I'm fighting. The last time I talked to Judy, she said she had some information on the house that would interest me. I don't know what it was, but I'm going to try to find out."

Larry was about to answer her when an ear-piercing shriek sounded outside her door. In an instant, Larry was on his feet, pulling on the door. Doreen ran past him, toward the spot at the bottom of the stairs where Tara stood screaming.

"Tara!" Doreen cried, grabbing for the little girl.

Tara went on screaming, pointing a trembling hand up the stairs.

"Oh, my God," Larry whispered.

Randy stood at the top, his small hand clutching the banister. Strange caterwauling noises came from his wide mouth. His clothes were shredded, blackened at the edges as if they'd been scorched. Thick fingers of blood oozed from beneath his long, dark bangs. His body began to waver back and forth.

Larry raced up the stairs, catching the child just as he fainted. Doreen came quickly behind him.

"What happened to him?" she asked, turning to Randy's twin.

"He was talking crazy!" Tara cried. "He kept saying we're all gonna pay for our sins! What sins, Doreen? What made him say that?"

The little girl followed as Doreen and Larry carried her brother to the bathroom.

"Get the first-aid kit, Doreen," Larry ordered. "Tara, tell Yolanda to call an ambulance!"

Larry had found some washcloths, and was pressing them to the cuts on the little boy's face. All the while, Randy kept on whining.

"What's wrong with him?" Doreen asked.

"I don't know," Larry said. "Randy, did you hit your head?"

Randy didn't answer. His wailing had ceased, but now he was talking softly, his sentences so rapid Larry couldn't make them out. Larry replaced the compress on the child's head with a new one, holding the boy close to him to stop the bleeding.

"Get me some bandages," he said.

Tara returned at that moment, gasping for breath.

"Yolanda's calling 911," she said.

Randy was mumbling something, staring at the seashell pattern of the wallpaper as Larry dressed his wound. Doreen leaned closer.

"Sinners all, since Adam's fall," Randy whispered. "Have to pay, have to pray, face the Lord on Judgment Day."

"Randy, stop that," Doreen commanded, straightening herself.

The little boy paid no attention, his lips still moving. Larry took another washcloth from Tara, who stood staring with round eyes, and replaced the bloodied one. He looked up at Doreen with concern.

"The sooner we get him to the hospital the better," he said. "I want a good look at the cut on his forehead, but there's too much blood now."

Doreen knelt down and put her hands on Randy's

shoulders. Leaning against Dr. Harlan, the little boy didn't
move to look at her.

"Come on, Randy," she said. "Want to tell me what
happened? Did you fall? Did you hit your head?"

"Paying for my sins," Randy said in a loud voice. "For
being bad."

"You aren't bad, Randy!" Tara cried.

Doreen reached for a towel and began to wipe the
streaks of blood from Randy's cheeks.

"Of course you aren't bad," she soothed. "Randy, did
someone do this to you? Did someone hit you?"

Randy cringed, pushing himself closer to the doctor.

"Randy, please tell me! Who did this to you? Tell me
who it was so I can make them stop hurting you!"

Now the little boy looked up at her, his expression so
malevolent that Doreen pulled back the towel she'd been
using to clean him.

"You'll pay for your wickedness," he snarled.

"Randy, how could . . . ?"

Larry waved a hand at her. "Get me a blanket, Doreen,"
he said. "I want this child ready when the ambulance gets
here."

Doreen moved to embrace Randy, but turned instead
and ran to find a blanket. On the way, she quickly looked
into Karen's room. Karen was asleep, oblivious to all the
commotion. She hurried into Randy's room, thinking she'd
grab one of his Space Warriors to keep him company in the
hospital. When she saw the twisted, blackened remains of
the toys, she felt something knot inside her.

She clutched one of the ruined figurines tightly and
threw her head back to yell at the ceiling, as if whatever it
was she wanted to fight was floating above her, in another
dimension.

"What do you want from us?" she screamed. "These are
just children! Go away and leave us alone! Just leave us
alone!"

"Doreen, how come you're yelling?"

Doreen turned with a start to see Harry-John in the doorway.

"And how come you're crying?"

"I'm just upset," she said. "Randy's very sick and I'm concerned."

"I—I came up to tell you the ambulance is here."

She heard Larry calling to her, and suddenly she remembered the blanket. Grabbing a corner of the comforter on Randy's bed, she pulled it toward her. She heard a soft *clump* and noticed a black book on the rug.

"What's that?" she asked.

Harry-John went to pick it up. "It says 'Holy Bible.' What's Randy doing reading a Bible?"

"I don't know," Doreen replied, extending her hand for the book.

But it might explain where he's getting all this religious talk from.

The ambulance attendants had come upstairs and were strapping Randy to a stretcher. As his sister sobbed in the background, Randy stared at the ceiling, still mumbling to himself. The paramedics carried him downstairs, with Larry close behind.

"I'll follow you in my car," Doreen said.

Downstairs, the other children gathered around Yolanda, watching the scene with anxious curiosity. Doreen hurried past them to her office. She left the Bible on her desk, grabbed her car keys, and headed for her car.

Pushing through glass doors marked OAKWOOD GENERAL HOSPITAL, Doreen said to a nurse, "Dr. Harlan just brought one of my foster children in. Can you tell me where to find him?"

The nurse pointed toward a green-and-white-striped curtain. Doreen went to it and called her friend's name.

A moment later, the curtain was pulled back. Larry unhooked his stethoscope and tucked it into his pocket. He shook his head, a look of complete bewilderment on his face.

"Is Randy going to be all right?"

"Physically, he's fine," Larry said. "I can't figure it out."

"What do you mean?"

"I mean, there isn't a mark on him. Doreen, you saw the blood as well as I did. But there isn't a scratch on that child's skin, let alone a cut big enough for that much bleeding."

"That doesn't make any sense."

"Unless it was someone else's blood."

Doreen's eyebrows went up.

"But whose?" she asked. "There was no one else upstairs when Tara called for me, except Karen, but she was asleep. And there's no way anyone could have gotten away without our noticing. And none of the other children were hurt!"

"I want to keep him overnight," he said. "I'm having the lab analyze a blood sample. And I think I'm going to recommend psychiatric evaluation."

"What?"

"I think it's necessary, Doreen. Until I gave that child a sedative, he did nothing but mumble religious nonsense. That isn't normal behavior for a ten-year-old, and certainly not for the Randy Welder I've always known! Something is happening to that boy, and I need to find out what it is."

"Not as much as I do," Doreen said softly.

She moved past Larry to the gurney, reaching out to touch Randy's forehead. The little boy didn't stir.

"You're not the Randy Welder I've known, either," she said. She looked at Larry. "Please make him right again?"

"I'll do what I can, Doreen. But until we find out what's going on here, nothing's going to change."

Doreen nodded. She took hold of Randy's small hand and brought it up to kiss it. In moments, the child's flesh was stained with tears that had begun to fall again, silently.

22

Dozens of questions crowded Doreen's mind as she drove home, each competing with the others and making it impossible for her to concentrate.

"All I want," she whispered, "is to sleep for about ten days."

Since few people lived along this route, there were no streetlights, and the only illumination on the mountain roadway was Doreen's headlights. Suddenly, a dark shape appeared in front of her car. With a cry, Doreen slammed on her brakes, bringing the station wagon to an abrupt halt. She was able to make out a woman's figure, hunched over and moving slowly across the road in front of her car. Angrily, Doreen rolled down her window and leaned out to scream, "Are you crazy?"

The woman turned to look at her, and to her dismay Doreen saw that it was the same person she'd seen crying in the woods twice before. She extended her hand toward Doreen, then gave a cry and ran, disappearing into the woods again.

With a heavy sigh, Doreen leaned back and said, "I don't need this tonight!"

She rolled the window back up quickly and started home again. The sudden appearance of the strange woman made her wonder again if she had anything to do with what had been happening. Though she looked small and frail,

there was something maniacal in her expression that sent
chills through Doreen.

"If you are the one who's been hurting my kids," Doreen said, "you'll be sorry!"

She pulled up in front of the house. As she walked up
the porch steps, she heard someone call her name; it was
Brendan, walking across the darkened yard.

"Good evening. I couldn't stop thinking about you, and
came to see if you're doing well."

"I'm managing," Doreen said. "Come in, Brendan. I
really need you tonight."

She was reaching for the door when Brendan wrapped
his arms around her and pulled her to him for a long, warm
kiss. He nuzzled her wheat-colored hair and whispered, "I
was so worried, to think how you've been hurt. I want to
protect you, my love."

Doreen's hands worked up and down his back.

"Brendan, I'm so afraid," she said. "I just took Randy
to the hospital. I don't know what's going to happen next!
And I have such a headache."

Brendan cradled her head in his large hands and began
to massage her temples, his callused hands moving in firm,
gentle circles.

"I don't want you to hurt," he said quietly. "Let the pain
go away. Let me help you."

"Oh, Brendan," Doreen breathed.

As his fingers massaged her, Doreen began to feel lightheaded. Shapes in the darkness around her began to waver,
as if the shadows had taken on a life of their own. Her eyes
closed, then opened again to slits.

For a split second she saw a small child with blond hair
standing near her car.

Her eyes opened wide, but he was gone.

"Who is that?" she cried, looking beyond Brendan's
shoulder.

"Who are you calling?" Brendan asked.

Doreen pointed to her car.

"There was a little boy standing there."

Brendan looked for himself.

"I don't see anyone," he said. "We're alone, my love. You're tired, and your eyes are seeing what isn't there."

Doreen closed her eyes and nodded.

"Of course," she said. "You're right."

"Is the pain gone from your head?"

Doreen paused for a moment. Then she looked up in amazement.

"Yes, it is! Brendan, you must have a magic touch."

She recalled the other times when he'd soothed her— once at the lake and the time after telling him of Judy's accident.

"How do you do that?" she asked. "Your touch is so soothing that it makes me forget everything."

"I love you," Brendan said, "and you can sense this when we're together."

"Oh, Brendan," she said, embracing him again, "I love you, too. You're the only good thing that's happened since we've moved here!"

Brendan nodded. "I'm happy that we've become more than neighbors."

His words made her think of another neighbor, the strange woman who'd walked in front of her car.

"Brendan, can you tell me about the other people who live in this area?" she asked. "One person in particular. There's a young woman with long, dark hair. She's very tiny, and I think she's about twenty years old. Do you know who she is?"

Brendan shook his head. "She doesn't sound familiar. Perhaps she's from one of the nearby farms? Why do you ask?"

Doreen told him what had happened on her way home that night, then told him about seeing the same woman in the woods before.

"I wonder if she might have something to do with the trouble we've had." Doreen said.

"She was crying out that someone was hurting her?" Brendan asked.

"But there was no one there," Doreen said. "I think she might be a little—"

Her words were interrupted by the sounds of shattering glass and screams. A lamp crashed on the gravel below them.

"That came from Karen's room," Doreen said, looking up.

She bolted into the house. Doreen's thoughts had turned completely to her children, and by the time she entered Karen's room Brendan was forgotten.

Karen was out of bed, leaning crookedly against the frame of her shattered window. The curtains had been ripped down and were lying in billowy piles around the teenager's ankles. Pieces of glass glistened on the windowsill.

"Karen, what happened?"

The young girl turned around, her dark eyes full of hatred. Doreen's heart jumped into her throat, and she took an involuntary step backward.

It was the same look Randy had given her after his accident.

"Why do you see him?" Karen demanded. "Why does he come to you?"

"Karen? What are you talking about?"

"That man!" Karen cried. "He doesn't belong here! You shouldn't be seeing him!"

"Karen Steiff, what business is it of yours who I see?" Doreen asked, annoyed now. "What on earth is going on with you kids, anyway? Look at that window!"

Karen turned to look at it as if she didn't know what had happened. Then her lower lip began to tremble, and tears poured from her eyes.

"I had to stop you," she said. "Had to stop you from giving yourself to him like a common harlot!"

Doreen could hardly believe what the young girl was saying. What teenager used expressions like *common harlot*? Feeling her anger rising, Doreen hurried over to

Karen, grabbed her by the elbow, and led her firmly toward the bed.

"My leg!" Karen protested.

Doreen ignored her, pulling her down until they were both seated on the edge of the bed. Then she took Karen's head in her hands and held it so that the youngster was forced to make eye contact.

"Karen, something is happening to you," she said. "Don't you see it? You've thrown out your makeup and fashion magazines. You've destroyed your perfume bottle collection—your only remembrance of your mother. And now you're acting as if my relationship with Brendan is something dirty and evil."

Karen nodded, moving Doreen's hands with her head. Doreen's fingertips began to feel warm as tears wet them.

"This isn't you, Karen," Doreen said. "Someone is teaching you these things, and I want to know who it is!"

Karen sniffled, but wouldn't reply.

"Sweetheart, listen to me," Doreen said, pressing on. "Randy is in the hospital tonight. Someone put him there! And I don't think Judy's death was an accident. Please help me! Tell me who's doing this!"

"Nobody," Karen whispered.

"Karen, please . . ."

"Nobody!" Karen screamed. "Leave me alone!"

She began to sob harder, her whole body shaking. Doreen took her hands away and tried to embrace the child. But Karen pulled back abruptly, shielding herself with a stuffed animal. She looked so hurt and helpless that Doreen wanted to hold her and rock her like a little child. But there was something more in Karen's expression, something so unnerving that Doreen simply stood up.

Karen looked as if she blamed Doreen for her pain.

"You can't sleep in here with that broken window," Doreen said softly. "Go down the hall to my room and use my bed."

Karen just stared at her, still crying.

"I'll sleep on the couch in my office. And we'll fix your window tomorrow."

A sharp pain went through her temples, and she realized that the headache had returned.

"I'm going to get some aspirin," Doreen said. "I'll be back to check on you in a few minutes."

Doreen left the room, closing the door behind her. Instantly, like a faucet, Karen's tears came to a halt. She stared at the door, her eyes focused on the red robe that hung there.

Slowly, the robe darkened to a black shape, and the shape took on a human form. With her gown floating like black gossamer, the apparition moved toward Karen's bed.

"You did well," she whispered. *"You've kept our secret."*

"Doreen doesn't think she's bad," Karen said.

"Of course not," the woman replied. *"No sinner recognizes herself. That's why we must help her, why we must punish her so that she will know her folly. The time is coming soon, young girl. You will reveal the true nature of your guardian to her superiors, as you did long ago, and you will end her sinful ways."*

"How?" Karen asked.

But the woman had disappeared, and the room was quiet. A soft breeze blew through the hole in the window, tossing Karen's hair and chilling her skin. The woman's words echoed in her mind, and she longed to call her back to explain them.

She had said "as you did long ago." But what did that mean? She'd never talked to Doreen's "superiors," whoever they were! She didn't even know Doreen a long time ago!

But she had come to trust the woman completely, and knew she'd return with an explanation when she felt the time was right.

Painfully, Karen pulled herself up to her feet and hobbled across her room to the door. She'd sleep in Doreen's room tonight, as instructed. But she would sleep on the floor, not in the bed where Doreen might have laid with wicked thoughts.

"I won't touch anything dirty," Karen whispered, moving slowly down the hall.

Faintly, Karen could hear the water running in Doreen's bathroom. She thought about going to wait in Doreen's room to talk to her. The woman said Doreen was dirty, but how could that be when she was washing herself right now?

"Only pain will cleanse away her sins."

Karen looked around, expecting the woman to be at her side. But the hallway was empty and quiet except for the sound of running water.

As Karen worked her long and difficult way down the hallway, Doreen was stepping carefully into the bathtub. The aspirin had yet to take effect, and the tension had moved down into her arms and legs. Slowly, cringing at the feel of steaming hot water against her skin, Doreen lowered herself into the tub. She rested her head against the tub's sloping back and sunk down as far as she could.

"Oh, Brendan, I shouldn't have sent you away," she whispered. "I wish those fingers of yours could be here now to get rid of this damned headache."

A picture of him smiling at her came to mind and brought an unexpected smile to her own face. With her eyes closed she dreamed of the kiss Brendan had given her out on the porch, so unexpected and as warm as this water.

She wondered what it would be like to make love to such a handsome, considerate, loving man.

"Doreen?" Karen shouted from the hall outside.

With a groan, Doreen grabbed the sides of the tub and pulled herself to a sitting position.

"What is it, Karen?" she called back.

When Karen didn't answer, Doreen reluctantly got to her feet and stepped out of the tub. The water was still hot, and her muscles still longed for its soothing ripples. But the children came first, and it sounded as if Karen needed help. Doreen pulled on her terry cloth robe, opened the bathroom door and walked out to the hall.

"Karen?"

The hallway was empty and quiet. Doreen walked across it and opened Karen's door, but there was no sign of the teenager. Maybe she had called out because she needed help getting to Doreen's room. Doreen walked back down the hall to her own room to make sure Karen wasn't in there. Maybe she was playing a little prank.

But the comforter was as smooth as it had been when Doreen made the bed that morning. Karen was nowhere in the room. Doreen closed the door again and began to look through the whole upstairs, checking each room with no results.

"Karen?"

She turned the corner into the shorter hallway and checked the rooms Judy had locked up. For a moment, she remembered that they'd thought Cindy was in one of them, only to have discovered she had been in the basement. Of course, Karen couldn't have gotten way down there with her cast.

But even as Doreen searched the upstairs rooms, Karen was fighting an invisible power that held her by her arms and dragged her along the downstairs hallway.

"Doreen!"

She shouted as loudly as she could, struggling against the captor she couldn't see, but no one responded. Her legs were splayed out, her cast thumping strangely over the carpet. Karen twisted and turned, shouting until her voice was hoarse.

"Help me!"

But no one heard her. Karen began to cry, grabbing awkwardly for the frame of the door through which she was dragged into the small triangular hallway by the cellar door. She looked desperately toward the kitchen, hoping

Yolanda would be working there, but the room was dark.

There was a scraping noise, and Karen lost all ability to scream as she saw the lock unfasten by itself. The door swung open, revealing the black abyss of the cellar. Karen began to whine, her throat sore and unable to make anything more than small, pathetic sounds.

And then she heard the voice of the strange woman.

"She wants to take over your soul," she said. *"She wants you to stay in her room so that she can influence you with her wickedness."*

"You're hurting me," Karen whimpered.

"I'm taking you to safety, girl," the disembodied voice said. *"Come into the darkness, and you will be protected from the evil of those who pretend to love you."*

Thump, thump, thump—Karen's cast pounded down the new wooden staircase, pain shooting up her leg each time her cast struck the next step. She closed her eyes, tears streaming down her face. Why didn't anyone hear her? Why didn't anyone come to help?

She was too weak to struggle, in too much pain to fight back. As they descended the staircase, the light from the hallway above grew dimmer, until it diminished entirely. Karen closed her eyes, terrified, and prayed for the strength to fight this thing that was so incredibly strong. The concrete floor felt cold to the backs of her legs, and cobwebs tickled her cheeks and arms.

"Come into the darkness, girl," the woman whispered. *"The darkness will keep out the influences around you. There, you will pray that the wickedness of your guardian has not blackened your soul. Pray, or the fires of hell will forever burn your young flesh!"*

They had reached a wall, and Karen thought she would be dropped here. But her body kept going, even when her shoulders struck the damp, moss-covered wood. The walls seemed to turn to liquid, consuming her. Threads of moss drew ice-cold lines across her skin, something gelatinous poured itself over her body. Karen opened her mouth to scream, watching her body pulled through the wall, watching the last view of the basement disappear as the wall closed around her feet.

The thing that had been dragging her let go at last, dropping her onto the cold, slimy floor.

23

It was terribly dark. Randy stood at his dresser and searched through the top drawer for his flashlight, the one his father had given to him long ago.

"What's the matter, son?"

Randy turned, hoping to see his father standing behind him, alive again. But there was only an open door leading to another, blacker room. Randy grabbed the flashlight and aimed it at the dark, walking ahead as if the beam itself were pulling him. He entered a long, unfamiliar hallway. The light bounced off a figure at the far end.

"Come here, son!"

Randy raced down the hall, arms opened wide.

But it wasn't his father waiting for him. Randy stopped short, screaming a soundless scream when he saw the woman in black standing there, her feet inches above the ground. She raised her arms up high, like a bird about to take flight.

"This house is mine!"

The scream startled Randy's body into semiwakefulness, and he rolled over, hitting the metal railing on the side of his hospital bed. Frantic, disoriented, he turned around and got on his knees. His hands raced over the twisted sheets and under the pillows. The Bible! Where was his Bible?

183

"Where's my Bible?" he cried.

"Go to sleep, kid," an unfamiliar voice said.

"Harry-John?"

"My name's Jamie," came the reply. "Calm down! You musta been havin' a bad dream or something."

Slowly, Randy took in his surroundings. He was in a large room, and there were three other boys in white-sheeted beds. All of the beds had the same metal railings, and there were odd-looking panels with wires and buttons behind each one. What was this place? Where was Doreen?

"Don't you remember coming here?" another child asked. "You're in the hospital. What's wrong with you?"

"I—I don't know," Randy said. "My head hurts a little bit."

He thought for a moment, trying to remember what had happened to bring him here, but his mind was a blank. Now that he was waking up completely, his head was really starting to hurt. Had he bumped it?

"You were yellin' something about a Bible," the second boy mentioned.

Randy frowned at him.

"A Bible?" he echoed. "What would I want with an old Bible?"

The second boy shrugged. "It was your dream, not mine," he said.

Randy threw aside his covers. He didn't like being in a place he didn't know, and he wanted to call Doreen to find out what was going on.

"I gotta find a phone," he said. "How do you get out of these beds?"

He took hold of the railing and started shaking it. What a dumb thing to put on a kid's bed, he thought, as if he were a baby!

"Try pushing that black button on the end," Jamie suggested.

Randy did as he was told, and the bed rail slid forward and down with a crash. Across the room the fourth child rolled over and cried out. "Shut up! Some of us got our appendixes out two days ago, you know!"

"Go back to sleep, Mike," Jamie ordered.

Randy climbed out of the bed, the tile floor chilling his bare feet. He was dressed in a light cotton hospital gown, and although it was summer he felt very cold.

"I don't know why you're bothering," Jamie said. "No one's going to let you use a phone in the middle of the night. Why don't you wait until your folks come in the morning?"

"'Cause I don't feel like it, " Randy snapped, looking around for something to put on over the hospital gown. "Where're my clothes?"

"They sent 'em home with your mom," Mike said from under his covers.

"She's not my mother," Randy growled.

"You can borrow my robe," the second boy offered. "It's the red-and-yellow one hanging on that hook."

"Thanks," Randy said, taking down the robe. He slipped it on, and even though it was several sizes too big he felt warmer. Someone had embroidered BILLY across the front pocket. "I'll be back in a little while."

"Don't let the nurse see you!" Jamie called.

Opening the door, Randy looked up and down the bright hallway. In an effort to cheer the place up, someone had painted candyland scenes along the wall. Flower baskets were hung from the ceiling between every two doors, and the floor had been tiled in bright white and orange. This floor felt even colder to his bare feet than the floor in his room. He could see the edge of the nurses' station just beyond the next corner, and he heard two women talking to one another. In the other direction, there was a big sign that said ELEVATORS. Randy decided to go that way, hoping to find a telephone. Maybe Doreen would be mad if he woke her up, but he just had to talk to her!

Randy found the elevator bank through a pair of swinging doors, but there were no telephones. Undaunted, he took a quick look around to be sure no one was watching,

then pressed each one of the four buttons. Two elevators
arrived, one with a man in a wheelchair in it. Randy chose
the other, empty one. He got inside, then glanced up and
down the number panel. Where would he go now that he'd
gotten this far?

"Four," he said, pushing that button. "That's a good
number."

He watched the numbers flash overhead, then moved
closer to the door as the elevator passed the third floor.
When the door opened, Randy stepped out, relieved to see
that this elevator bank was deserted, too. Now all he had to
do was find a phone.

He heard someone talking just then, and ducked behind
a large plant. Randy watched as two young men in lab
coats went to stand by the elevators.

The elevator opened and the men disappeared. Randy
came out of his hiding place. Where to now? he wondered.
Where would he find a phone? He looked up at the big
plastic letters on the wall and read: INTENSIVE CARE.

Wondering what that meant, Randy pushed open one of
the swinging doors, ignoring the sign that said AUTHOR-
IZED PERSONNEL ONLY.

This floor was different from the one where he'd been.
There were no pictures painted on the walls, just a few
framed posters from the last Olympics. The floor was plain
white and the walls light green. It was noisier here, too.
Randy could hear phones and bells ringing, and from
somewhere far off a voice called for a Dr. Abramson.

Slowly, he walked down the hall, looking all around
himself. He saw a recessed area up ahead and wondered if
there would be a phone there. He could hear some nurses
talking to each other, and he hoped they wouldn't see him.

Curiosity made him read the names posted outside the
doors, and he wondered what was wrong with the people in
the rooms. Some of the doors had been left open, and
Randy stopped to look into one room, its occupant an old
woman hooked up with wires and hoses. He shuddered,
turning quickly away. But when he got to the next room,

he stopped again. One of the door signs said TREVOR CRANE.

"Wow," Randy whispered.

He knew that this was the man who had fallen from the ladder at the house. And he also knew that Doreen had been trying her best to find out how he was doing. Wouldn't she be pleased if Randy was able to answer her questions? He wouldn't bother the guy. He'd just take a look at him.

Randy glanced quickly up and down the hall, then entered the room. There was a very old man sleeping in the bed nearest the door, and Randy tiptoed past him. He found Trevor asleep on the bed next to a flower-lined windowsill. Randy didn't really want to look at the sick man, so he busied himself for a moment with one of the numerous Get Well cards. He could hear something clicking with a steady rhythm and the lulling sound of slow breathing.

Biting his lip, he turned to face Trevor's body.

"You don't look so bad," Randy whispered, letting himself breathe again.

Trevor had more wires connected to him than the old lady next door, and there was a monitor at his side that make a long series of squiggly lines. Randy knew from listening to Doreen and Dr. Harlan that Trevor was in a coma, and that this meant he was sort of asleep. Doreen was worried that he might never wake up, and Dr. Larry had said there'd been no progress. But Trevor didn't even look sick!

Carefully, Randy leaned closer to the man and looked at his face.

Trevor's eyes snapped open, and he stared up at Randy with a frightened expression.

"Oh, gee!" Randy cried, backing up.

Trevor's hand shot out, grabbing the little boy. The man struggled against the IV tube in his arm, turning onto his side. His breathing was labored, but his grip was surprisingly strong when Randy tried to pull away.

"I—I know you," Trevor gasped.

"Let me go," Randy begged, wide-eyed.

"You have to listen," Trevor said, struggling with each word. "It's dangerous to—to—to stay at that house. Get out! Get out before she k-k-kills you!"

"Let go of me!" Randy shouted, jerking away.

He ran out of the room, not looking where he was going. Someone grabbed him from behind, and as he struggled to get away he heard a woman say, "What on earth are you doing here? It's nearly eleven P.M.! How did you get on this floor?"

Randy looked up at her. There was a name tag on her shirt that read A. FREDERICKS.

"That man's awake," he said, pointing into Trevor's room. "He was talking to me!"

The nurse abruptly let go of him and hurried into her patient's room. But Trevor was as quiet as he had been when she'd left him a short while earlier, still breathing through the tube in his nose. She checked the monitor, but it didn't indicate any recent changes in his brain activity. Surely he hadn't been awake!

She stormed out of the room, ready to reprimand the little boy, but he was nowhere to be seen.

"Well, I'll just make a call down to Pediatrics," Nurse Fredericks said, "and tell them they'd better keep a closer watch on their little ones!"

In the meantime, Randy had raced as fast as he could to the elevator bank. His heart was pounding, and he rocked nervously back and forth on his bare feet as he waited for an elevator. When one finally came, he hurried inside and begged the door to close before the nurse caught up to him.

If he could just make it down to his room, and jump quickly back into bed, he could pretend he had never left!

But there was just one problem, he didn't remember where his room was.

He decided to punch every number. Then he'd only get out if the floor looked familiar. The elevator bell rang loudly each time the doors opened, and Randy peeked out to see where he was. Maternity, Ear-Nose-Throat (they called it ENT), Radiology—it seemed he'd never reach the floor with the children's ward.

Then, at last, he saw the big plastic letters that read PEDIATRICS.

He jumped out of the elevator and ran to the swinging doors. But this time, rather than pushing through them, he stood on tiptoe and looked through the small window to be sure the coast was clear. He saw one of the nurses in the hall, and waited until she'd gone into a room before entering the ward. Every muscle in his body was tense because he anticipated getting caught, but by some miracle he made it back to his room unseen.

"Mrs. Varon was just in here checking on us. She knows you were up," Jamie said.

"Did you find a phone at least?" Billy asked.

Randy shook his head. He had found something else, but he didn't want to talk about it. Shaking all over, he slid under his covers and turned away from the other boys. He didn't feel like talking. He just wanted to figure out what had happened. How come Trevor was awake? And what was he talking about? Why were they all in danger?

Bit by bit, memories came back to him. He saw images of his Space Warriors figurines, all black and twisted. He saw his sister pointing at him, screaming. Then Dr. Larry running up the stairs and Doreen shouting something at him. But why? What had happened to him?

"What did you find out there?" Jamie asked.

Randy pulled his covers up over his head.

"Nothing," he lied. "I don't wanna talk right now."

He was not only frightened, he was also angry with himself for not finding a phone. Trevor had said they were in danger, and Randy wished he could have called Doreen to warn her. He didn't know why, but a sense of dread was starting to fill him, and he was terrified that something very, very bad was going to happen back at the house.

24

Doreen had thoroughly searched all of the upstairs rooms, but couldn't find a sign of Karen. The other children were sound asleep in their own rooms, alone. Completely bewildered, she longed for the simplicity of the old ranch house. Maybe it had been crowded there, but it had been safe. This place had so many rooms and closets that Karen could be hiding anywhere!

"No!" she said out loud. "I won't allow myself to be turned against our new home!"

A door opened with a soft creaking noise, and Tara came out into the hallway, rubbing her eyes. Her bare toes poked out from beneath the ruffle of her long blue nightgown.

"What's going on?" she asked groggily. "I thought I heard Karen yelling. Is she okay?"

"Of course she is," Doreen lied. "Go back to bed."

Instead, Tara shuffled over to Doreen and wrapped her arms around the woman's waist. Resting her head against Doreen, she said, "I was dreaming about Randy. He was yelling for help and I couldn't get to him! Then I woke up and I heard Karen. It sounded like she was downstairs."

She looked up at Doreen.

"But that's silly, isn't it? Karen couldn't be downstairs!"

But where else can she be? Doreen thought.

"Go back to bed, Tara," she said. "You'll need your rest so you can go to pick up Randy tomorrow. Would you like that?"

Tara smiled, nodding.

"I miss my brother," she said. "I wish he didn't get hurt. I wish I could figure out what happened!"

"Dr. Harlan said Randy's just fine," Doreen replied, wanting Tara to leave her so she could continue her search. She coaxed the child back into her room, helping her under the light coverlet on her bed.

"Good-night, Tara," she said. "And have good dreams this time."

"G'night," Tara murmured, turning onto her side.

Doreen left the room, hurrying down the stairs. Maybe it didn't make sense that Karen could be downstairs, but she was certainly not on the upper floor. She began to call out the young girl's name, her body tense with fear that something had happened to the teenager.

Karen could hear Doreen's voice calling out to her, but she made no attempt to answer her guardian. She sat on the cellar floor, her back against the wall and her two legs straight out in front of her. Her ankle throbbed, but it was more annoying than painful. All Karen could see was the faint white outline of her cast, but it didn't even seem to be part of her.

Strangely, she didn't feel frightened. The cold, damp darkness enveloped her like an embrace, and she felt safe here.

If she went upstairs, if she answered Doreen, she wouldn't be safe any longer. She knew that Doreen was the enemy, a soldier of the devil who would twist her soul until the Lord had no more use for her. In the strange, dark room where she had knelt and prayed, an all-consuming hatred of her guardian developed, and fear had turned to strength. She had willed herself back into the dimly lit cellar, and now here she sat, listening to Doreen's desperate cries. But she wouldn't answer.

Two pinpoints of yellow light appeared in one of the

shadows, and tiny feet scampered across the cement floor. A rat's squeal pierced the darkness, but Karen didn't move. She just stared at the retreating shadow, turning her head to watch it go. As she did so, her cheek brushed something soft and moist. Karen reached up to touch the wall behind herself, feeling the damp strands of moss. She closed her eyes and breathed in the foul aroma, not at all repulsed.

She heard the upstairs door open, and heard Doreen arguing with Yolanda.

"She must be down here," Doreen was saying. "There's no place else to look!"

"But how?" Yolanda asked. "She couldn't have walked with that cast!"

Doreen came down the stairs, but Karen couldn't see the beam of the flashlight as it moved around the cellar.

"I wish Sam's people had fixed the wiring down here before they took off on us," Doreen griped. "Karen? Karen, are you down here?"

Now Harry-John came down the stairs, dressed only in his pajama bottoms. He leaned against the sturdy wood railing that had been installed after Trevor Crane's accident. Then he pointed and said, "There she is, Doreen!"

Doreen gasped, turning to look behind herself.

"Harry-John, you scared me!" she cried. "What are you doing out of bed?"

"I came down to get a glass of milk. And I heard you talking to Yolanda. But look, Doreen, there's Karen! How come she's in the basement?"

Doreen shined her light in the direction he was pointing.

"Oh, my Lord," she cried. "Karen, how did you get down here?"

"Please, leave me in peace," Karen said softly.

Doreen ignored her. She knelt down beside the teenager and put a hand gently against her cheek. Karen simply stared ahead.

"What happened, honey?"

"She's freaked out," Harry-John said.

"Go back to bed, HJ," Doreen ordered.

"But I want to stay and watch!" The child protested.

"Damn it! For once, would you just listen and stop giving me a hard time?"

Harry-John took a step back, not knowing what to say. He'd never seen Doreen so angry.

"Get upstairs!" she cried.

Without another word, Harry-John turned and raced up the stairs.

"He's just as frightened by all this as you are," Yolanda said in a gentle voice.

"HJ will be fine," Doreen insisted. "Please, help me get Karen back upstairs."

"Keep your hands off me, heathen witch!" Karen hissed, backing away.

"Karen, why . . . ?"

Yolanda touched Doreen's arm.

"Don't get upset," she cautioned. "We can't find out what happened until we get the child upstairs."

Doreen nodded. "Take her ankles, but be careful of her cast."

"Let me go!"

"Hush, Karen," Yolanda said.

Together, the two women managed to lift the young girl. With Karen hung between them like a hammock, making animal-like sounds of protest, they struggled toward the newly built staircase.

"No, let me go," Karen begged in a weak voice.

"Shh," Doreen said. Walking backward up the stairs, one step at a time, she said to Yolanda, "Thank God this staircase was rebuilt. However Karen got down here, it would have been dangerous with those old stairs!"

"Let's just get her upstairs," Yolanda said breathlessly.

At last they reached the kitchen, where they carefully sat Karen down in a chair. Yolanda pulled a stool over and propped Karen's leg on it, and Doreen wrapped a sweater around the child's shoulders. She noticed the green marks on Karen's face, and touched them gently.

"What's that?" she asked.

She pulled a long, wet strand from Karen's hair, then threw it to the floor with a cry of revulsion.

"Ugh! What is that slime?"

"I heard one of the workers say there's mildew growing downstairs," Yolanda said. "Something to do with it being wet there."

"And probably full of germs," Doreen said worriedly. "Karen, why were you down there? Why didn't you call for help?"

Karen said nothing. She seemed to be studying the checkerboard pattern of the plastic tablecloth.

"Karen, please talk to me," Doreen begged.

"That child isn't going to say a word," Yolanda said. "Doreen, if I were you I'd call the police. Now, we know there's no way Karen could have gotten downstairs by herself."

Doreen stood up, walking toward the phone.

"You're right," she said, dialing the number. "Once and for all, I want them to find out what's happening here!"

When someone answered, Doreen described what had happened and asked for help. To her surprise, a squad car appeared fifteen minutes later. It contained the same two officers she had talked to after Judy's accident.

"There must be some way to put an end to this," Doreen said, leading them into the kitchen. She waved a hand at Karen, then Yolanda. "This is Karen Steiff, one of my foster children. You met Yolanda Berle, my housekeeper."

"Hi, Karen," the male police officer, the one named Shaver, said. He turned to Doreen. "I'm going to take a quick look through the house."

The policewoman, Officer Haines, sat down at the table with Karen.

"Doreen says you got all the way from your room down to the cellar," the officer said. "Tell me how you managed that, Karen."

"I don't remember," Karen whispered.

Doreen took the teenager's hand, but Karen's fingers remained limp in her own.

"Did someone help you?" Officer Haines asked.

"Don't know."

"Karen, have you seen anyone different around here lately? Someone you've never seen before?"

Karen turned at last, glaring at Doreen.

"She's got a new friend," the teenager growled.

"A neighbor," Doreen said to the policewoman. "His name is Brendan Delacorte."

"Where does he live? We might need to question him."

"I'm not exactly sure," Doreen said. "I mean, I don't know his exact address. I do know he lives on one of the nearby farms. But what does Brendan have to do with this? Someone helped this child down those stairs, and I want you to find out who it was!"

"Does this Delacorte fellow have access to this house?"

"Of course not," Doreen said. "I'm very fond of Brendan, but even so I don't give spare keys out to people I've only recently met."

Very fond. The words sounded too superficial, but somehow Doreen didn't feel comfortable telling the police that she had a new boyfriend. Maybe they'd be critical of her, condemning her for falling in love when so much tragedy was happening all around her. Still, she didn't want them dwelling on Brendan, and was grateful when the other police officer returned.

"Not a sign of anyone," he said. "The doors are all locked, and the windows that are open have fans in them. If there was anyone here, he's long gone."

"Did Karen here tell you anything?" he asked of Doreen.

"She can't remember what happened," Doreen said. "Is there any way I can get police protection until we find out who's doing all this?"

"This is a small community," Officer Haines said. "I doubt we have the manpower to provide you with a guard. Besides, there's no definite evidence there was someone here tonight."

"Definite evidence!" Doreen cried. "Look at her! Someone must have helped her down those stairs! What more 'definite evidence' do you need, for God's sake?"

The police officers looked at each other.

"Well, it's amazing what kids can do when they're determined," the policeman said softly.

Doreen could tell by his tone that he was as unconvinced as she was.

"I took one of my other kids to the hospital tonight because he had been struck on the head. Now, maybe he fell and hit it. But he was absolutely terrified, and off in another world the way Karen seems to be right now. Children who have accidents, or who do things by their own willpower, do not act as frightened as these kids."

The two cops thought for a few moments, then Officer Haines looked up.

"I have an idea," she said. "If you really think someone's been lurking around here, bothering the kids, then why don't you have one of them hypnotized? Sometimes children are too frightened of an adult to rat on him, but under hypnotism they can feel free to tell what's happening."

"I'm not so sure about hypnotism for a thirteen-year-old," Doreen said. "Not after all Karen's troubles."

"Well, talk to your doctor about it," the policewoman said. "It's the best I can offer."

"Right now, there's no one in the house," the other officer said. "But if one of your neighbors somehow has access to the place, your best bet would be to find out who it is and stop them."

"Don't you think I've been trying?" Doreen replied.

"The kids know who it is," Yolanda said. "But they can't seem to tell us. Talk to Larry, Doreen. Ask him what he thinks about this hypnosis idea. It seems to be our only hope!"

Doreen sighed, placing her hands on Karen's shoulders. The child tensed up visibly.

"All right," Doreen said. "I'll do it. If it means saving my kids, I'll try anything!"

"Well, then that's all we can do," the policewoman said, standing. "We should be getting back to headquarters."

Doreen walked them to the front door.

"Thank you for coming so quickly," she said.

"For what it was worth," Officer Shaver said. "I'm sorry we can't do anything more, but I'm sure you'll be safe for the rest of the night."

Doreen said good-bye to them, wishing as they walked to their car that his words were true. Then she turned and walked back to the kitchen. Karen's head was down on the table.

"She fell asleep, the poor thing," Yolanda said. "Doreen, I don't see how we can carry her up that big flight of stairs to bed."

"She was going to sleep in my room," Doreen said. "And I was going to stretch out on the couch in my office. Looks like it'll be the other way around."

Carefully, she slid her arms around Karen and lifted her up.

"Don't you need help?"

"It's just a short walk to my office, Yolanda," Doreen said. "I think I can handle her."

Yolanda walked close behind her, turning off the kitchen light as they left.

"She looks so sweet," the housekeeper said. "Who could hurt a beautiful child like that?"

"Or a good kid like Randy," Doreen said. "I don't know, but when I find him, he'll be sorry."

Yolanda reached past Doreen at the door to the office and flicked on the light. Doreen carried Karen to the couch and laid her down. The child mumbled something, but didn't wake.

"I'll get a blanket," Yolanda said.

Doreen sat on the edge of the couch, holding Karen's limp hand in her own. She looked around the room, and her eyes rested on the black book she had placed on her desk earlier that evening. She remembered the Bible now, walked across the room to retrieve it.

Doreen flipped open the back cover, revealing a page completely filled with minuscule writing. She shuddered when she read the line at the bottom: "If darkness washes away evil, then the child shall be consumed in darkness."

What on earth was Randy doing with something like this? Doreen turned a few dozen pages at once, coming to the end of the Bible text itself. The next page was headlined FAMILY HISTORY, and all the pages that followed were completely filled.

"Interesting," Doreen said.

"What's interesting?" Yolanda asked, entering the room with the blanket.

"I found this old Bible in Randy's room," Doreen said. "It has a diary in the back of it. If Randy's been reading this, it may answer why he's been so obsessed with religion lately."

"Reading old journals isn't right for a little boy," Yolanda said.

"I'm going to take a closer look at this," Doreen said under her breath.

She left her office, walking to the staircase and up to her room. As she got ready for bed, she thought about what a crazy night it had been. She felt exhausted by it all, but at the same time she was too interested in finding out what the diary had to say to go to sleep. Propping her pillows behind her back, Doreen sat up in bed and began to read. The first page revealed a family tree, and she skimmed quickly over the names. The family that had once lived here had been named Winston, with Miles Winston the father and Charity Winston the mother. They had no children, but one adopted daughter was listed: Vanessa.

"Vanessa," Doreen said out loud. "That sounds so familiar, but why?"

Shrugging, she turned the page and began to read. Miles Winston had been a preacher, and had run a home for orphaned children. Doreen thought this was a fascinating coincidence. There was a lot of scribbling with religious overtones, but nothing that would have turned Randy's mind around.

The writing was so tiny that Doreen had to struggle to read it, and the headache she'd been fighting earlier started to come back again. She finally closed the book, after reading only a few pages, and put it on her nightstand. Then she turned off her light and closed her eyes.

Moments later she heard footsteps in her room, and she opened her eyes to see a small silhouette in the moonlight.

"Frankie?"

"You shouldn't have this," someone whispered in a voice that couldn't be Frankie's. "Daddy will hurt you if he finds it."

Doreen reached up quickly to turn on the light.

There was no one in the room at all, and the Bible was missing from her nightstand.

25

Larry arrived at the hospital early the next morning, anxious to look in on Randy. His rounds didn't officially begin for another half hour, but the strangeness of this case had kept him up all night. The injury to Randy's head had been obvious back at Addison House, but somehow the cut had miraculously healed on the way to the hospital. Larry had racked his brains trying to decide if he had actually seen a cut at all, or just a lot of blood. With the thought that all that blood might have come from someone else, he'd sent a sample down to the lab. Now he weaved his way through the corridors of Oakwood General, passing other doctors, nurses, and interns just going off the night shift. He entered a room marked HEMATOLOGY.

A gray-haired man looked up at him, pushing a pair of wire-framed glasses to the tip of an upturned nose.

"Dr. Harlan," Patrick MacGrady said. "I was just cleaning up. My shift is almost over."

"I came early to talk to you," Larry said. "Were you able to look at that blood sample?"

"The blood type is A positive."

"And the Welder boy is O negative," Larry said. "So the blood wasn't his."

"Was there a fight?" Patrick suggested. "Was the blood from another child?"

Larry shook his head. "Not likely. But I have no idea where it came from. I'll have to talk to the boy when he wakes up."

He took the file Patrick handed him and started to leave.

"Just wait a second, Larry," Patrick said, grabbing the elbow of Larry's lab coat. "There's something I want to tell you. I noticed the patient's address. It's that old house just outside the west end of town, isn't it?"

"I guess so," Larry said. "Why?"

Patrick pushed his glasses up his nose again.

"Well, now," he said, "I might just be a superstitious old man, but there have been strange occurrences there over the years."

"What kind of occurrences?"

"There was a suicide there about twenty years ago," Patrick said.

"What does that have to do with Doreen Addison and her kids?"

"Maybe nothing, but there's something you should know. Aaron Howell, the man who lived there last, shot himself in the mouth after smothering his wife and young son."

Larry grimaced. "I remember that old story. You bring back memories of the nightmares I used to have when my big brothers would tell it to me."

Patrick turned to him.

"There's something more," he said. "Something that never came out in the papers. I know because I was on the forensic team assigned to the case. Howell left a note saying he had killed his family to protect them from evil, that voices told him he had to do it. Apparently, the man had gone slowly out of his mind. He wrote that there were other presences in the house, voices he had no choice but to obey."

"He sounds crazy," Larry said. "But I still don't see the connection."

"Word gets around fast in a small town like Oakwood," Patrick said. "And there's been talk of strange happenings up at the mansion since Addison House relocated there. We know about that worker who died when a weather vane fell from the roof. Then there's the young woman who worked at the house before her fatal accident."

Larry nodded. "Her funeral is this morning."

He looked at his watch.

"I really should make an appearance," he said. "Doreen's going to need all the support she can get."

"This Doreen is a good friend of yours," Patrick said. "If you really want to help her, get her out of that house. Because whatever drove Aaron Howell to murder and suicide will surely turn her in the same direction."

"That tragedy happened a long time ago," Larry said. "And it has nothing to do with today. I appreciate your concern, Dr. MacGrady, but I don't believe in supernatural phenomena."

Patrick opened a door, pulling out a news clipping. He handed it to Larry.

"Before you make any judgments," he said, "this is an article about the Howell murder-suicide. When I learned your young patient was from that house, I went through the coroner's files in the basement until I found the Howell file. This was mixed in with copies of the coroner's report. Let your friend read it and make her own decisions on what to do."

"I'm sure Doreen will be as unimpressed as I am," Larry said, folding the clipping into his pocket without looking at it.

He left the office, feeling a little unnerved. "Forget it," he said, poking an elevator button. "I'll figure this out on my own, and the supernatural will have nothing to do with it!"

He got off at PEDIATRICS and went to the nurses' station. Martha Varon wearily held up a handful of folders.

"One of your patients kept me busy last night!"

"Really?" Larry said, opening the top file.

"You know what that Welder kid did? He went upstairs to intensive care! Mrs. Fredericks called down here all

upset because he'd walked into one of her patients' rooms.
A man named Trevor Crane?"

"Uh-oh," Larry said, closing the file. "I'd better go
have a talk with him."

Larry pulled back the green-and-white-striped curtain
surrounding Randy's bed. The little boy sat up straight,
smiling.

"Hi!"

"Good morning, Randy. "How's your head feeling?"

"Okay," Randy said, brushing back his long, dark
bangs. "Can I go home?"

"Maybe this afternoon, if you look okay."

He pulled an ophthalmoscope from his pocket and
looked into Randy's eyes.

"I hear you went exploring last night."

"How'd you know?"

"The nurses around here have eagle eyes and superhu-
man hearing," Larry said. "Want to tell me what happened?"

"I just wanted to find a phone to call Doreen," Randy
said. "But you know what happened? I found Trevor
Crane's room. He's the guy who fell in our basement!"

"I know," Larry said, looking into Randy's ears.

"He woke up, Dr. Larry!" Randy said. "He grabbed
hold of my arm and told me we'd better get out of that
house, or else!"

Larry unhooked the stethoscope he'd just put into his
ears.

"The man is in a coma, Randy. He can't talk."

"He talked to me! It's true!"

"Nobody's calling you a liar, Randy, but I'll look into it.
Now hold still and let me take a good look at you."

As he examined the little boy, Larry worried that the
story about Crane might have been based on an hallucina-
tion that had seemed very real. Was Randy imagining
things as a result of his head injury?

"How do you feel this morning?" he asked.

"I already told you I feel fine," Randy said. "And I want to go home."

"Randy, can you remember what happened yesterday? Can you tell me how you got blood all over yourself?"

Randy shook his head no.

"What's the last thing you can remember? Think hard, Randy. This is important. Did you have a fight with someone?"

Randy closed his eyes. He could hear the sounds of the cartoon Jamie was watching, and a phone ringing somewhere. His mind was a blank about the previous day.

"I don't know," he said.

"Give yourself a minute," Larry suggested.

Randy sighed. He'd already tried to figure out what he was doing in the hospital, but had been unsuccessful.

And then, suddenly, an image rose in his mind. It was a woman's face, twisted in anger. She was screaming something he couldn't hear . . .

He quickly opened his eyes.

"What happened?" Larry asked.

"Nothing!"

"Don't tell me 'nothing,'" Larry said, taking hold of the boy's wrist. "You've lost all your color and your pulse is working like a triphammer. What did you see when you closed your eyes?"

Randy squirmed. "I didn't see anything, honest!"

Larry patted him on the shoulders with both hands.

"All right," he said. "This will come in good time. But I think I'm going to keep you here for a while until we're sure you're okay."

Randy began to whine.

"I'm okay!" he cried. "I want to go home!"

Larry stood up.

"As soon as you can, I promise. I'll look in on you later, Randy."

He left the room, wondering just what kind of home Randy wanted to return to, where so many evil things had happened. But he was beginning to sound like Patrick. He had other children to look at this morning, and they didn't need to see he was worried.

There were dark circles under Doreen's eyes when she looked in the mirror that morning. She sighed, turning the water on cold and splashing it over her face in an effort to wake up completely. She'd stayed up late trying to locate the missing Bible and the child who had taken it. But all her young charges were innocently asleep in their beds, and the Bible was nowhere to be found.

"Maybe I'm going crazy," she mumbled, reaching for her toothbrush.

As she readied herself for the funeral service, Doreen thought about the previous day. Was Randy up yet, she wondered? And did he remember anything? She would drive to the hospital when the service was over to see if Larry thought the boy could come home. Doreen couldn't wait to talk to her friend, to find out what he thought of what had happened to Karen. He was so sensible, maybe he could find a logical answer to all of this.

After applying a subtle touch of makeup, just enough to hide her fatigue, Doreen chose a brown cap-sleeved dress with a drawstring waist. It wasn't fancy, but it was somber enough for the occasion. She smiled to think how Judy preferred bright colors. Then she clasped a short gold chain around her neck and left her room.

Doreen passed her office on the way to the kitchen, and saw that Karen was still asleep on the couch. Carefully, she went into the room to check on her. She stroked her hand along the child's dark cheek. Karen mumbled something, turning away from her. Her breathing was slow and even.

"Sleep," Doreen said. "Then I know you're safe."

She left her office, heading toward the kitchen. There she found the other children eating fruit and cereal. The usual morning chatter that had always greeted Doreen was gone. The youngsters ate in silence, frowning at their bowls. Yolanda stood at the counter, mixing cups of hot coffee. She turned and handed one to Doreen.

"I think it would be best if I stayed home with Karen and the little ones," Yolanda said. "I see no reason for Cindy or Frankie to go, and of course Karen can't attend. Tara and Harry-John are already dressed."

"I hate funerals," Harry-John growled, tugging at the bow tie he had clipped to the collar of his white shirt. "How come so many nice people have to die?"

Doreen took a long sip of coffee, giving her mind time to meet the almost impossible challenge of the child's question. Why, indeed? How could she explain it to him when she couldn't figure it out for herself?

"Life's just unfair sometimes," she said.

"Why?" Tara asked. "How come both my mommy and daddy had to die? And I liked Judy so much! Why does God take the people you love so much?"

Cindy looked up, wide-eyed.

"Are you going to die, too, Doreen?"

Doreen felt her heart skip a beat.

"Of course not," she insisted. "I intend to be around for a long, long time."

Trying to find an escape from this morbid line of questioning, she looked up at the clock. Setting her cup down on the counter, she said, "It's time to get going."

"HJ and Tara," Yolanda said, "get your rain gear from the front closet. It's drizzling outside."

The children pushed their bowls away, climbing from their seats. There was no enthusiasm in their steps when they left the kitchen. Doreen gave Frankie and Cindy a kiss good-bye, then followed the older children.

"I'm scared," Tara whispered as Doreen snapped the hood of her red poncho.

"I'll be with you," Doreen said. "It's just a quick service, to say good-bye to Judy and ask God to take care of her."

She opened the front door and led them out to the station wagon.

"No, I mean I'm scared of this house," Tara said, climbing into her seat.

"Everybody around here's acting so creepy," Harry-John put in. "What was Karen doing in the basement last night, anyway? How'd she get down there?"

"I really don't know, HJ," Doreen said with a sigh. She turned the key and set the windshield wipers in motion. Then she looped around the yard and headed out to the road.

"Can we look for another house?" Tara asked. "I don't like this place. It hurt Randy."

"Houses can't hurt people, Tara," Doreen insisted.

How can you be so sure?

Doreen gave her head a slight shake, wondering where the thought had come from.

"Besides," she went on, "we have no place else to go. Don't you remember what happened when we had to leave the other house? I was so afraid you kids would be taken from me and put into a state shelter."

"Yuck," Harry-John said. "I'm not going back to one of those scuzz-joints!"

Doreen turned onto the main highway, her car joining others. The sight of heavy machinery made her shudder, as she remembered that Judy had rammed her car into a rock crusher. Unbidden, the horrid thought came to mind that her friend's blood might still be staining the metal.

She focused her eyes on the road straight ahead, ignoring the construction to either side.

"That's exactly why I want to keep Addison House going," she said, answering Harry-John's comment. "I opened it to help the kids in Oakwood County, and nothing is going to prevent me from doing that."

"I hope I stay with you forever, Doreen," Tara said, putting her head on Doreen's shoulder.

"Me, too," Harry-John put in.

Doreen smiled. "Thanks. But you know this is just a foster home. Someday, you'll go to live with people who will love you too."

"Nobody wants us," Tara pouted. "Not two kids together like Randy and me."

"And not somebody who's nine like me," Harry-John put in. "You and Yolanda and Judy are our real family now. I mean, you and Yolanda."

He kicked the dashboard.

"I wish she was still here," he said.

"Oh, so do I," Doreen whispered, feeling tears rising. It was rare that her children spoke so candidly of their feelings. She recalled what she had felt like as a foster child, and could feel the pain all over again when Tara and Harry-John spoke like this.

"You're crying," Tara said. "We're sorry."

"We didn't mean to make you cry, Doreen," Harry-John insisted.

Doreen wiped at her eyes.

"I'll be okay," she said softly.

For the rest of the trip no one spoke. Doreen was relieved when the exit for Judy's hometown finally came into view. After finding the church, she parked the car and turned off the ignition. When they got out, she took each child by the hand. Together, they walked up the short flight of stone steps, through the vestibule, and into the sanctuary. There were a lot of people there, and she quickly picked out Judy's parents in the front row. An usher motioned them toward one of the pews, and they slid into it.

The service was a quick, dignified one. When it was over, Doreen led the children up to Judy's parents to offer their condolences.

"My daughter couldn't stop talking about you," Fred Wagner said. "She was fascinated by that old house, too."

"I wish she could still be with us there," Doreen said. "I'm so sorry, Mr. Wagner."

She gave him a hug, then embraced Judy's mother, who returned a slight pressure to Doreen's arms, then quickly let go to turn to the next person. Doreen wanted to say more to her, but thought better of it and led the children from the church. The rain had burned away, and the sun was shining brightly. She noticed Larry Harlan standing at the bottom of the steps.

"Larry!" she called, walking over to him. "It was so sweet of you to come. I know you were on duty."

"I thought you might need a friend," Larry said. "Hi, kids."

Tara and Harry-John waved to him.

"Is my brother okay?" Tara asked.

"He looks great, Tara," Larry said. He looked at Doreen. "As a matter of fact, he went exploring last night. Gave the nurses a hard time."

Doreen laughed a little, despite the strain of the funeral.

"Sounds like the real Randy Welder," she said.

Larry breathed deeply. "It's getting hot, isn't it? I think I'll take my jacket off."

He unzipped the jacket and peeled the arms back. As he did so, the newspaper clipping Patrick had given him fell to the ground.

"Let me get that for you," Doreen said, bending to retrieve it.

As she reached to pick up the clipping, a gust of wind blew back the fold, revealing a large photograph. With a gasp, Doreen grabbed at her chest. A sharp pain shot through it, and her legs and arms went instantly numb.

"What is it?" Larry asked, helping her back to her feet. "Doreen?"

She handed the paper back to him quickly.

"Nothing!" she insisted. "I'm okay! There was something about that picture that frightened me, but I don't know what it was. Forget it, Larry. Let's just go home."

Larry put the clipping in his pants pocket. Something about it had frightened Doreen, but there was no way she could have known what the article was about. Not in the few seconds she had had to see it!

"Do you want to go to lunch?" he asked. "I know a nice diner on the way home. You could follow me there."

"Can we, Doreen?" Harry-John asked. "Please?"

"Sure," Doreen said. "Lead the way, Dr. Harlan!"

She walked with the children back to the car, trying to

keep her fear off her face. There was something strangely familiar about the people she'd seen in the news clipping, something that had sent ice through her veins. But the feeling of terror was so strong that she wasn't certain she wanted to find out what it was that she couldn't remember.

26

"You look tired," Larry said. "I think the strain of all of this is getting to you, Doreen."

He poured himself a cup of coffee from the thermal pitcher the waitress had brought to their table. Tara and Harry-John seemed so engrossed in their own conversation that Larry felt able to talk privately with Doreen.

"I just buried one of the sweetest people I've ever known," Doreen said.

"What are you going to do now?" Larry asked. "There's only two of you to care for six kids. Will you be looking for new help?"

"I suppose I'll have to. But who would want to work for me? Once somebody learned about the strange accidents that have been happening at that place, and about what happened to Judy, any potential employee would turn tail and run."

The waitress appeared and with a smile served each person at the table. Harry-John went right into his scrambled eggs and sausage, but Tara poked gently at the food on her plate, trying to decide what to eat first.

"I'm just going to have to make it on my own, with Yolanda's help," Doreen said. "This doesn't faze me, Larry. I've done well enough on my own before and I can do it again."

"Besides, I have friends," she continued. "There's Yolanda and you, of course. And there's Brendan Delacorte, my neighbor. He's been very helpful, and I know I can turn to him if I really need someone."

Larry started cutting up his ham, his hand moving forcefully.

"You can call on me, too," he said. "I'm your friend. And you always know I could be more than that."

"How come you aren't Doreen's boyfriend?" Tara asked, picking up this last sentence of Larry's. "I like you. You could get married, then adopt all of us, and . . ."

Both Doreen and Larry managed to laugh at this.

"Larry and I are just friends, Tara!" Doreen said.

"Why?"

"Yeah, how come you're not all mushy together like some grown-ups?" Harry-John asked.

Doreen shook her head. "It's just not something that ever happened between us. Now come on, eat your breakfast. We want to pick up Randy in a little while."

"How much do you know about this Brendan Delacorte?" Larry asked.

"I know he's kind, gracious, and handsome," Doreen said. "I know he's always there when—"

She stopped herself, looking up at Larry.

"What are you, my newest foster father?" she asked. "What do you care about my love interests?"

"I care a lot, Doreen," Larry said. "You should know that."

"Well, don't worry about Brendan," Doreen said. "He's wonderful. In fact, I'll make it a point to introduce you two sometime soon. You'll like him. He seems like the athletic type, and he's got horses."

"Good for him," Larry said without enthusiasm.

Doreen knew that Larry was jealous, and this worried her. Their relationship had grown in a platonic way, and she couldn't imagine falling in love with Larry Harlan. He was a good friend, one of the few people she could label a best friend, but she didn't want romance to get in the way of that.

"I'm finished," Harry-John announced.

"Me, too!" Tara cried.

Larry signaled the waitress.

Harry-John rode with Larry to the hospital, and Doreen and Tara got into the station wagon. Tara sat as close to Doreen as she could, resting her head on Doreen's arm.

"I want to be close to you," Tara said. "Doreen, is it okay to be afraid to see my brother?"

"Why would you be afraid, Tara?"

"Randy's been acting so weird lately. He's always reading that stupid Bible and—"

"What do you know about that, Tara? Do you know who gave it to him?"

Tara sat up straight, looking out the front window.

"We found it in my closet the first day we moved in. It had a picture of a tree in it with all these weird names."

"A family tree," Doreen said. "Lots of old Bibles have them."

"Anyway, it sort of gave me the creeps. But Randy thought it was neat. One night I went into his room 'cause I heard him having a nightmare, and he started reading it to me. I didn't like it, Doreen."

Doreen felt a chill running over her skin.

"I'm sure you didn't," she said. "But, Tara, why would Randy just start reading a Bible on his own? That's not something a ten-year-old boy normally does."

"Not my brother, anyway," Tara said. "But Randy isn't normal anymore. He's wacko! And I hate it. I hate it 'cause he doesn't want to play with me. He just wants to read that stupid Bible."

Doreen reached over and patted the child's knee, poking out from the hem of her red dress.

"You don't need to worry," she said. "I took it out of his room and I have no intention of giving it back."

If I can find it myself!

"Tara, I have a question for you," Doreen went on. "Have you seen any strangers around our house lately?"

"No," Tara said. "Why?"

"Think, honey," Doreen said. "What about Randy? Has he talked to any adults without my knowing of it?"

Tara looked down at her hands.

"Well, he said something about a lady," she answered softly.

She didn't want to tell Doreen that Randy liked this strange woman better than his guardian.

"What about her?" Doreen asked, growing excited.

"He just said she's beautiful and smart."

"Does she have a name?"

"Randy didn't say. But I don't think I'd like her. She tells Randy bad things."

Thank God, at last someone's shedding a light on all this!

Excited, Doreen pressed the child for more details.

"What sort of bad things?"

Tara squirmed.

"Tara, please answer me."

"Well," Tara drawled. "She said you're a bad lady. But I told Randy that's dumb and that you're our best friend."

"Thanks, Tara," Doreen said, signaling that she intended to turn into the upcoming exit. "I don't know why that woman thinks I'm bad, or even who she is, but I mean to find out. And when I do, I'm going to tell her to stay away from our house!"

"Good," Tara said. "Then maybe Randy will be my twin again and not a big weirdo."

What kind of monster filled little children's heads with lies and made them turn against their caretaker? Doreen wanted to find this strange woman and punch her for what she had done to Randy and Karen. And heaven only knew, but Cindy's adoption of an imaginary mommy might also have something to do with this stranger.

"You walk on ahead with HJ, Tara," Doreen said as they entered the hospital after parking the car. "I've got something to tell Larry."

As the children skipped toward the elevators, Doreen took Larry by the arm.

"Tara says Randy's been talking to some woman," she said quietly. "Apparently, she's been telling him negative things about me."

"Who is she?"

"I have no idea, and I don't know what she has against me. But when I get home tonight, I'm going to try to find her."

The elevator doors opened, and they all stepped in.

"Let me make a suggestion," Larry said. "Don't let Randy know you found out about her. I'm not sure I want him to be confronted in that way."

"I'll save it for when we get home," Doreen said. "How soon will he be out?"

"Check-out time is eleven A.M. Once I sign his papers he'll be yours again."

Tara pointed to the nameplate outside her brother's room.

"Here he is!" she cried.

"Go on in," Doreen said. "I'll be right there."

She turned to Larry.

"Will you help me deal with this woman? If I need you?"

"What about Brendan?"

Doreen frowned. "Sorry I asked."

"Okay!" Larry cried. "Call me if you want. You know I'm always there to help you."

He looked at his watch. "Let me get to those papers. I'll see you later, Doreen."

To Doreen's surprise, he kissed her on the cheek before walking away. She watched him, then turned to walk into Randy's room. He was sitting up in bed, smiling, and pointing to the other boys in the room.

"That's Jamie, and that's Mike," he said. "And that's Billy. Guys, this is my twin sister, Tara. And my buddy Harry-John."

He cocked his head at Doreen.

"That's Doreen."

"Are you his mother?" Billy asked.

Doreen smiled. "No. Randy and Tara live with me."

She went to Randy's bed and sat on its edge, reaching out to brush back his long, dark bangs.

"Hi, honey," she said. "How do you feel today?"

"Great," Randy said. "I'm sure ready to blow this scuzz-joint."

Doreen laughed. He *did* look fine, more like the Randy she had known back at the ranch house. She hadn't noticed it before, but she realized now that in these past days Randy had grown paler, his eyes lackluster. But here in the hospital, a glow had come back to his cheeks.

"Well, Dr. Larry's getting things ready," Doreen said. "I'm very proud of you, Randy. It isn't easy to stay alone in a strange place. Maybe you'd like something special when you get home?"

Randy shrugged, smiling. "Okay, but I'll have to think first."

Tara leaned forward, her hands pressed down on the white sheet.

"How about your Bible?"

Randy looked bewildered.

"My what?"

"Your Bible, silly!" Tara said. "Oh, brother, it's all you've been reading lately."

"You're nuts," Randy said with a click of his tongue.

Doreen felt something lighten inside her chest. It seemed as if Randy didn't even remember all his religious talk! Well, maybe his accident had finally put an end to that nonsense.

Randy bounced a little on the mattress. "I know what I want! A new Space Warrior. There was this neat one on TV this morning, and I don't have it yet for my collection."

Doreen bit her lip. He really didn't remember what had happened, did he? He didn't know that all his figurines had been mysteriously destroyed.

"If that's what you want," she said.

"Lucky," Harry-John said. "Wish I'd get sick or something so I could have a new toy."

Suddenly a nurse walked into the room. Without a word, she went to Randy's bed and pulled the curtain closed around it.

"Oh, no," Randy groaned. "Not another test!"

"No, a few questions," the nurse said. "I'm the head nurse for this shift up in intensive care. Anne Fredericks left a message about what you did last night."

Randy slid under his covers until just his face showed, looking guilty.

"Randy?" Doreen asked.

"I didn't hurt anyone!"

"I didn't say you did," the nurse replied, looking stern. "But you did talk to Trevor Crane last night."

"Oh, Randy, you didn't!" Doreen cried. "How did you find him?"

"Well, I just went looking for a phone and there he was," Randy said, looking guileless.

"You told Mrs. Fredericks that he spoke to you," the nurse went on. "If this is true, we need to know what he said. It may be of some importance to his family, or it may give us a clue as to what exactly happened to him."

Doreen saw Randy curl up his knees, and watched as his eyes rounded with nervous fear. Angry that the nurse was bothering a sick child, she cut in before Randy could speak again.

"What does this have to do with Randy? Why are you pestering a little boy like this?"

The nurse glared at her.

"Because this child was the last person to speak to Mr. Crane."

"The last person?" Doreen echoed.

"That's right," the nurse said, turning back to Randy. "Trevor Crane is dead."

27

Frankie sat in Doreen's office chair, his feet dangling, using his hand as a lever against the desk to swivel himself back and forth. She had been gone for hours, and he wanted her to come back home again. He felt scared and alone, but here in her chair, at least, he could pretend she was with him.

A short while earlier, he had watched as Yolanda picked up the telephone. He could only lip-read a few of the words she spoke, but he caught his own name and *parents*. What was going on? Was someone calling about his parents? It couldn't be! He didn't want to ever see them again, not ever!

Afraid, he laid his head down on the desk and began to cry. Moments later, he felt a tap on his shoulder. He looked up, into the eyes of the strange blond-haired boy. The child shook his head, bringing a finger to his lips. Frankie put his head back down and went on crying.

Go away, he thought.

The child grabbed Frankie's sleeve and gave it a tug. Frankie tried to brush him away, but the boy kept on pulling, forcing Frankie to get up. He shook his head, his eyes asking the other child what he wanted. The blond boy beckoned him to follow with a sweep of his arm.

Frankie left Doreen's office, walking down the hallway to the front door. The blond boy opened it, gesturing for

Frankie to follow him. Though it had been gray and cloudy
that morning, the afternoon sun shone brightly, and Frankie
had to cover his eyes against the glare. He could barely see
the little boy in front of him, but still he followed. They
crossed the meadow, walking on the path that cut through
the woods to Marty's place. But when the run-down metal
shack came into view, the blond boy pointed to his left and
turned off the path. Frankie made his way, pushing aside
low-growing branches and pulling an occasional burr from
his shirt. At last they entered a clearing, an overgrown
patch of grass and wildflowers at the base of a hill.

Frankie stopped. He shook his head, his expression full
of confusion. The blond boy pointed, and soon Frankie
understood what he wanted to show him. There was a cave
here, almost hidden behind vines that dripped over its entrance. The blond boy spoke to Frankie for the first time.

"Hide here," he said. *"Hide here, or they'll get you!"*

Frankie took a step toward the small cave. He could
hide there, couldn't he? And then they couldn't send him
back to his parents!

He turned to smile at the other boy, to thank him for
helping. But the other child was nowhere in sight. Frankie
turned a complete circle, looking around in confusion.
How could the other child have disappeared again so
quickly? Frankie stood still in wonderment, wishing he
knew what made his strange friend so magical.

Doreen pulled into the driveway, her knuckles white as
she gripped the steering wheel. She had been tense all over
since hearing of the strange woman who'd been lying to
Randy. But the news about Trevor Crane's death had made
her nerves as taut as a bow.

Larry had reprimanded the nurse after hearing that she
had terrorized Randy, but Randy seemed no worse for the
wear, having spent the entire trip home chattering about his
adventure in the intensive care ward.

"Go on and play," she said to the children. "Yolanda
will call you when dinner is ready."

Tara gave her a hug.

"Don't worry, Doreen," the child said. "We're gonna be okay!"

Harry-John scrambled out after Tara, but as she opened her own door Doreen realized that Randy hadn't moved. He sat staring at the house, suddenly silent, his eyes wide.

"Come on, Randy!" Tara cried.

Randy shook his head vigorously.

"I'm not going in there," he said in a quiet, firm voice.

"Randy, what is wrong?" Doreen asked, reaching across the seat to touch him.

He shrank away from her.

"I'm not going in there!" he cried. "I hate that place! I hate it!"

Suddenly the child who had been so cheerful a few moments earlier burst into tears.

"Oh, Randy. What is it?"

She slid across the seat, taking him into her arms. He was shaking all over.

"I'm afraid, Doreen," he said. "That's a bad place, and something is going to happen to me in there! Trevor Crane said so!"

"Randy," Doreen cooed, hugging him tightly. "Don't pay any attention to what Trevor Crane said. He was a sick man, and his mind was doing crazy things. Nothing bad will happen!"

But bad things already have happened.

Doreen tried to push the thought aside.

"Randy, come inside with me," she said. "I won't leave you alone, okay?"

Randy shook his head.

"You can't stay in the car," Doreen said, more firmly.

Tara climbed in behind Doreen, looking at Randy over Doreen's shoulder.

"Randy, let's play a game up in my room, okay?" she said. "I want to go in the house with you 'cause you're my twin."

Randy sniffled, wiping his eyes with the backs of his hands.

"Okay," he said softly. "But I don't want to be alone!"

Everyone got out of the car, and the twins held hands as they walked on ahead of Doreen. Seeing the way Randy's head hung broke her heart, and she wondered if she wasn't just being stubborn in staying here. If the kids hated it that much . . .

But there was no time to think of that. No sooner had she walked into the front foyer than Yolanda came hurrying up to her.

"Oh, I've been waiting for you!" the housekeeper cried. "Someone called from Social Services. It seems they've gotten word about the accidents at this house, and they're going to do an investigation!"

Doreen strode into her office, wondering what else could possibly happen.

"Frankie's parents have also heard what is happening," Yolanda went on. "And they're talking about taking him back again!"

Doreen's eyes widened.

"Oh, how nice," she said with bitter sarcasm. "They must've finished their rehabilitation and want another shot at him. No judge would return a child to parents who'd done that to him—no sane judge, anyway."

Yolanda shook her head. "What are we going to do?"

"I don't know!" Doreen cried. "Everything's going wrong! First Carruthers takes our old house from us, then when we find a place that seems wonderful and it turns out to have a jinx on it!"

She sat down hard in her chair, angrily swiveling it back and forth.

"And I just heard that Trevor Crane died this morning!"

"Oh, no . . ."

Doreen nodded. "What happens if his family decides to sue? They'll take everything I have, and I'll lose Addison House for certain! I can't let that happen!"

"We have to get a good lawyer," Yolanda said.

"We can't afford a good lawyer," Doreen replied.

She reached for the message pad on her desk, where Yolanda had scribbled the name of the social worker who wanted to talk to her. Barbara Clayton. Well, that was a relief. She and Barbara were longtime acquaintances. But the idea of being put under the microscope of Social Services, even by a friendly associate, made Doreen shudder.

"When are they coming?" she asked.

"The day after tomorrow," Yolanda replied. "Doreen, I think we should sit down with all the children and discuss this. We must present a united front, or heaven knows what will happen!"

Doreen nodded. "Good idea. We'll talk at dinner. If they can convince Barbara that they're happy here . . ."

There was a knock at the door, and Cindy entered.

"Doreen, there's a man outside looking for you," she said. "He says his name is Brendan."

"Oh!" Doreen cried, standing quickly. She waved at the housekeeper. "Excuse me, Yolanda. I really need to see him!"

She hurried toward the front door. When she opened it she saw Brendan standing on the porch, holding a bouquet of wild roses. Taking the flowers, she threw her arms around him and held him tightly.

"You always come when I need you," Doreen whispered. "Brendan, the whole world is going crazy around me. Please help!"

"My love," Brendan said, "it hurts me so much to see you afraid."

"Let's go inside where we can talk," Doreen said.

They entered the house, Doreen's head against Brendan's upper arm. She led him into the parlor, where they sat together on the couch. Doreen kept her body close to Brendan's, needing the warm security of his presence. The aroma of horses that seemed to surround him like an aura once again comforted her.

"Brendan, I'm in trouble," Doreen said. "Social Services is coming to do an investigation because of all the things that have happened here. They might bring a case against me to close Addison House, and I don't know what to do!"

"They could never take this place from you," Brendan said. "It belongs to you."

Doreen pulled back, laying a hand on his arm.

"It isn't the place I care about," she said. "Its the children! I can't lose them!"

She frowned.

"You know, that's the first negative thing I've said about this house," she said. "I do care about it! But so many terrible things have happened . . ."

She sat back into the couch, staring across the room at the cold fireplace. There was a solution, wasn't there? Just leave this place!

"I could find another home," she said softly. "A safer home."

"You would leave?"

Doreen looked at him.

"If it means keeping the children," she said. "It's my only choice, unless I can find out who's been causing all this trouble."

Reminded of the information Tara had given her, she placed both her hands on Brendan's arms.

"Maybe you can help me," she said. "I know I've asked you before about our neighbors, but now I need more information."

"Whatever I can do for you," Brendan said.

"It's a young woman," Doreen went on. An image of the girl who had run in front of her car came to mind. "She's very young, with dark hair. I think there's something wrong with her mentally. She may be the one who's been frightening the children!"

Brendan looked down at the rug, thinking. He shook his head.

"I'm sorry," he said. "But she still doesn't sound familiar."

"But I have to find her!" Doreen cried. "Don't you see?

It's the only way I can save the children. And I don't know what I'd do if they made us go away!"

Tears had begun to rise, blurring her vision. Brendan put his arms around her, pulling her close, kissing her over and over.

"You won't go away, my love!" he cried. "Not ever! No matter what it takes to help you, I'll do it!"

As the two embraced, someone else watched from the doorway of the parlor. Though Tara and Harry-John were coming down the stairs together, neither one could see the woman enshrouded in black gauze. She glared at Doreen and Brendan, her heart full of hatred.

"Tonight," she whispered. *"Tonight, I will destroy you and take what is rightfully mine!"*

Doreen pulled away from Brendan.

"What did you say?" she asked.

"Not a word," Brendan replied.

Doreen looked around the room.

"Funny, I thought I heard someone talking," she said.

Tara and Harry-John entered the room. They both glanced at Brendan, their expressions solemn. Doreen knew they weren't happy about her having a boyfriend, and she smiled to reassure them.

"Say hello to Brendan," she said.

Both children waved and mumbled a greeting.

"Doreen, we can't find Frankie," Harry-John said.

"Is he with Yolanda in the kitchen?"

"Nope, and he isn't in his room or the classroom," Harry-John replied.

"Or in the backyard," Tara went on.

Now Doreen stood up, worried.

"Oh, God, Brendan," she said. "Something else has happened!"

"Don't worry," Brendan said, rising himself. "I'm sure the boy is fine. If you'd like, I'll start looking for him in the woods."

"I'd appreciate that," Doreen said. "In the meantime, you kids look again through the house."

The children turned and ran from the room, the adults walking behind. In the hall, Brendan pulled Doreen close and kissed her once more.

"Don't be afraid," he said. "I would never let anything happen to you."

Doreen smiled a little. "At least I have you, Brendan. I don't know what I'd do without you!"

Brendan opened the front door.

"If I find him," he said, "I'll bring him directly back here."

"Thank you, Brendan," Doreen said.

After he left, she walked straight down the hall to the cellar, where both Cindy and Karen had been found. Could Frankie have somehow made it down there, too? The latch was thrown shut, but still Doreen opened it and reached in to turn on the light. She opened her mouth to call to the little boy, but remembered that he couldn't hear her.

But Frankie wasn't in the basement. He was hiding in the little cave the blond boy had shown him, curled up in a ball and shivering with cold despite the heat of late June. Frankie intended to stay there forever, or at least until someone told him his parents didn't really want to take him back.

He closed his eyes, praying, but images of his father's angry face filled his mind. His parents had hated him so much, beaten him so often. Why did they want him back again? Why didn't they just leave him alone?

Slowly, with silent tears falling down his cheeks, the little boy nuzzled back into the soft dirt floor and fell asleep. As the summer wind blew the vines that curtained the cave entrance, deepening the darkness surrounding him, Frankie began to dream.

Running as fast as he could. Sounds of screams all around him, and cries of anger.

He leaped into his bed, the circus figures on his wallpaper seeming to come to life. Clowns laughing uproariously. Elephant trunks swaying. Dogs jumping through hoops.

Then one of the dogs turned to him and growled, red blood pouring from its mouth.

Frankie screamed, and then there was someone in the doorway of his room, a massive figure.

His daddy. His daddy was going to hurt him again.

But this man wasn't his daddy. This was a strange man with short blond hair. The man climbed into his bed, grabbing him by the neck. He began to squeeze, harder and harder, until Frankie gasped desperately for air. . .

Frankie's mind forced an abrupt end to the dream, and with a cry he threw himself to the side, as if trying to get away from the man in his dreams. His body landed against a pile of hard and long things.

Sticks, Frankie thought, shaking all over. *Why are there sticks here?*

But he realized that he could use one of the sticks to defend himself if anyone came to get him. Frankie grabbed for one and, holding it like a weapon he pulled back some vines to look outside. The sun was pretty low in the sky, but its rays were at just the right angle to illuminate what was in the cave.

When Frankie saw the skull and the bones, he began to scream.

28

While the others searched for Frankie, Karen sat on a chair in the library, one foot propped up on an ottoman. She could hear them calling the child's name, and when she looked out the window she saw Harry-John wandering around the side yard. Doreen had been fretful, crying out how sick and tired she was of the children wandering off. She had checked the basement first of all, but Frankie had not been there.

"Of course not," Karen said out loud, squirming to make herself more comfortable. "He's not down there. He wasn't called down."

But Karen wanted to go back to the cellar again, to the cool, comforting darkness. She wanted the beautiful woman in black to come to her . . .

"Come get me?" Karen called, plaintively. "I need you! Please come for me!"

Suddenly, the curtains began to stir, moving more and more rapidly until they flapped straight out from their rods like flags. Small statues on the mantel started to dance in circles and the furniture began bumping up and down. Karen's dark hair blew helter-skelter. The bitter cold wind that filled the room had no definite source, and it carried a low-pitched wail from somewhere far off.

"Where are you?" Karen cried. "I want to go back! Come get me!"

Then, just as quickly as it had started, the wind stopped
and the room grew deathly still. Karen felt two hands on
her shoulders, and she turned her head with a smile to see
the woman in black standing behind her chair.

"Come, child," the woman said. "The time has come
for you to join me forever. To leave the wicked around you
while you still might be saved!"

She took Karen's hand and pulled her up. As easily as if
she had no cast on her leg, Karen followed the woman
down the hall and to the cellar door. Karen looked at the
lock, but the woman did not reach out to unlatch it. Instead, she walked right through the wood door, pulling
Karen behind her.

After half an hour of searching, Doreen and the others
met in the kitchen for dinner. The children were pale and
somber, as full of worry as the adults.

"I'm not hungry," Cindy said, pushing her plate away.

"Me neither," said Randy.

"Please eat something," Doreen said. "You just came
home from the hospital, and I don't want you to get sick!"

Randy looked up at her.

"Trevor said something bad was gonna happen at this
house!" he cried. "And it did! Frankie's gone and we can't
find him!"

"We will find him. We just have to rethink our strategy.
Come on, hurry up and eat. We've got another two hours
of daylight."

Yolanda checked to be certain that everyone had eaten
dinner. There were three empty place settings—her own,
Karen's, and Frankie's. The housekeeper had hoped the
little boy would come back on his own in time for supper.

"I'm going to get Karen," she said softly.

She left the kitchen and went down the hall to the library, where Karen had been left during the search. When
she opened the door, she saw that Karen was nowhere in
the room. Yolanda felt a sinking in her stomach as fear
rushed through her. Quickly, she turned and ran back to the

kitchen. She leaned into the kitchen, one hand holding the doorjamb.

"Doreen, Karen's managed to get herself up again," she said, breathlessly. "She's not in the library!"

Randy jumped up and down in his seat.

"You see! You see!" he cried. "It's getting too weird!"

"Be quiet, Randy," Harry-John growled.

Doreen was already out of her seat, opening one of the cabinet drawers to remove a flashlight.

"You kids stay here with Yolanda," she ordered. "Not one of you is to move from this room."

"Doreen, I'm scared!" Cindy cried. "I want my mommy!"

Doreen ignored her, pushing past Yolanda. She reached for the latch on the basement door, never stopping to think that Karen couldn't have thrown the lock again from the inside. Switching on the light, she hurried down the stairs.

"Karen!" she called. "Karen, are you down here?"

Stopping halfway down the stairs, she aimed the flashlight in all directions. It illuminated the washer and dryer, the oil burner, and stacks of boxes. But there was no sign of Karen.

The beam caught something on a far wall and made it glitter. Curious, Doreen continued down the stairs and to the back wall. She saw at once that the glistening came from wet, dripping moss. Now she remembered being told that there was a water leak down here. Somehow, she had never had the chance to ask someone to fix it. But right then her first concern was for Karen, and it was obvious that she was not down here again. Doreen went back upstairs.

As she closed the basement door and locked it behind herself, she heard a knock from the front door at the far end of the hall. Yolanda appeared in the kitchen doorway, ready to answer it, but Doreen stopped her.

"Stay with the children," she said. "I don't want them out of your sight!"

She turned and hurried to answer the door. Brendan,

returning from his search without Frankie, greeted her with
a rueful smile. At the sight of him, tears began to fall from
her eyes.

"What's wrong?" Brendan asked, taking her into his
arms.

"Everything! This house is what's wrong! Now Karen
and Frankie are *both* missing."

Brendan looked past her, down the hall.

"Where are the others?"

"In the kitchen," Doreen said, blinking away the last of
her tears. "Yolanda is keeping watch over them. Brendan,
please help me find the children!"

"We spent half an hour looking for Frankie after you
left," Doreen said. "But the kids were getting worn out and
I knew they needed a break for dinner. When Yolanda went
to help bring Karen into the kitchen, she was gone!"

"Then she just left the room . . ."

"A child with a cast on her leg?" Doreen asked. "Brendan, someone helped her! It's that crazy woman the children have been talking about! I've got to find Karen and
Frankie and pack our bags and get the hell out of here
and—"

Brendan took her face in his hands, moving closer to
kiss her and stop her from talking.

"Shh," he said. "You must calm yourself. Don't talk
about leaving this place."

"I've been stubborn about it," Doreen said. "I need a
shelter for my children, or Social Services will close down
Addison House!"

She rubbed the side of her head in a gesture of worry.

"They're coming here in two days," she said. "What if I
can't find the children? What if something else happens?"

"Nothing else is going to happen," Brendan assured her.

"But . . ."

"Hush, my love," Brendan said, brushing tendrils of
wheat-colored hair from her face. He began to stroke her,
the massaging action soothing her nerves. Doreen began to
grow sleepy, despite all her worries. "Don't think about

anything. Relax, and I'll help you. You must relax, or you'll never be able to find the children."

"I have to get up," Doreen said. But she made no attempt to move. Her bones and muscles had suddenly gone numb.

"Shhh . . ."

Doreen's eyelids grew heavy, and within moments she had fallen asleep, her head on Brendan's lap. She began to dream at once.

There was a flash of light, then a child's scream from one of the bedrooms. Doreen began running to it, hoping one of the children had been found. Instead, as she reached the top of the stairs, she saw a big man with close-cropped blond hair lumbering down the hall.

"WHO ARE YOU?"

But he didn't answer. He opened one of the bedroom doors and entered the room, bellowing something that Doreen couldn't hear. She ran down the hall, screaming at him to stop. But she didn't move quickly enough.

When she entered the room, the man was standing at the side of the bed with a pillow in his hands. There was a child in the bed, strangely pale and still.

Doreen began to scream.

But it wasn't one of her children, and her cries stopped when she saw this. Curiously, walking on legs made of gelatin, she moved closer to the bed to see a little blond-haired boy in a red flannel sleeper.

Doreen woke up with a cry, grasping at her chest as pain twisted her insides.

"Oh, my God, Brendan," she said, looking at him with wide eyes. "We've got to find the children! There's something evil in this house and we have to get out fast!"

"There's nothing evil in this house," Brendan insisted.

"Yes, there is," Doreen said, standing. "Brendan, I just had a dream, and it answered a question that's been nagging at the back of my mind."

She told him about the newspaper clipping concerning

the Howell suicide and murders that had dropped out of Larry's jacket.

"Brendan, I saw those people in my dreams before I ever saw that newspaper photograph!" Doreen cried. "And just now I dreamed that I saw the same man murder his own child in this house! How could I have known what those people looked like when I'd never seen them before?"

"There must have been a picture somewhere in the house—"

"Never!" Doreen cried. She started to leave the parlor. "I'm going to call the police. I need help!"

Though Brendan had been sitting on the couch when she started for the door, he was suddenly behind her, grabbing her.

"You're making a terrible mistake," he said.

"Let go of me, Brendan," Doreen commanded. "I have to get to the phone!"

"No!" Brendan cried. "Don't you see? If the police hear that two of your children are missing, what do you suppose they'll think? After all that's happened, wouldn't the authorities remove the other children from this house?"

Doreen hesitated, one part of her desperately needing help, the other part fearful of losing all that she'd worked for.

"I—I don't know what to do."

"How long have the children been gone?"

Doreen shook her head. "A few hours, I guess. I'm not exactly sure."

"Not very long," Brendan pointed out. "They could be most anywhere, and in that short time, what harm could have come to them?"

"I don't even want to imagine," Doreen said. "But Brendan, we've looked everywhere!"

"We'll look again," Brendan said. "Go on now, tell the others. There's still time until dark, and I'm sure we'll find them."

Doreen smiled, just a little.

"You know," she said, "having you to help us really makes me feel better!"

"Only this time," she said, "we'll be a little more organized. Harry-John, your job is to look upstairs. Under beds and in closets, too."

"We already did that!" Harry-John protested.

"Please, HJ, just do as I ask?" Doreen said. "Now, Randy and Tara, I want you to check this whole floor. Yolanda, would you mind searching the woods at the front of the house?"

"I'll look over every square inch!" Yolanda promised.

Cindy jumped up and down in her seat.

"What about me? What about me?"

"You come with me, Cindy," Yolanda said.

"And Brendan and I will search the woods at the back of the house," Doreen said. "In fact, I'm going to talk to Marty Laudon. Maybe he knows something!"

"That nut probably won't even want to talk," Harry-John said.

"He'll talk to me," Doreen insisted. "Now come on. We'll all meet here in the kitchen when the sun goes down."

Yolanda nodded. "Let's get going," she said. "Before it gets too dark to see!"

Cindy took Yolanda's hand. The housekeeper opened the back door and led the child out, saying, "You stick right by me, you hear? We don't need you getting lost again, too!"

Cindy skipped along at Yolanda's side, looking up at the woman.

"I won't get lost," she said. "How come Frankie got lost? How come Karen got lost? Are we gonna find them? Will Doreen give me a reward if we find them?"

"My, you ask a lot of questions!" Yolanda said. "I don't know how they got lost, and I don't know if we'll be the ones to find them. But I'm sure if we do, you'll get a reward."

"Maybe something from the special toy closet," Cindy said.

The little girl gazed off toward the woods, and Yolanda could tell that she was imagining what she'd choose. Yolanda looked up at the sky and saw the sun low on the horizon. Not too much time until dark . . .

"Here we are," she said as they reached the driveway that cut to the road through the woods in front of the house. "Let's walk along here, okay? We'll call as loud as we can, and then we'll walk through the trees."

"I can yell loud," Cindy said. "Listen. Kaaarrreen!"

Yolanda cupped her hands over her ears.

"Perfect," she said. "But remember, Frankie can't hear you, so you must keep your eyes open for him."

Cindy let go of Yolanda's hand, running to the opposite side of the drive. While keeping her eye on the little girl, Yolanda joined Cindy in calling out Karen's name. She prayed that Frankie was with the older girl, that somehow Karen had gone out to find him on her own and had succeeded. Maybe her leg was hurting her, and she couldn't get back home!

"I see something!" Cindy cried suddenly.

She bolted into the woods, ignoring Yolanda's commands to wait. The little girl had noticed something moving through the trees. Maybe it had been Karen! Wouldn't Doreen be proud if she found her friends?

She stopped when she saw the person again. But it wasn't Karen or Frankie. Cindy smiled.

"Mommy!" she cried. "Can you help us look for Karen and Frankie?"

The woman smiled back, opening her arms.

"They are safe," she said. *"Come with me, child. It's dangerous here."*

Cindy looked over her shoulder, hearing Yolanda call out to her.

"Well, I better tell—"

The woman grabbed her, pulling Cindy up into her arms.

"No, you must not tell anyone!" the woman cried.

"But Mommy!"

"There is nothing to worry about, little one," the woman said.

Cindy smiled up at her beautiful mommy, but the smile vanished in an instant.

The last rays of sunshine had made their way through the leaves, casting light on the woman's face. And Cindy was looking into the empty eye sockets of a skull.

Just a few yards away, Yolanda turned abruptly at the sound of the child's screams. She hurried toward them, calling out in panic.

"Cindy? Cindy, where are you?"

But, just as she came to a clearing, the screams stopped and the woods were silent once again.

"Oh, dear heaven," Yolanda moaned. "This can't be happening! Not another child!"

She turned a complete circle.

"Cindy! You answer me!"

But she heard only a bird chattering.

Yolanda didn't hesitate. She started back to the house, planning to call the police.

But she didn't even reach the driveway. Something smoky and sinuous rose from the ground, blocking her path with heat so intense that Yolanda was reminded for an instant of a hot, open oven.

The blackness swirled, wrapping around her like a tornado. Yolanda began to scream herself, but her screams were short-lived, and she collapsed, unconscious, onto the forest floor.

29

There was a padlock on Marty's steel door. He hadn't bothered to lock up his house before this, and Doreen felt a little uncomfortable at the thought that he knew she had been poking around his things a few days earlier. The smell of recently cooked game, something that always seemed to surround Marty's shack, lingered heavily in the air.

"He's been here recently," Doreen said to Brendan. "I can smell the food he was cooking."

She shuddered. "Ugh! The man lives like some kind of savage."

"A man like that could be responsible for your troubles," Brendan said.

"I've considered it," Doreen said. "And I think he has something to do with it. But the children keep talking about a woman. If I could just find Marty, I'd insist he tell me about her."

She sighed. "But obviously he's not here. Brendan, what time is it?"

Brendan shook his head. "I don't know. But we've been searching these woods for quite some time."

"Then we should probably get back," Doreen said. "The others will be waiting for us at the house."

She took Brendan's arm, and he walked her to the edge

of the woods. There they stopped, and Brendan hugged her.

"Don't worry," he said. "I know we'll find them. In fact, I'll stay out and continue searching. I've lived in these woods for many years, and I know them well. Perhaps I can find them myself."

"Thank you," Doreen said. She pulled away. "Maybe you'll have better luck alone."

She walked back to the house. As she neared it, she saw Tara standing at the kitchen door, looking out. The little girl had a frown on her face that told Doreen Frankie and Karen weren't back yet.

When Doreen opened the back door, Randy and Harry-John turned quickly away from the refrigerator, looking guilty and holding cans of soda behind their backs. But Doreen didn't have the heart to challenge them for taking the drinks without permission.

"No luck?" she asked.

Randy shook his head.

"We looked everywhere," he said. "They aren't here."

"It's like they just disappeared," Harry-John said. He opened his can of soda. "All that running around made me thirsty."

"You worked hard, I know," Doreen said. "Haven't Yolanda and Cindy come back yet?"

"I didn't see them," Harry-John said.

Doreen frowned, gazing through the window at the purple sky.

"It's pretty dark," she said. "And we were supposed to meet here when the sun went down."

"Maybe they found Frankie and Karen!" Randy cried hopefully. "Maybe they're bringing them back right now!"

Doreen sighed, nodding. It was cold in the house, even though it was a warm summer evening. A familiar sense of foreboding began to fill her, and she turned away from the children so they wouldn't see the worry reflected on her face. For a few minutes, Doreen busied herself at the sink, washing dirt from the woods off her hands.

She swallowed, braved a smile, and turned.

"It's getting late," she said. "You kids go on up and get ready for bed."

"But I want to stay up until Karen and Frankie come back!" Harry-John cried.

"I don't want to be alone," Tara said.

Randy took her hand.

"You can stay in my room tonight," he said.

Tara looked at Doreen. Doreen nodded her approval. She knew Randy needed his twin with him as much as Tara needed her brother. She opened her arms.

"Hug me, you guys," she said.

The three children hurried to her, crowding to embrace her. Tara looked up, her brown eyes wide with worry.

"Is everything gonna be all right?" she asked.

"Everything's gonna be fine," Doreen insisted. "You go on and get ready for bed. I'll be up as soon as Cindy and Yolanda get back."

After the children left the kitchen, Doreen suddenly realized that she hadn't included Frankie and Karen among the people she was waiting for.

Harry-John turned to the twins at the top of the stairs.

"You know what I think?"

"What?"

"I think we need more help," Harry-John said. "How come Doreen isn't calling the police? That's pretty dumb!"

"Doreen isn't dumb," Tara retorted. "She knows what she's doing."

Harry-John sneered at her.

"If she knows what she's doing, how come Karen and Frankie aren't back yet?" he asked.

"And how come Cindy and Yolanda are gone now, too?" Randy put in.

Tara looked down the stairs at the tightly closed front door.

"I'm scared, Randy," she said. "I think something bad happened."

"Me, too," Randy said. "Maybe they were all kidnapped!"

The children walked to their rooms.

"If they were," Tara said, "I bet that lady you were telling me about did it!"

"What lady?" Randy asked with a frown.

"The one you said was your new friend," Tara said. "Before you went into the hospital."

Randy felt something twist inside him, but he drove away his feeling of dread with a click of his tongue.

"You're nuts," he said. "I don't know what you're talking about."

"Forget it," Harry-John interrupted. "I've got a plan. Maybe Doreen doesn't want to call the police, but we can get Dr. Larry to come help."

"Sure," Randy said. "That's a great idea!"

"Don't you think Doreen should call him?"

"Why wait?" Harry-John said. "We can call him ourselves. Doreen will be really proud that we helped, won't she?"

Randy shook his head.

"I don't know," he said. "Maybe she'll be mad 'cause we told Dr. Larry what happened."

"Well, I'm not going to sit around just waiting for Karen and the other guys to come back," Harry-John said. "I'm going to sneak into Doreen's room and make a phone call to the hospital."

"What if Dr. Larry isn't there?" Tara asked.

"Then I'll leave a message," Harry-John said. "I'll tell them it's important. So are you going to come with me or not?"

Randy and Tara looked at each other.

"Somebody should stand guard," Randy said. "To make sure Doreen isn't coming."

"I'll do it," Tara said.

As Tara stood at the top of the stairs, the boys hurried to Doreen's bedroom. Harry-John went to the nightstand beside her bed and picked up the phone.

"What's the number of the hospital?" he asked.

"How should I know?" Randy said.

"Oh, great! It's probably in Doreen's office," said Harry-John.

Randy pointed to the drawer of the night table.

"Look inside there," he said. "Maybe there's a phone book."

Harry-John pulled open the drawer.

"Bingo," he said.

He flipped through the book until he found the number of the hospital. He dialed the number and listened to the phone on the other end of the line ring a few times. When the switchboard operator came on, Harry-John said, "Is Dr. Harlan there?"

"Just a moment, please."

Harry-John tilted the phone so that Randy could hear, too. A woman's voice said, "Pediatrics. May I help you?"

"Uh, yeah," Harry-John said. "Is Dr. Harlan there?"

"Who shall I say is calling?"

Harry-John looked at Randy.

"Harry-John Little," he said. "It's real important."

"I'll see if I can find him," the woman said.

There was a long pause. Harry-John danced back and forth in his sneakers, nervous energy making it impossible for him to stand still.

"I hope he's there," Randy said.

They heard a click.

"What's up, HJ?"

"Dr. Larry, we need you," Harry-John said. "Something really weird's going on, and Doreen isn't even going to call the police!"

"Tell me what happened," Larry said urgently.

"Well, Frankie disappeared this afternoon," Harry-John said. "And then, while we were having dinner, Karen took off, too! We all went out looking for them, and you know what? Yolanda and Cindy haven't come back yet! We were supposed to meet in the kitchen at sundown."

"And you say Doreen isn't calling the police?"

"Nope," Harry-John said. "So we figured we'd call you. Can you come here, Dr. Larry?"

"Well, I'll try," Larry said.

"We really need you!"

"Okay, okay," Larry said. "I'll be there as soon as possible. Good-night, HJ."

"Thanks, Dr. Larry," Harry-John said.

"He's coming as soon as he can," he told Randy.

"Good," Randy said. "Now, let's get out of here before Doreen comes."

In the hall, they told Tara what Dr. Harlan had said and then hurried to their respective rooms.

In his own room, Randy undressed and put on his coolest pajamas. Through the door that joined their rooms, he could hear his sister singing. Randy guessed that it probably made her feel better, the way people sometimes whistled when they were afraid.

He blew a tune through his own lips, but it didn't help. It didn't drive away the strange feeling in his stomach. Four people were gone! Frankie and Karen and Cindy and even Yolanda! Somebody took them, for sure, and somebody was going to come get him.

I'll bet it was that lady you told me about who did it!

What lady had his sister been talking about? Randy couldn't remember making friends with any lady! Especially not one who would hurt his friends!

Still, there was a chilling sense that he should know what Tara meant. His twin would never make up a story like that. And something bad had happened to put him in the hospital overnight. Somebody had hurt him! He brushed toys from his bed, pulled back his covers, and climbed in.

"Whoever it was," he whispered to the darkness. "I think she's coming back!"

"Tara. What are you doing? You said you'd sleep in here tonight."

Tara didn't answer. *Maybe she is mad because I*

didn't remember the lady she was talking about, he thought.

For a few minutes Randy shivered under his covers, afraid of what he couldn't see in the shadows. The flashlight his father had given him sat invitingly on the dresser across the room. Taking a deep breath, Randy got up and hurried to it, grabbing it. He switched it on as he turned back toward his bed.

The beam caught something on his covers, a small black rectangle.

Randy's eyes widened and his jaw dropped. He had cleared his bed off, hadn't he?

And that meant someone was in the room with him.

"Who . . . who . . . ?"

He couldn't choke out the words. The room was very still. Randy's dresser stood between the door to the hall and the door to Tara's room. For a moment, he debated which one was closer, then bolted toward Tara's. He turned the knob, but it jammed hard.

"Tara!"

His sister went on singing, as if she couldn't hear him.

"Tara, open this door!"

The little boy's screams went unheard. Without thinking, he bolted toward the hall door. But it, too, was locked tight. Randy began banging on it, shouting for help.

"HJ? Doreen? Somebody!"

Something pressed hard on his shoulder. Randy stiffened. This was it! He cringed, tears spilling from his eyes. He didn't want to be hurt! Why wasn't anyone coming to help him? Where was Doreen?

"She doesn't care about you," a voice said.

There was something familiar about it, something that made Randy tremble all over.

"Turn and look at me, child."

Slowly, unable to resist, Randy did as he was told. He found himself gazing into the shining eyes of a woman dressed in a long black gown. Randy backed away from her, doubling over as he began to retch.

Everything came flooding back to him in a rush of painful memories. The black rectangle on the bed was the Bible, and this woman was the one who had put him in the hospital!

"You—you leave me alone," he croaked, his throat raw as he wiped spit from his lips. "Go away!"

"I won't hurt you, child," the woman said. *"It is she who wishes to hurt you."*

"Don't talk to me!" Randy cried, covering his ears.

He turned back to the door, only to find that it was still locked.

The woman put both her hands on his shoulders.

"Come with me, child," she said. *"I will protect you."*

"I don't need protection," Randy sneered. "Tara!"

"She can't hear us," the woman told him. *"Boy, listen to me. Don't you know the authorities are coming? Don't you know the woman you call Doreen plans to lie to them, to tell them all is well here?"*

"She wouldn't lie!"

"She will!" the woman insisted. *"She has done it before, other times when she has come here to take what is rightfully mine! She has lied for her own gain, and she will do it again!"*

"You're nuts!" Randy screamed. "Let me out of here!"

He suddenly felt himself being lifted from the ground, his body floating toward the ceiling. Too frightened to scream, Randy squeezed his eyes shut. It felt like he was on the whirly ride at the amusement park, where you were suspended in midair and your guts were six inches higher than they were supposed to be.

She was going to kill him. She was going to throw him out the window like she threw that weather vane off the roof, like she pushed Trevor Crane from the ladder, like she probably killed Judy. . .

But he was set down on his feet again. When he dared to open his eyes, he found himself looking out the window.

"Look toward the trees, boy," the woman said. *"Do you*

see her? Do you see what your beloved guardian is doing?"

Randy squinted, making out two figures in the distance. One of them was Doreen, and she was hugging the other one. Randy smiled, thinking she had found Yolanda. But the smile faded when Doreen backed up a step. It was a man she was with, not the housekeeper.

"Do you see what she does, boy?" the woman in black whispered. *"She throws herself into the arms of a man while those she supposedly cares for wait in danger! Is this the woman you all love so much? Who cares more about her own passions than the welfare of her charges?"*

Randy shook his head. He didn't understand why Doreen was with a man, but he was certain there was a good reason. They were more important to her than that man was, no matter what this crazy woman said!

"No!" he cried. "He—he's just helping her."

"Foolish child!"

She took his head in her hands, turning him abruptly to face her. Her eyes were yellow, like two glowing coins in the dark.

"You will come with me," she said, her voice forming frost despite the warm summer air. *"I will show you the evil ways of your guardian, and protect you from her."*

"No," Randy whispered.

"Yes," the woman said simply. *"Come with me, boy. Come with me, or you'll die. She'll kill you!"*

"No!"

"She'll kill you! She's evil!"

Randy covered his ears again and squeezed his eyes shut.

"Leave me alone!"

A door opened up beneath him, and with a scream he felt himself falling, falling . . .

"Help me!"

Randy didn't open his eyes as the cold air rushed past him on his fall into nothingness. He was going to die! She was going to kill him!

"Help!"

Something grabbed him, strong arms holding him close.

"Let me help you, boy," the woman breathed into his ear. *"Let me save you."*

"Save me," Randy croaked, defeated.

"She is evil."

"She is evil," Randy parroted, no longer in control of his own mind.

30

Doreen had given Yolanda and Cindy fifteen minutes, and when they still didn't return she went out looking for them. By then night had fallen and the moon was up, and it was difficult to see beyond the shadows of the trees. Though she gripped the flashlight tightly, her hands were still trembling.

Go back home and call the police, Doreen! Don't be an idiot!

She ignored her conscience. She couldn't bring the police into this—not two days before the Social Services representative was due!

What are you trying to prove, Doreen?

"I'm not trying to prove anything!" Doreen cried out loud, her voice thin on the night air. "I can handle this myself! I know I can! I won't ruin Addison House by involving the police!"

She heard a whispery sound in the trees and turned to aim her flashlight.

"Yolanda?"

The housekeeper did not answer her.

You're a failure, Doreen. You never could do anything right.

Doreen's heart jumped. It wasn't her own voice that spoke in her mind, but Mrs. Stone's! How many times had she heard that same line from her foster mother? Maybe

she had been right. Maybe Doreen had no business caring
for children—not when she let them become endangered!
Just because she stubbornly refused to take them away
from this house!

"Oh, Mrs. Winters," Doreen whispered, speaking to the
foster mother who had last cared for her, the one who had
left her the money to start her work, "how I wish you were
here!"

She walked farther along the path, but there was no sign
of Yolanda or Cindy.

Don't be crazy, Doreen! Call the police!

"I will! I will call the police!" she said out loud. "I don't
care what happens to me; the welfare of my kids is too
important!"

As she turned back toward the house, she came face-to-
face with Brendan.

"Brendan!" she cried. "Where did you come from?"

"I found them," Brendan said.

"Who?" Doreen cried, excited and relieved. "Which
ones did you find? Where are they?"

Brendan put an arm around her and started to lead her
down the path to the road.

"I found all of them," Brendan said. "It's quite a story.
It seems Frankie fell and hurt himself. Karen went looking
for him when she overheard you talking about him."

Doreen shook her head, bewildered.

"How? She had a cast on her leg!"

"You'll have to ask her to explain," Brendan said.

"But what about Yolanda?" Doreen asked. "And
Cindy?"

Brendan frowned at her, for just a moment. Then his
eyes became softer.

"Oh!" he said. "The others. They're at my place, too. I
met them as I was looking for the boy and girl. They're all
well, my love. If you want to come see them . . ."

"Why didn't you bring them home?"

"The boy, Frankie, is hurt," Brendan said. "I thought he
shouldn't walk. I think he twisted his ankle."

"Then he should see a doctor immediately!" Doreen cried, tugging at Brendan's arm. "Come on, take me to them!"

She was walking slightly ahead of Brendan, pulling him along in her excitement. What a relief to know that everyone was safe!

"Your housekeeper didn't want to leave the children," Brendan said. "That's why I've come back. Listen to me —are you going to leave the other children alone in that big house?"

Doreen stopped short. The lights of the mansion were just pinpoints through the trees now. And Tara, Randy, and Harry-John were alone in there . . .

"Oh, dear," she sighed. "What should I do? Frankie needs me, but I don't think the other children should be left unattended. Not after all the things that have happened!"

Brendan took her by the shoulders.

"Then don't leave them alone," he said. "Go back to them, and in the morning I'll return with the others."

Doreen hesitated, not knowing what to do. She wanted to go to Frankie, to be sure he wasn't very seriously hurt. But if she left the other children unsupervised and something happened . . .

"Well, Yolanda is with them . . ."

"Your housekeeper is a trustworthy woman," Brendan said.

"Oh, I don't know what to do!"

She looked up into Brendan's dark eyes. He gazed at her solemnly. Instantly, Doreen felt herself grow lightheaded. She blinked, breaking eye contact, and looked down.

"What is it?"

"I felt a little dizzy. It's nothing."

She looked up at him again. His eyes were so deep and dark, so full of love for her. Everything around Doreen suddenly went dim, and all she could see was the moonlight reflected in his eyes. Something was happening . . .

"Brendan?" she whispered.

"Hush," Brendan said. "Listen to me, my gentle butterfly. They are all safe. I will take care of them and bring
them to you in the morning. Go home now, go to sleep,
and dream of me."

"I'm going home," Doreen mumbled.

"The children are safe," Brendan said, his voice deep
and rich.

"Safe," Doreen echoed.

"I love you," Brendan said. "Nothing will hurt you."

"I love you, Brendan," Doreen said.

He leaned down to kiss her, his embrace almost crush-
ing her.

"Go home, gentle butterfly."

"Brendan . . ."

When she opened her eyes he was gone. She looked
around, feeling numb all over, but did not wonder how he
had disappeared so quickly.

When she got back to the house, she locked all the
doors and went upstairs. She began to get ready for bed.
Like a robot, she methodically washed and dressed in her
nightgown. Then she climbed into bed, and within moments she was sound asleep.

Hours went by filled with dreams of the children, of Mr.
and Mrs. Winters, of other foster homes. There was a brief
nightmare about the Stones that brought Doreen to wakefulness at three A.M. But sleep quickly claimed her again.

In time, there was another dream.

She was sitting by a fire, her back erect, a Bible open in
her lap. But she wasn't herself. She was a woman with
waist-length black hair. She felt afraid.

"I know what you do, wicked thing," someone was saying. *"I know the lust in your heart! But he is mine! And if
you try to have him for yourself, you'll be punished!"*

She spoke, but it wasn't her own voice. It seemed she
had become someone else in the dream.

*"I—I don't know what you mean, Mother! There is no
lust in my heart! I've remained pure, I swear it!"*

"I've seen you with him! I shall tell your father, and

*he'll put you in the dark room, so that you may think of
your sins!"*

She began to cry.

*"I don't want to go in there, Mother! I hate that place,
so cold and dark . . ."*

*"Far from distractions that will keep you from thinking
of your evil ways!"*

"Don't send me there!"

"Tell him you'll never see him again."

"I can't!"

"Tell him!"

And then the older woman was gone, and a man stood
in her place. Doreen couldn't see his face; she could only
make out his silhouette, created by the light of the fireplace.

*"Don't be afraid. I won't let her hurt you. Don't be
afraid, my gentle butterfly . . ."*

There was a ringing noise.

Doreen woke up, startled by the ringing phone. Nine
A.M.! How could it be so late?

"Did I wake you up?" Larry Harlan asked. "You sound
so tired."

"I must have overslept," Doreen said groggily. "What's
up?"

"I'm calling to ask you the same question," Larry said.
"Is everything okay over there? HJ called me last night to
tell me about Yolanda and the children."

Doreen shook her head, confused. "Yolanda and the
children? Why would he call about them?"

"He said they were missing," Larry explained, wondering why Doreen sounded so befuddled. "That Frankie
wandered off and Karen followed him."

"Oh!" Doreen cried. "I understand! Larry, I'm sorry HJ
scared you. Everyone's fine here. Frankie got lost in the
woods, but he's okay now. We're all okay. There's nothing
to worry about."

"Do you want me to come out? I promised HJ I'd come
last night, but I got stuck here at the hospital."

"No, I don't need you," Doreen said. "Everything's under control. The children are okay. They're safe, I swear it. Really, we're just fine."

"Are you sure?"

"I'm sure!" Doreen insisted. "We're okay! Don't worry about us, Larry! We're fine!"

She hung up the phone and got out of bed. How could she have slept so late? The children were probably wondering what happened to her, and no doubt Brendan was ready for her to come get his houseguests. Doreen dressed quickly and left her room. The house was very quiet, but the silence didn't bother her. It was rather pleasant to have peace in the morning.

"Children should be seen and not heard," she whispered.

Now where did that crazy statement come from? she wondered.

Doreen knocked on Randy's door, then Tara's, calling to them. Harry-John's room was closed, too. Funny that the children had also slept late. Doreen expected them to be anxious to get their friends back.

She heard a click, and turned to see Tara wander into the hall, dressed in a white eyelet nightgown. Harry-John's door opened, too, and he came out rubbing his eyes.

"Boy, am I tired!" he cried. "I wanna go back to bed!"

"Me, too," Tara whined. "I kept having bad dreams all night."

They came up to Doreen, and she put her arms around their shoulders. They walked to the stairs together.

"We're all pretty worn out," she said. "It was quite a scare we had, wasn't it?"

"Did Yolanda come back?" Tara asked.

"And Frankie, and Cindy, and Karen?" HJ put in.

"They're all at Brendan's," Doreen said. "He found them last night. Frankie fell and hurt himself, and Brendan didn't think he should be on his leg. So they spent the night there. We'll get them after breakfast."

"Boy, I'm glad that's over," Tara said. When they

reached the top of the stairs, she looked back over her shoulder. "Now, I wonder why that brother of mine isn't up yet?"

"He's just as tired as the rest of us, I suppose," Doreen said. "You go wake him up, Tara. Tell him I want breakfast over with quickly so we can hurry to Brendan's."

Tara went to her brother's room and knocked on the door. When he didn't answer, she turned the knob and walked in. The room was in a shambles. His sheets and comforter were torn from the bed, and his curtains were down. But it wasn't until she saw the wall right next to her that Tara began to scream.

There was a long, tapering splotch of black, like soot. It was as if someone had set a fire in the night! And nearby, spattered on the wall, spots of blood still dripped.

"Doreen! Doreen!"

Doreen came out of the kitchen as the little girl raced down the hall, in tears and waving her arms frantically.

"It's Randy! He's gone and there's blood all over the place!"

Doreen patted the child's head.

"I'm sure there's nothing to worry about," she said. "Randy's just fine."

"Randy's *not* fine!" Tara wailed, stamping her foot. "Nothing's fine! This whole place is crazy! I want my brother!"

Doreen simply shook her head.

"Don't fret so, Tara," she said. "I know Randy's fine. I'm sure that wasn't blood you saw—"

"It was! It was!"

Tara began to cough, her voice hoarse from screaming. Hearing all the commotion, Harry-John came from the kitchen, still holding a glass of orange juice. Doreen turned away from Tara, seemingly oblivious to the girl's cries.

"I'll fix breakfast," she said. "Then we'll go straight to Brendan's. Randy's there, I'm sure."

She brushed past Harry-John, who immediately hurried to Tara's side.

"What're you crying for?" he asked. "What's going on?"

"It's R-Randy," Tara stammered. "He isn't in his room and there's—there's b-blood all over! And Doreen d-doesn't even c-care!"

Harry-John whispered, wide-eyed, "What's the matter with her? I think she's been acting sort of funny since we got up."

Tara wiped her nose.

"I d-don't know," she said.

"Well, I'm gonna call Dr. Larry again," Harry-John said. "I don't care if Doreen gets mad. I'm gonna ask him to come here and do something about all this crazy stuff!"

The two children went into Doreen's office.

"You stand by the door," Harry-John said, "and tell me if you hear the kitchen door opening."

He found the telephone book on the corner of Doreen's desk and looked for Dr. Harlan's number. He dialed the phone and waited.

"It's me again," he said.

"H-J . . ." Larry said with a sigh. "Doreen says everything is okay."

"It isn't okay at all!" Harry-John insisted. "Now Randy's gone, too! And Doreen doesn't even care!"

"Of course she cares," Larry said. "She loves you all very much."

"Then how come she isn't looking for Randy?" Harry-John asked. "There's blood all over the walls of his room."

Larry thought about this. Harry-John was mischievous, but not the type of child who would make up a story like this. But Doreen had insisted that everything was under control.

That thought set off an alarm in his mind, just as it had in his earlier phone conversation with Doreen. She had been almost *too* insistent, repeating over and over that they were all fine. Doreen didn't usually talk like that.

"Harry-John, where are the other kids?"

"At Brendan's. They stayed there all night."

Harry-John explained the situation as it had been explained to him.

"Wait a minute," Larry said. "Doreen didn't mention Frankie's being hurt. I think I will come over. Don't worry, kids. I'm on my way."

HJ hung up, and as they left the office, Tara said, "I think Doreen's lying to us. I don't think the others are okay at all."

When they entered the small triangular hallway on their way back to the kitchen, they heard a click, and the cellar door slowly began to open. The children looked at each other, an unspoken question between them. Hadn't the lock been latched just a few minutes earlier?

"You are right, little one. She is lying."

"Who said that?" Tara whispered. The voice had come from the cellar.

"I don't want to know," Harry-John said in a shaking voice, reaching for the kitchen door.

"She is lying to you! Your friends are all dead! She killed them! She will lie to the authorities! She hates you! Come down here and I will protect you! Come down into the darkness!"

"Close the door!" Harry-John cried. "That crazy lady Randy told us about must be down there!"

He reached past Tara to slam the door shut, but Tara pushed his arm away.

"No!" she cried. "If she's down there, then Randy must be with her!"

She threw the door open wide and flicked the light switch but nothing happened. Some light from the kitchen illuminated the new staircase, but very little of the basement below.

"Tara, are you nuts?" Harry-John cried. "Doreen! Doreen!"

"Don't you call her!" Tara screamed, striking her friend. "I'm going to get my brother!"

She started down the stairs.

"Randy! Randy, are you down here?"

Harry-John stood in the doorway.

"Please, come back!" he cried, tears welling in his eyes. "Don't go down there! She's crazy! She'll kill you!"

Tara ignored him.

"Randy! Raaannddyyyyyy!"

As she cried out her brother's name, Harry-John watched in horror the two gnarled hands that suddenly shot through the space between two of the new stairs. Talonlike fingers locked around Tara's ankles. The little girl fell forward, screaming, twisting her body to reach up to Harry-John.

"Help me!"

"Tara, no!"

He watched in horror as Tara's body was pulled into the stairs, actually pulled *through* the wood! She screamed and screamed, disappearing into something glistening and dark.

"Harrrryyyy-Joooohnnnnn!"

The boy stood frozen, not knowing what to do.

"HJ, help m———...!"

She never finished the word. Her head disappeared under the stairs, and suddenly they were solid wood again.

Harry-John's knees buckled underneath him, and it was only Doreen's quick hands that kept him from falling down the stairs.

"What are you doing?" she asked.

Harry-John tried to speak but couldn't.

"Let's have our breakfast, HJ," Doreen said. "Then we'll go to Brendan's house."

Harry-John cowered, suddenly very much afraid of his guardian.

31

Worried about the children at Addison House, Larry grabbed his keys and headed for his car. He couldn't make sense of Doreen's behavior, especially her lying to him. She had always been so concerned about the children! Why hadn't she told him Frankie had been hurt?

Well, he'd find out soon enough. The mountain roads were almost clear of traffic, and he thought he could be at her place within twenty minutes. But suddenly, as he rounded a curve, he saw a big yellow backhoe in the road ahead.

"Damn!" he cried, putting his foot on the brakes.

He thought of Judy, and of how she must have tried her own brakes when she saw the rock crusher.

A woman was waving a red flag, bringing the few cars that were on the road in front of him to a halt. Larry drummed his fingers on the steering wheel impatiently, waiting for the backhoe to move out of the way.

"Why aren't you eating, HJ?" Doreen asked. "I'm not as good a cook as Yolanda, but I don't think anyone can mess up scrambled eggs."

Harry-John glowered at her, not speaking.

She's crazy! She doesn't even wonder about Tara!

"Well, okay, young man," Doreen said. "If you don't

261

want to eat, you can go hungry until lunch. Don't think I'll let Yolanda give you anything when she gets home!"

She's not coming home! Don't you see that? She's not coming home!

Doreen patted Harry-John's head.

"Come along now," she said, her voice unusually sweet. "Let's put these dishes away, and we'll be off to Brendan's house to get the others."

"We aren't going to get them," Harry-John growled, speaking at last. "They're all dead."

Doreen simply shook her head, laughing at him.

The feel of wet sheets brought Frankie to wakefulness. He moaned, embarrassed that he had wet the bed like a baby. He hadn't done that in years!

But this wasn't his bed—or his room. It was dark and cold in here. He tried to see, but there was only the smallest ray of light from a tiny window above the bed. He turned to pull himself from the bed, but he couldn't move.

Frankie realized to his horror that his leg had been chained to a footrail.

When the backhoe finally backed off the road, Larry followed the wave of the red flag and hurried past the construction site. He had lost fifteen minutes already, and he could see more machinery up ahead.

"God, don't slow me down," he prayed. "Those kids need me. Something tells me they aren't going to be safe until I get there!"

But within a mile he had to stop and wait for yet another truck, a bulldozer this time.

Cindy clung to Yolanda; the feel of her arms and the housekeeperish smells of vanilla and cinnamon and pine and soap made the little girl feel just a little less afraid of the dark.

"I don't know where we are, child," Yolanda whispered. "But as soon as I can see a thing, I'll get us out of here!"

"Get up and find a light!" Cindy said.

Yolanda's voice was tremulous.

"I—I can't," she said. "My chest is hurting terribly. I think my ribs are—"

Silence!

The booming voice filled the infinite darkness. Yolanda felt Cindy jump, and pulled the child closer.

"You will never leave! You will not leave until you learn that she is wicked! Until you help me regain what is rightfully mine!"

"Mommy?" Cindy asked, her voice shaking.

"That's not your mommy," Yolanda said.

"It sounds like Mommy," Cindy insisted. "Is that you, Mommy? Are you going to take me home again? Please, Mommy!"

Laughter filled the air, high-pitched and maniacal.

"Tell me the one called Doreen is a whore, and I will let you go!"

"Doreen is not a whore!" Yolanda snapped. "Who are you? Where are we? You'll go to jail forever for this!"

"Say Doreen is a hussy and you shall be free! Say she is a liar and a cheat and you shall be free!"

"I want to go home, Yolanda."

"Shh, Cindy," Yolanda said.

"She left you! She let you be hurt!"

Cindy considered this.

"Maybe Doreen really *is* a bad lady," she said.

Yolanda hugged her.

"No, child! No! You're cold and frightened and hungry! It's making you talk silly!"

"Say she is a whore! Say it! Say it! Say it!"

Cindy started to cry.

Doreen opened her front door and beckoned to Harry-John. He hung back near the kitchen, afraid to go with her, wondering what she had in mind. A frightening thought had occurred to him. Maybe the weird lady Randy had been talking about was really Doreen in disguise! Maybe she wasn't so nice after all, and just ran Addison House so she could catch little kids and hurt them!

"HJ, what's wrong with you?" Doreen asked. "Will you hurry, please? I really do want to get to Brendan's house."

Harry-John took a hesitant step forward.

"We'll all have a picnic this afternoon, okay?" she said, walking toward him. "Come on, HJ. Don't be afraid. You don't think *I'd* hurt you, do you?"

Suddenly, Harry-John gave a yell and ran into the kitchen. Moving as fast as his jellylike legs could carry him, he crashed through the back door and started across the meadow. He didn't know where he was going, or how he'd find help, but he had to try!

Why hasn't Dr. Larry come yet? Where is he?

Harry-John raced toward the woods, oblivious to Doreen's shouts.

"Meet me at Brendan's, HJ!"

Yolanda tried to keep Cindy's ears covered, but the strange voice that filled the darkness was far too loud. It had been going on incessantly, demanding that they turn against Doreen. But why, the housekeeper wondered? Who could hate such a sweet woman as Doreen Addison?

"Doreen's bad," Cindy lisped.

"Don't say that!" Yolanda cried.

"I want to go home!" Cindy said. "And that lady's gonna take me home if I say Doreen's bad! So I'm gonna say it!"

Suddenly Yolanda felt Cindy being yanked from her arms. She frantically reached for the child, but couldn't find her in the dark.

"Doreen's bad! She's wicked! She's a hoo-er!"

"You don't even know what those words mean!" Yolanda shouted into the blackness that surrounded her.

The laughter went on and on.

* * *

Frankie cried loudly, but no one seemed to hear him. He couldn't see, and of course he couldn't hear. But his dominant sense was smell, and he detected something strangely familiar in the air. It was pungent and sweet at the same time, but he couldn't quite figure out what it was.

He reached through the darkness and touched the strap around his ankle. It was very wide and made of leather, and Frankie could feel a heavy buckle on it. It was twisted once around his leg and again around the post of the bed, secured with a padlock. Frankie tried painting his toes to make his foot straight, but he still couldn't put it through. Twisting at the buckle did no good.

Frankie began to cry again.

But if anyone answered his cries, Frankie could not hear.

Randy sat with his head tucked into his knees and his arms wrapped around his legs. He rocked back and forth, humming a song. He was cold, tired, and hungry, but he needed the music to drown out the voices that had been filling his head all night long.

The last thing he remembered was going to bed. He had no idea where he was, or how he had gotten there. It was so dark that he couldn't see, and he was too afraid to feel his way around. Wherever he was, he knew he wasn't in the house. The floor was made of dirt, and the air was musty-smelling and dank.

And he was afraid to find out where the voices were coming from.

All night long, they had been crying out to him.

"Say she is wicked! Say she is a whore!"

"You must tell the authorities that she is evil. She must be driven away from here!"

"The woman named Doreen has come to steal what is rightfully mine! She must be stopped!"

Sometimes the voice sounded like the woman in black, and when he heard her speak, Randy stiffened and covered his ears. Her voice frightened him most of all.

"Say Doreen is a whore, and you shall go free!"

He wanted so much to get out of there. He couldn't stand the voices anymore! They'd been going on all night long, never stopping, never letting him sleep.

"I want to go home!" he cried out to the darkness.

"Say she is wicked!"

"She's wicked!" Randy yelled. "Let me go!"

"Say she is a whore! Say she is evil!"

"Doreen's a whore and she's evil!" Randy cried. "She brought us to this stupid house and she let us get hurt and I hate her, I hate her, I hate her so much and I want my mom and dad!"

Somewhere in the darkness, Yolanda heard the screams and turned her head to listen. But they were abruptly cut off, and her strange prison was silent once again.

Larry was furious. Road construction in upstate New York had been going on for a long time, but never had it taken him so long to get to Addison House. And something inside made him sure the kids really needed him this time. Harry-John's phone calls, Doreen's lie, the things that had happened in the past weeks, all made him sure that today the children were in real danger.

At last, with a sigh of relief, he turned on to the road that led to Addison House. With nothing in his path and not a state trooper in sight, Larry gunned the motor. But he yanked his foot from the gas pedal and slammed on his brakes when he saw Harry-John limping alongside the road.

"HJ?"

Harry-John was bent slightly forward, his arms crossed over his chest. When he looked up, Larry saw tears in his eyes. Harry-John threw himself into the doctor's arms.

"You came!" he cried, gasping. "You came!"

"You've been running, HJ," Larry said. "And you're white as a sheet. What's going on here?"

Harry-John shook his head.

"I don't know!" he cried. "It's so crazy! Tara disappeared right after I called you and Doreen doesn't even care!"

Larry turned the boy toward the car.

"Come with me," he said. "I'll get some answers."

"Tara went into the stairs," Harry-John mumbled.

Larry opened the passenger door and helped the little boy inside.

"There's something down in the basement," Harry-John said.

"I don't understand, HJ," Larry said. "You're talking nonsense."

"It's not nonsense!" the child cried. "I saw her! A lady's voice called Tara down into the basement and she went down and something pulled her into the stairs! It's true!"

Harry-John was sobbing. Larry patted him and drove to the house.

"Doreen's not there," Harry-John said. "She went to Brendan's to get the other guys."

"That figures," Larry grumbled. "I think this Brendan and I are going to have it out."

He glanced sideways at his passenger.

"Do you know where Brendan lives?"

"Nope."

"Well, keep your eyes open," Larry said. "Tell me if you see a house through the trees."

Larry turned the Bronco around in the driveway and drove back to the road.

Through his tears, Harry-John tried hard to see beyond the woods. After about a mile, he spotted a quick flash of movement. The little boy tapped the doctor's arm.

"There she is!" he cried. "There's Doreen!"

Larry stopped the car and got out. Harry-John followed him.

"Doreen?" the doctor called.

"Larry?" her voice came back.

Larry waited until she ran up to him. Her hair was a mess, and her eyes were round, as if she had just woken up. She looked completely bewildered.

"What is going on, Doreen?"

She combed her fingers through her hair, frowning.

"I don't know, Larry," she said. "The children are at Brendan's, but I can't find his house."

"HJ told me about Frankie," Larry said. "Why didn't you let me know he'd hurt himself?"

"He's fine, Larry," Doreen insisted. "I just have to get to Brendan's house so I can take him home!"

"And the others?" Larry asked. "HJ says Randy and Tara disappeared since last night. Are they at Brendan's, too?"

Doreen shrugged.

"I don't know," she said. "Help me find them, Larry. They're my kids! If anything happens to them . . ."

Harry-John watched her, feeling hopeful for the first time that day. Doreen was finally showing some concern instead of acting in the crazy, uncaring way she had earlier.

"Tell me where this Brendan lives," Larry said.

"I—I don't know," Doreen said. "I've tried to find his house, but I can't."

"Maybe it's far away," Larry suggested. "Let's get in my car and—"

"No!" Doreen cried. "He was always walking when he came to my house. He told me he lives right here!"

She looked back toward the woods. She felt so strange, as if she'd been injected with novocaine and it was wearing away and the pain was slowly returning. Part of her sensed the danger her beloved children were in, but part of her kept insisting they were fine. She didn't know what to believe!

"They're okay," she said again.

"I'm not so sure," Larry answered. "Doreen, think—did he ever give you any clue as to where he lived?"

Larry thought, *If he hurts those kids, I'll break every bone in his—*

"Yes!" Doreen cried. "I remember now! We once walked to a beautiful lake, and he said his home was just near it!"

Larry took her by the arm.

"Then let's find that lake," he said.

They started into the woods with Harry-John close behind.

Frankie couldn't cry anymore. His eyes burned, and his hands hurt where he had pounded them on the wall next to the bed. Wherever he was, there was no one with him at the moment. The strange, familiar aroma still lingered in the air. Frankie closed his eyes and breathed it in, trying hard to remember where he had smelled it before.

When he closed his eyes, a picture of the skeleton he had found in the cave came into view. Frankie's eyes snapped open and focused on the window overhead. His eyes had adjusted to the darkness by then, and by the little bit of light that shown in he could just make out a small dresser on the far side of the room. There was a lamp on top, and a vase of some kind. Frankie wished he could reach the lamp and light it. He wished he could take the vase and use it as a weapon. He would just clunk his captor over the head when he came into the room.

But where was his captor? And who was he?

Doreen led Larry and Harry-John through the woods in the direction where she was certain she'd find the lake. After half an hour of searching, she came to a halt and shook her head.

"I'm lost," she said. "I thought it was this way, but I can't find it."

"We've got to keep trying," Larry said. "Did he ever say how big his house was? If it's just a little cabin, it could be hidden farther up the mountainside, in the trees."

"He told me he has six horses," Doreen said. "You need a lot of land for horses, but there doesn't seem to be any clearing in sight."

"All right, let's keep going," Larry said. "We aren't going to find the lake or your friend's house by standing here."

They walked on, Larry between Doreen and Harry-John. The little boy wanted it that way, not quite trusting his guardian.

Suddenly, Doreen cried out.

"This is the way! I recognize this tree from the marks where a bear clawed it years ago. The lake is just a little distance from here."

"When we get to it," Larry said, "we'll probably find a path that cuts through the woods to Delacorte's. If someone dug this lake out, like you told me, there has to be—"

Doreen stopped so abruptly that Larry walked into her. She covered her mouth to stifle a gasp, unable to believe what she was seeing.

"I thought you told me it was filled," Larry whispered.

"It was!" Doreen cried. "I swear it was! There were swans . . . and lily pads. And the most beautiful weeping cherry trees!"

Larry scratched his head. "There's nothing here now."

He was right. Doreen looked with amazement at a dry lake bed. It was impossible! Lakes didn't dry up overnight!

"I was wrong," she said. "It must be somewhere else! Brendan and I went to a lake, I swear it!"

She hurried ahead of the others, looking around. To her dismay, she suddenly came upon the flat rock where she and Brendan had rested. She sank down to it, touching it carefully as if afraid it, too, would vanish.

"There was a lake here, Larry," she whispered. "I swear it. I was with Brendan—he brought me here. I'm not crazy, Larry!"

Larry sat next to her. Harry-John kept his distance, scuffing the dirt.

"You're not crazy," Larry said. "But this Delacorte guy might be."

"Brendan?" Doreen said. "Never! He's the kindest, most helpful—"

"Did he ever give you anything, Doreen?" Larry interrupted. "Did he ever give you anything to drink or to eat?"

"What are you talking about?"

"Drugs, Doreen!" Larry cried. "Don't you see? He might have given you something laced with hallucinogens!"

Doreen shook her head vigorously.

"No way!" she cried. "He wouldn't hurt me! Besides, he never gave me a thing." *But,* she thought, *maybe kissing him affected me somehow—I felt so tired afterwards.* . . .

She gazed toward the mountainside that sloped into the spread of dirt and weeds. Though the trees had been emerald-green the other day, today they seemed gnarled and faded. Had it all been an illusion? Was she out of her mind?

She put her arms around Larry.

"What am I going to do?" she asked. "I'm so scared! I want my children back!"

Larry gave her a hug, then stood up and pulled her after him.

"This is more than we can handle," he said. "I don't care what you say, I'm calling the police. Come on, Doreen, let's go back to the house."

Doreen nodded, letting herself be pulled along.

"Yes," she said, her voice lifeless. "Yes, let's call the police."

She had the sound and slow mannerisms of someone who had been given Demerol, making Larry believe she had been given drugs. It made sense, since her personality had changed so completely. He wished he could find Brendan Delacorte, because if he had given Doreen something to do this to her Larry would make him pay.

They came out of the woods and cut across the meadow to the house. The closer they got to it, the slower Harry-John moved.

"Don't be afraid," Larry said. "I won't let anything hurt you."

"She's in there," Harry-John said. "The lady who took Tara and Randy is in the basement. I don't want her to get me, too!"

"You see, Larry?" Doreen said. "It's a woman who's after my kids, not Brendan!"

They reached the house, entering through the back door.

"Listen to me, Doreen," Larry said. "Get on the phone and call the police. In the meantime, I'll check out the basement."

Harry-John looked from the doctor to his guardian. He didn't want to stay with Doreen, but he was more afraid of the basement.

"Don't go down there," he said. "Something bad will happen!"

"Not if I can help it," Larry said, opening the cellar door. He reached in and switched on the light and saw it didn't work. "I'll be up in a minute."

He heard the sound of the phone being dialed as he went down the stairs. The kitchen light illuminated a little of the cellar, but when he got to the bottom of the stairs, he switched on the flashlight he had brought with him.

"There's nothing down here, HJ!" he called up the stairs.

"Tara went down and something grabbed her!" Harry-John yelled back. "I saw it! I did!"

As he listened to the child's cries, Larry was suddenly aware of another voice, sounding as if it came from far away. He cocked his head to one side and listened hard.

It wasn't his imagination. It *was* a voice, and it was coming from a definite direction. Larry moved toward it and realized it wasn't far away at all.

It was muffled by a wall, a wooden wall with a thick growth of moss on it.

32

Yolanda tried to move, but each time she did her ribs felt like two sharp knives. She knew that she and Cindy weren't alone, because she had heard Randy's voice shouting from somewhere in the blackness. And whispers in what sounded like Karen's voice kept repeating, over and over, "She is evil. She has taken what is not hers."

Yolanda had called out to the teenager, but there was no reply.

She reached up, groping for Cindy. The little girl was there, but she had moved away, taking up Karen's chant with her babyish, lisping voice.

"She is evil," Cindy was saying.

"Doreen is a whore," Karen added.

"Stop it!" Yolanda cried. "Don't talk that way!"

Randy went on shouting, but Yolanda could not understand his words. She tried to pull herself along the floor, hoping she could find a way out of this dark prison. But her broken ribs were too painful and refused to let her move.

All of a sudden, through all the talking, Yolanda heard a pounding noise. It sounded like someone knocking on a door!

"Who's there?" she shouted. "Help! Help!"

Karen and Cindy began to chant all the louder, drowning out both the knocking and Yolanda's voice.

Frankie had fallen asleep. He tossed in the bed, nightmares plaguing his mind.

"No, daddy! No!"

"You're wicked, filled with the devil! I must drive him from you! I must save you!"

"Daddy, please!"

A man with very short blond hair leaned over the bed, pressing one strong arm across the boy's shoulders. The child thrashed about, trying to get free, but he was trapped. The man reached for a pillow with his other hand . . .

Frankie woke up screaming, looking into a pair of blue eyes. Someone was standing over his bed, pressing his shoulders down into the mattress so that he couldn't move.

Larry turned away from the wall, his knuckles stained green where he had been knocking on the moss-covered wood. It had had a hollow sound to it, and the voices that seemed to come from the other side had grown louder before finally stopping altogether. He went to the staircase. Harry-John was still standing at the top holding on to the doorknob.

"Get Doreen," Larry called up. "Tell her to bring me an ax."

Moments later, both Doreen and Harry-John came down the stairs. Larry gave the child a questioning look.

"I didn't want to be alone," Harry-John said.

Doreen handed the ax to Larry.

"Are the police coming?"

"The phone's dead," Doreen said.

Larry growled. "That figures."

"What are you going to do?" Doreen asked.

"That wall," Larry said. "I hear voices behind it. Didn't you ever wonder why there would be one wooden wall and three stone ones?"

"I thought there had been shelves there at one time," Doreen said. "That the wood had been put up over the stone."

Larry picked up the ax and swung it into the wood. The pounding noise filled the basement, and when he had broken through one of the slats he reached out and pulled it back. It broke easily, and as Larry pulled it away a great rush of cold, foul-smelling air came into the cellar.

"Oh, my Lord," Doreen whispered. "What's back there?"

"That's what I mean to find out," Larry said, smashing the wood.

Some time later, he had created a hole big enough to walk through. The flashlight he held illuminated the dripping stone walls of an ancient passageway. There were sconces on the walls encased in cobwebs.

"What do you see?" Doreen asked, unable to look around Larry's shoulder because the hall was so narrow.

"Not much," Larry said. "It seems to go on forever." There was a squeaking noise.

"What was that?" Harry-John asked.

"A mouse?" Doreen asked.

"Sounded like a child crying."

Doreen grabbed Larry's arm from behind.

"Is one of my kids in there?" she asked. "Hey! Who's there? Tell me where you are!"

"Doreen! Help us!"

"That's Yolanda!" Harry-John said.

"We're coming!" Larry shouted. "Hold on!"

The light picked up something pink in the distance, and as Larry got closer he realized it was a ribbon from Cindy's hair. He began to run. Doreen kept right behind, with Harry-John doing his best to stay close. Suddenly there was a loud *thwump!* as Larry slammed into something and sprang backward into Doreen. Even as this happened, softly glowing lanterns lit up all at once, revealing a small room.

"What the hell was that!" he cried.

He had struck something solid, but the passageway to the children was clear!

"You—you must have hit a low ceiling," Doreen said. "Larry, let me get to Cindy!"

She tried to move around him, reaching toward the room's entrance. Her hands stopped short.

"There's a glass door here!" she cried. "Give me something to break it with!"

"That's not glass," Larry said, rubbing his aching head. "My body would have shattered it."

Doreen pulled a loose stone from the wall and began to pound at the strange, clear barrier. As she tried to break it, she saw Yolanda, Cindy, Karen, and Randy on the other side.

"I don't see Tara or Frankie!" she cried.

Karen began to laugh.

"Tara hasn't learned her lesson yet!" the teenager shouted, her voice muffled by the barrier. "She won't accept the truth—that you're evil!"

"Don't listen to her, Doreen!" Yolanda cried, looking up from her prone position. "There's a madwoman here and she's making them say crazy things!"

Doreen pummeled the obstruction harder, tears of frustration rising.

"Leave us, you whore!" Cindy cried, her curled lips making her look like a snarling animal.

"Cindy, why . . . ?"

Larry pulled her away.

"Let me try that," he said. "If it's a window of some kind, it has to have a weak point."

He shouted to Yolanda through the barrier, "Can you stand up?"

She shook her head. "I think my ribs are broken. Please, please get us out of here!"

Larry put the rock down and waved Doreen and Harry-John away from him.

"Stand back," he said.

He gave himself some distance, then ran shoulder-first into the barrier. Nothing happened. He tried it again.

When he struck the invisible door this time, a great flash of white light surrounded him. Blue streaks, like lightning, jagged away from his skin, outlining his body. Larry screamed, smoke pouring from his mouth, and collapsed unconscious.

"Larry!" Doreen cried.

She began pounding on the barrier with both fists.

"Doreen, don't touch that!" Harry-John cried.

"Open this up!" she screamed. "I want my children!"

"Leave us alone, you hussy!" Karen cried.

Through the obstruction, Doreen could see another flash of white light, this one column-shaped.

Harry-John squinted his eyes, unable to stand the brightness.

Then the brilliance was gone, and a woman in black was standing in the center of the room with the children.

"Fool!" she cried. *"Did you think you could come back here, to take what is rightfully mine? I fought you before, and I shall fight you again!"*

"Who are you?" Doreen demanded, still pounding on the barrier. "What are you talking about?"

"Brendan!" the woman shouted. *"You have come back to take him from me, but you won't!"*

Doreen shook her head, confused.

"What do you have to do with Brendan?" she demanded. "And why are you hurting my kids? Let me have them back, whoever you are."

"Don't you understand?" the woman asked. *"I'm educating them. I'm educating them as you were educated. Don't you remember this room? It's our meditation room, where we sent the children we cared for—the very children you taught—to reflect upon their sinful ways! You spent your last hours here, thinking of the haughty, lustful things you did to win our stablehand's love. But Brendan is mine, and will always be mine!"*

Doreen heard Larry groan. He began to move and slowly pulled himself to his feet.

"I—I don't understand," she said to the woman. "Brendan never mentioned another woman! And you have no right to hurt my children!"

The woman threw back her head, laughing maniacally. A tunnel of smoke gushed up from her mouth. It drooped down around her, surrounding her, swallowing her.

She was gone.

"Come on, Doreen," Larry said, pulling her. "Whatever that is, we can't fight it!"

"Larry, my kids!"

"There must be another entrance!" Larry said. "We just can't get through this one! But we've got to hurry!"

Reluctant, but realizing that he was right, Doreen followed the doctor down the hall. She could hear Yolanda crying out, begging them not to leave her. But Karen's voice rose above the housekeeper's: "You are evil, Doreen Addison! Evil! Evil! Evil!"

The word echoed over and over as they raced up the stairs.

Doreen screamed, pointing to the back door. Larry turned to see a man looking in the window.

"It's Brendan!" Doreen cried.

She hurried to the door, pulling it open. She threw herself into Brendan's arms, sobbing.

"My love, what has happened!"

"You tell us," Larry said, glaring at the other man.

Doreen pulled away.

"Brendan, there's a madwoman holding my children hostage," she said. "She's got them in a secret room in the basement, and we can't get to them!"

Brendan nodded. "She's doing it again, I see."

"What?" Doreen's question was breathless.

"She's trying to turn the children against you, as she did before," Brendan said.

Doreen stepped away from him.

"You know about this woman?" she asked, incredulous.

"Brendan, you said you didn't know anyone who might be hurting the children. You lied to me!"

Brendan moved toward her, taking her arms with his big hands. Doreen's body stiffened. She suddenly didn't like the feel of him near her.

"My love," he said. "Don't you see? She's teaching them to tell lies about you, as they did long ago! They'll tell the authorities that you are unfit to care for them, and they'll drive you away. I can't let that happen again, my Vanessa, I can't!"

Doreen jerked away from him, hurrying toward Larry. Her friend put an arm around her, restraining himself from sending Brendan Delacorte through the kitchen door.

"Why did you call me Vanessa?" she cried. "Who is Vanessa? I thought you loved *me*, Brendan—Doreen Addison!"

"Oh, no," Brendan said, shaking his head. "Doreen Addison is only the name you were given in this life. But you are truly Vanessa Winston! I know this to be true—for you came to this house as a teacher, just as you did long ago! And the way that you accepted my affections—you must love me! Only my Vanessa would touch me so! They've poisoned your mind, my love, made you forget your true destiny."

"Destiny?"

"To be with me," Brendan said. "You are my Vanessa, and we belong together! So many times you've come back to me, and each time she's frightened you away. No more! I won't allow her to harm you again!"

Brendan took a step toward Doreen, but stopped when he saw Larry pull her to the side.

"Don't touch her," Larry said in a threatening tone.

Brendan's eyes flashed.

"You have no claim to her," he shot back. His eyes were imploring when he looked at Doreen. "My love, don't you see? They've hurt you so much, you don't even know who you are! But you're my beautiful butterfly, my Vanessa! You've tried to come back to me, but I've always lost you!

Not this time! This time you won't be taken from me!"

Tears were falling from Doreen's eyes.

"You're insane," she said. "I'm not Vanessa! I'm not! And I want my children back!"

She turned to Larry.

"Do something!" she cried. "Make him tell us what's happening here!"

Larry rushed toward Brendan, his hands reaching out to grab him.

"Listen, you son-of-a-. . . ."

But the moment he touched Brendan, the other man seemed to turn into a cloud of steam, and disappeared into thin air. Doreen cried out in dismay.

"Oh, God," Larry whispered in disbelief.

He took Doreen by the arm. Then he reached for Harry-John, who had been cowering under the kitchen table.

"Come on, we have to get out of here!"

"No!" Doreen cried. "My kids are trapped downstairs!"

"Doreen, we can't get to them from here!" Larry shouted. "Hurry! We have to find another way into that room! God knows what we're dealing with here!"

With Doreen crying in protest, Larry pulled her and the little boy from the kitchen. When they were a distance from the house, the trio turned to look back at it. It looked so innocent, the brick exterior hiding the evil within.

"We've got to get help!" Larry said. "We need to search every inch of this land. Chances are pretty good there's another entrance to that room, a secret passage from the outside."

Harry-John tugged at Doreen's pants leg. "Maybe that nutty old guy named Marty knows where one is?"

Doreen looked at Larry. "I—I don't know. He's so eccentric!"

"We don't have much choice," Larry said.

They began to run to the old man's shack. Though she had previously thought Marty was crazy, Doreen desperately hoped he'd be willing to help her. She didn't know what else to do!

"I see smoke," Harry-John said. "That means he's home."

They hurried to the shack, and Doreen pounded on the door. It swung open a few moments later, revealing Marty standing there with a hunting knife in his hand. Larry pulled Doreen back, strangely feeling that Marty might use the knife on *her*.

"We need help," Doreen said breathlessly. "There's a madwoman after my children! She's got them locked in a basement room, and we can't get to them!"

Marty tilted his head back, looking down his nose at his visitors.

"Now you want me," he said. "Few weeks back, you was telling me to keep away."

"Don't argue with her," Larry said. "Can't you see we need help?"

Marty rubbed his jaw.

"Yep, I can see," he said. "I saw it comin' for a long time, just like with the others. Like with that guy who killed his wife and little boy. I knew they'd be comin' back again, those evil spirits that made all the blood rise before. Tried to tell you." Marty trailed off.

He noticed Harry-John moving closer, toward the doorway, eyeing something inside. Marty stepped aside to block the child's view.

"Hey, I saw somebody moving in there!" Harry-John cried. "I think it was Frankie!"

"Nobody's here but me!"

Harry-John turned to Doreen and Larry.

"It was Frankie! I saw him!"

Larry grabbed the old man's arm and pulled him out of the way. With Doreen behind him, he rushed to the slightly open door at the back of the shack. Doreen cried out when she saw Frankie on a sheetless bed, his ankle cruelly shackled to the footrail.

"What have you done!" she screamed at the old man.

Larry went to Frankie, who was lying unconscious, and began to revive him.

"Had to do it!" Marty cried. "He would have gone back to the house, to the danger! I had to keep him here, safe!"

"This is kidnapping!" Larry said. "Get the key to that lock and free him!"

Marty turned over the vase on the dresser. A key dropped out into his hand.

"It was the only way I could keep him safe," he said. "I would have gotten to the others, too, but there was no chance! And it sounds like she's got them under her spell again!"

"Again!" Doreen said. "You talk as if this has happened before."

"It has," Marty said, unlocking his captive.

Larry took the boy into his arms. Frankie's eyes fluttered, and he mumbled something, cuddling against the doctor's chest.

"We don't have time to talk about it now," Larry said. "I don't suppose you have a phone . . ."

"Never needed one," Marty said. "But it ain't a phone that's gonna help you."

Doreen's eyes were red-rimmed, and her voice was thin and shaky.

"Then suppose you tell us just what we *should* do!"

"Get the kids and get out," Marty said. "Like I told you before. It's not safe stayin' in that house!"

"I know that!" Doreen cried. "But don't you see? I can't get my children! She won't let me have them!"

"Then you gotta give her something she wants," Marty said. "A trade."

Doreen looked at Larry, who stood rocking back and forth from his heels to his toes, Frankie cradled in his arms.

"B-Brendan," she whispered, suddenly understanding. She turned back to Marty. "But why does she want him?"

"It's a long story," Marty said. "But I been watchin' her come and go since I was a kid. Saw her by the house when the murders took place. It wasn't Aaron Howell that did them. It was her!"

"Do you know any way we can fight her?" Doreen said.

Marty shook his head. "She's too powerful, too fulla meanness. You just gotta give Brendan back to her, then pack up your things and leave."

Doreen sighed deeply. "I suppose it's the only way..."

"Wait a second!" Larry cried. "What are we fighting here? You haven't told us yet who these people are!"

"Ain't you guessed yet?" Marty asked. "They're spirits —ghosts! They've been walkin' this land since my daddy was a boy. He used to tell me about 'em."

"There's no such..."

"Things as ghosts?" Marty finished. "Smart folks believe in 'em. Smart folks know you can't fight 'em."

"Ghosts?" Harry-John said in disbelief. He had been listening with wonder to the adults' conversation, and suddenly he moved closer to Doreen, afraid.

"Nonsense," Larry said.

"Larry, you saw Brendan disappear!" Doreen cried. "You saw that strange glass wall!"

She reached out to Marty.

"Please, tell us about them," she said. "Anything you can tell us will help!"

Marty sighed, sinking into a splintery wooden chair.

"Far as I know," he said, "there was a couple of folks named Miles and Charity Winston who lived in that house over a hundred years ago. The place was an orphanage— sort of like your place. They had an adopted daughter named Vanessa..."

Doreen gasped.

"She was a schoolteacher there, and Brendan Delacorte was a stablehand. One day, some of the kids came and told Miles Winston that Vanessa had been foolin' around with Brendan. 'Course that sort of thing wasn't acceptable then the way it is today."

He rubbed his knuckles under his nose.

"It's all there in the Bible," he said. "There was an old family Bible I saw once when I was a kid—one of the times that the house was empty. But my daddy caught me with it and walloped me for trespassin'. I never read any more."

"Randy's Bible!" Doreen cried. "Larry, we have to go back to the house and find it! It might have the answers we need!"

"I'm not going back there!" Harry-John cried.

"I can't leave you alone," Doreen said.

Marty stood up.

"Let 'em stay here," he said. "I won't let 'em get hurt."

"It's strange," Doreen said. "But somehow I believe you. Harry-John?"

"I'd rather stay here than go back to that crazy house!"

Larry put Frankie down. He wobbled a little, his eyes blinking. Then he ran to Doreen.

Don't go! Don't go! he signed frantically.

Doreen knelt down and quickly signed an explanation to him. He really didn't understand, but he trusted her enough to realize that she believed Marty had only been trying to help in his own way.

"Come on, Larry," she said. "We've got to find that Bible."

Back at the house, it was deathly quiet. Where children's laughter had once been, the house seemed all the more eerie. Doreen stood near the cellar door, leaning against her friend.

"I took the Bible from Randy's room," she said. "And after that it disappeared from my office."

"Maybe he took it back again," Larry said. "Let's go look in his bedroom."

There was a strange smell of smoke in the air when they opened Randy's door. When she saw the blood spattered on the wall, fear-edged anger rose in Doreen. How could anyone hurt small children like this?

"Here it is! Something's working in our favor, at last," Larry said.

Doreen sat on the edge of Randy's bed and began to flip

through the ancient pages, so quickly that pieces began to flake off and sail to the floor.

"There must be a family record of some kind," she said as she turned the pages. "I've got it. Here's the family tree—Miles Winston, wed to Charity Jefferson on July 10, 1810. It doesn't say they had any children."

"Marty said the girl named Vanessa was adopted," Larry reminded her. "Do you see any reference to her?"

Doreen scanned the pages, turning them more carefully now. Her finger snaked down the pages, her eyes catching a few words here and there. Then she stopped, her finger resting on the first mention of Vanessa's name.

"Her real parents were members of the local church," she said. "Whey they both died from smallpox, she came to live with the Winstons."

She went on reading.

"Vanessa started teaching here when she was seventeen," Doreen said. "The children really loved her. Apparently, Miles Winston looked upon her as a daughter. He says some pretty nice things about her. But he sounds as if he was a strict father, too. He keeps talking about a meditation room, where the children were sent from time to time."

"The room downstairs?"

Doreen nodded and continued reading. Suddenly, she gasped.

"Brendan?" she whispered.

"What?"

"Brendan's name is in here!" Doreen said. She started skimming again, her eyes moving frantically. "He came to work as a stablehand, and the two fell in love. Miles disapproved and . . ."

"And what?" Larry demanded.

Doreen jumped up. "There's no time to explain! We've got to get downstairs again! We've got to get to the children!"

With Larry close behind, she raced through the hall and

down the stairs, crying out at the top of her lungs, "Brendan! Brendan, I need you!"

"Doreen, what are you doing?" Larry asked, chasing her down the cellar stairs.

Doreen ignored him. "Brendan, help me! I need you! Vanessa needs you!"

She entered the secret passageway, her voice bouncing off the wet walls. When she came to the glass barrier, she started pounding on it, screaming. She could see Tara and Randy embracing each other, watching her with cold expressions. Cindy was shifting back and forth, clenching and unclenching her fists. At the child's feet, Yolanda cried silent tears.

"Wicked hussy!" Karen screamed. "Leave us alone! We are at peace now!"

"We don't need you!" Randy cried.

"No!" Doreen cried. "You're my kids! She's made you all crazy!"

Doreen turned her back to the glass barrier, screaming into the dark tunnel.

"Brendan!"

Larry covered his ears.

"Doreen, he can't hear you."

"He has to hear me, Larry!" Doreen cried, tears falling from her hazel-colored eyes. "He's the only one who can fight her."

Her eyes widened.

"Brendan . . ."

Larry felt pinpricks of ice at the back of his neck, and knew without turning that she had conjured up the ghost of Brendan Delacorte. Silently, he backed away, watching as Brendan went to Doreen with open arms. She embraced him so warmly that Larry wondered how much she understood of what was happening. But he said nothing, unable to make sense of it himself.

"My love, you're crying," Brendan said.

"Don't you know why?" Doreen said. "Look what she's done to my kids! She's turned them into monsters!"

"She has influence," Brendan said.

"I want my children back!"

Brendan nodded, reaching over her shoulder to the barrier. There was a pop, and a sizzling noise, and the obstruction melted from the inside out as if it were plastic that had been touched by fire. A blast of cold air filled the tunnel, escaping from the hidden room.

Larry pushed past Doreen, running to Yolanda.

"We've got to get them out of here!" he said. "Yolanda, can you stand?"

"If you help me . . ."

Carefully, he supported the housekeeper as she got to her feet. She winced, holding her side. It hurt badly, but Yolanda knew she had to get out of there before the woman in black returned.

"Brendan, help us!" Doreen cried, unfastening the shackles that held Karen to the wall.

The teenager drew back her head and brought it forward again, spitting at Doreen as she did so.

Doreen wiped her face with the back of her hand.

"Larry, I can't pick her up," she said. "But that cast . . ."

"Leave Karen to me," Larry said, lifting the child. "Brendan can take Randy or Tara . . ."

They looked around the room, but Brendan was nowhere to be seen.

"Where did he go?" Larry demanded.

"I—I don't know," Doreen said, confused herself. "I don't care! I just want to get out of here!"

"Not me!" Randy cried. "I'm not coming!"

"Be quiet!" Larry snapped. "Doreen, you carry Cindy and go first. Then Yolanda, then the twins. I'll bring up the rear with Karen."

"You're trying to tempt us!" Randy cried. "To lead us into temptation!"

"I don't want to go!" Cindy cried, struggling in Doreen's arms. "I want my mommy!"

The adults, ignoring the children's protests, led and carried them through the dark tunnel and into the basement.

Once Larry had come through, he looked behind them.

"That was too easy," he said. "She's got to be around somewhere."

"Then we'll fight her," Doreen said. "But this time, she won't get my children back!"

Laboriously, burdened by reluctant children and Yolanda's injury, they made their way upstairs.

"Let's get out of this house," Larry said. "Put the kids in my Bronco, and I'll take them and Yolanda to the hospital."

"Larry, I need you here!"

"We've got to get the kids away from this place!" Larry said. "Don't you see what she's doing to them!"

"And what do we do when they come back?" Doreen cried. "She'll still be here, and she'll hurt them again!"

"Doreen, we can't come back," Yolanda protested weakly.

Cindy and Tara were sobbing. Randy stared at the kitchen floor, mumbling something. Larry was teetering under Karen's weight, the teenager either unable or unwilling to help support herself.

"We *can* come back!" Doreen cried. "This is my house! Mine! I'm not going to let some hundred-year-old witch take it from me!"

"Doreen, face it!" Larry shouted. "How do you fight something so powerful? Something so unnatural? I took an oath to become a doctor, to help people. If I let the children stay here, I'd be breaking that oath!"

Doreen waved a hand at him.

"Then go!" she cried. "Get them out of here, far away! But I'm going to fight for the house and my life."

"Doreen, please," Yolanda begged.

But Doreen had already opened the back door and walked to her car. She was halfway down the road in her car before she looked in her rearview mirror and saw Larry helping the last of the children into his Bronco. He was right, she knew, but so was she! And she knew there was only one way she could put an end to all of this.

She had to get Brendan and Vanessa together again.

"Please, God," she prayed. "Let me find the place where I saw that woman the other day!"

She realized that the young woman she had seen crying in the woods had been a ghost too. She must have been Vanessa Winston! Approximating where she had seen her, Doreen pulled off the road and got out of the car. She walked into the woods, calling out the woman's name, praying her idea would work.

"Vanessa?"

Only the birds answered her.

"Vanessa Winston, please answer me! I'm your friend! I want to take you back to Brendan!"

For fifteen minutes Doreen walked through the woods. But Vanessa's spirit would not be raised as easily as Brendan's.

I didn't raise Brendan's spirit. He was near the house and he heard me calling!

Suddenly Doreen smelled a strange but familiar odor, and she knew Marty's shack was near. Her mothering instinct took over, and Vanessa was forgotten for the moment as Doreen hurried to check on Frankie and Harry-John. Marty was outside when she reached the clearing around his place.

"You're calling that girl?" he asked. "She won't come. She's too scared."

"How do you know?" Doreen asked.

"She's tried to come back before," Marty said. "But that other one always scares her away. Never lets her near Brendan."

Frankie appeared at the door just then. When he saw Doreen, he ran up and hugged her around the waist. Harry-John came out, too.

"Where's Dr. Larry?" he asked. "Where's everybody else?"

"They're all safe, thank God," Doreen said. She looked at Marty. "I read the Bible, and I know what happened to Vanessa. I think the only way I can stop all this is to let

Brendan know what happened. I'm sure Brendan and Vanessa have been trying to get together, but Charity Winston always stops them. I've got to find Vanessa! Her body must be somewhere on this property."

Frankie, who had been looking up at her and reading her lips, backed away and started shaking his head vigorously.

No body! he signed. *No cave!*

"What cave?" Doreen asked, her hands signing the words.

Frankie bowed his head, frowning.

"That's where I found him. In a thicket," Marty said, "just outside a low cave. He was shakin' so bad I knew the spirits had gotten him, so I brought him here."

Doreen looked at Marty.

"What cave is that?" she asked. "Could Frankie have seen something there?"

"Only one way to find out," Marty said. "C'mon, I'll show you."

Harry-John took a step forward.

"Don't leave us!"

"You watch Frankie," Doreen said. "You'll be all right."

She followed Marty into the woods, to a clearing that was thickly overgrown with weeds and grass. The old man pointed to a spot where the ground was raised just a few feet. On closer inspection, Doreen could make out the opening of a low cave behind a curtain of vines. It was too small for an adult to climb into, but a child could easily have fit.

"How on earth did he find this?"

Marty shrugged.

"Well, help me pull these vines away!" Doreen ordered, starting to rip at the heavy foliage.

The work was hard, but after a few minutes the opening to the cave was clear. Doreen got on her knees, and could see a long, dark tunnel at the cave's opposite side. Its destination was lost in blackness. Doreen stood up, and as she did so she realized she was facing the house.

"This must be the secret passageway!" she cried. "It must lead back to the house!"

Marty tapped her arm.

"Look at that," he said.

She bent down again. At first, it seemed she was looking at a gnarled piece of log. Doreen gasped when she realized what she was really seeing.

"My God," she said. "It's a body! A mummified body!"

The figure in the cave was on its stomach, one hand reaching out as if trying to grab something. All that was left of the dress it had once worn were fringed pieces of rag and spiderweb remnants of rotted lace.

"It's a brown dress," Doreen whispered.

The young woman in the woods had been wearing a brown dress.

"It's Vanessa!" she said, standing up. "She's here! The poor thing must have crawled from that hidden room, only to have collapsed when she reached this cave."

Once again, Doreen began to shout the woman's name.

"Vanessa! Vanessa Winston, please come! I want to help you!"

Marty shook his head, scratching the back of his neck.

"Darn fool . . ."

Doreen hushed him.

"Vanessa? Brendan is looking for you! Let me take you to him!"

"Well, I'll be!" Marty cried. "Look over yonder!"

Doreen looked in the direction he was pointing. There, a few yards away at the edge of the woods, stood a small figure in a long brown dress. Doreen took a step toward her.

"Vanessa . . ."

The young woman began to sob, backing away.

"Don't be afraid!" Doreen cried. "I'm here to help you. Brendan wants you, but Charity won't let him get to you!"

The woman nodded.

"He left me!" she cried. *"He left me to die!"*

"Oh, no!" Doreen said, wanting to take this frail little

spirit in her arms. She was so pathetic, so much like the children Doreen had known over the years. "Brendan didn't know what happened to you!"

Vanessa finally looked up, her brown eyes doelike.

"I'm so afraid!" she said, her voice almost melodic on the summer wind.

"Don't be!" Doreen said. "We must get you back to Brendan. We must fight Charity!"

"Nnnnooooo!"

Vanessa's high-pitched scream sent birds shooting to the sky.

"She won't hurt you!" Doreen cried. "Brendan won't let her!"

"She's too powerful," Marty said. "Vanessa's tried to come back, but Charity keeps scarin' her off. Saw it when I was a boy, saw that woman in black—"

He was interrupted by a childish cry.

"Doreen! Help us!"

Doreen looked around, and she caught her breath when she saw Frankie and Harry-John coming out of the woods. They weren't with anyone, but something unseen was holding them both two feet off the ground.

"Make her put us down!" Harry-John cried.

Doreen started running toward them.

"Let them go!" she cried to what she couldn't see. "Let my children alone!"

Maniacal laughter filled the air.

"Leave us alone!" a voice said. *"Leave Brendan to me and send that hussy back to her grave!"*

"She's no hussy," Doreen said through clenched teeth. "Vanessa is innocent. I know what *you* did, Charity Winston! I read your husband's journal! You poisoned the minds of the children in your orphanage, locking them in that dark room until they agreed to lie about Vanessa and Brendan. You made them say the two of them were lovers!"

Harry-John and Frankie thumped to the ground. When

they tried to run, it seemed they were tied by invisible ropes to the trees.

Moments later, Charity appeared, a mist with only a suggestion of human features.

"They were lovers," Charity hissed.

"That's not true!" Vanessa cried.

Charity seemed to not hear her.

"No, Charity," Doreen said, her outwardly calm voice belying the terror she felt inside. "Brendan and Vanessa loved each other, but they never consummated that love. Vanessa remained pure until the day she died. Your husband believed your lies about Vanessa and Brendan, and thought the devil himself had made Vanessa give herself to a man who was not her husband. He locked her in that basement room, refusing to give her food, expecting her to pray for forgiveness."

Vanessa was crying openly. Harry-John and Frankie were begging Doreen to help them, but for the moment she ignored the boys. Marty just stood back, watching in amazement.

"He left her there, Charity!" Doreen cried. "He ignored her cries for help and left her in that room! Vanessa starved to death! She tried to crawl through the tunnel to escape, but she was so weak she collapsed! And no one came to help her!"

"Liar!" Charity screamed. *"She deserved to die! The Lord punished her for her wickedness! There is no room on this earth for whores like Vanessa Winston!"*

"No room on earth for whores like *you*!" Doreen yelled "Get away from this place! Leave us alone! Leave Vanessa alone!"

Charity threw back her head and started to laugh. Her body seemed as solid as if it were alive. Doreen watched her, horrified at what she saw.

"Leave Vanessa alone," Charity mimicked. She snarled, her smile gone. *"I'll never leave her alone. I'll send her to hell, where she belongs!"*

Charity's body began to waver, as if Doreen were looking through water. In an instant she was gone, and a moment later, Vanessa started screaming.

"Help me! Oh, please help me! She's hurting me!"

Doreen ran toward Vanessa, but Marty caught up to her and grabbed her arm.

"Let me go!" Doreen cried. "She needs help!"

"How you gonna fight that?" Marty demanded. "Don't be a darned fool!"

Vanessa had disappeared, too, but her screams still filled the air.

"Somebody has to help her!" Doreen cried.

She started yelling as loudly as she could.

"Brendan! Brendan!"

Vanessa and Charity reappeared. Charity had Vanessa by the hair, and she was glaring at Doreen.

"Stop!" she hissed. *"Stop, or I'll kill the children."*

But Doreen wouldn't be stopped. She knew the only way to fight Charity was through Brendan's strong love for Vanessa.

"Brendan!"

"There he is!" Marty shouted.

Brendan had appeared a short distance from the two women.

"Leave her alone, Charity," he demanded.

"Brendan, you've come back!" Vanessa cried.

"I've always been here, my love," Brendan said. "I've always tried to find you. I thought I had found you, but those others were imposters!"

"Vanessa is the only imposter," Charity hissed. *"I am your only true lover!"*

"I never loved you, Charity," Brendan said.

Charity wailed.

"You did love me!" she cried. *"I gave you horses and fine clothes and money! I gave you myself! You are mine!"*

"Never!" Brendan cried. "How could I love a married woman! I was just a naive boy when you took me, but through the years I have grown wiser. I don't love you, Charity! I hate you!"

He opened his arms, and a moment later Vanessa was in his embrace.

"I know what you did to my sweet Vanessa!" Brendan said. "I know how you made the children lie to your husband, and how you made him lock this sweet girl in that dark room. But you won't hurt her again. Now that Vanessa is with me, you'll never hurt her again."

A catlike yowl came from Charity's red mouth.

Vanessa turned away in fear, burying her face in the shoulder of Brendan's white shirt.

"Don't let her hurt me," she whimpered.

"Leave this place, Charity Winston!" Brendan shouted. "You are not welcome here. I don't love you. I love Vanessa! Vanessa! Vanessa!"

Each time he shouted the name, Charity cried out, ripping at her own flesh with gnarled hands. Unable to stand the reality of Brendan and Vanessa's love, she was destroying herself. The strong woman who had been standing at the edge of the woods was now a hunched-over old hag with pointed teeth and dark circles around her eyes. With one last gasp, Charity pointed toward the lovers, then went up in a column of flames.

The flames disappeared as quickly as they'd come.

"She's gone," Doreen whispered.

Frankie and Harry-John ran to their guardian. Keeping her eyes on Brendan and Vanessa, Doreen put her arms around the boys.

"I waited so long for you, Brendan," Vanessa was saying. *"I didn't know if you'd ever come back for me!"*

"No one told me," Brendan said. "They said you had gone away to visit someone. I didn't know what they had done to you."

"I was so frightened!" Vanessa cried. *"It was so cold, and dark!"*

"I'm with you now," Brendan said. "It will never be cold and dark again."

Seconds later, the two lovers were consumed by a great cloud of billowing blue smoke.

For a few moments, Doreen just stood there, watching the place where the strange scene had just occurred. Marty swore under his breath, unable to believe what had happened.

Then Doreen collapsed, sobbing from relief and exhaustion, holding Frankie and Harry-John as if she'd never let them go.

Epilogue

Two Days Later

"It's the most amazing transformation I've ever seen," Larry said, watching the children playing tag behind the big old house. "Just about an hour after I got them to the hospital, the kids were acting completely normal."

"About the same time the spirits left," Doreen said. She shook her head. "I still can't believe it happened, Larry. I was so taken by Brendan! How could he have been a ghost?"

"Beats me," Larry said. "But he's gone now. And so is Charity. I can feel it. This place is at peace."

"All the spirits are gone," Doreen said. "There was a child that I kept seeing. He must have been Donny Howell, the boy that was murdered by his father. Poor little soul. He was just wandering the earth in search of someone who would help him. But now that the evil has been driven away, I'm sure he's gone, too. This house is going to be a happy one, the way it should have been from the start!"

"Thank God for that," Larry said. He pointed out the window of Doreen's office. "Look who's arrived. Is that the woman from Social Services?"

"That's Barbara," Doreen said with a nod. "I wonder what she's saying to the children?"

Outside, Barbara Clayton had stopped to talk to the children before entering the house. She believed that she could learn so much more from the candid little ones than by interviewing their guardians.

"How did you hurt your leg, dear?" she asked Karen.

Karen smiled shyly.

"Dopey me," she said, tugging at one of the clips she'd put in her hair. "I was looking around in the attic and I fell."

Karen did not remember being pushed down that ladder.

"Come look what I can do!" Randy cried. "I can swing upside down from this tree branch!"

He jumped for it and did a flip. Barbara clapped.

"Do you like it here?" she asked.

"It's the best!" Tara cried. "Doreen's the greatest."

"Yeah, it's a neat place," Harry-John put in.

Of all the children, he was the only one who seemed to remember everything that had happened in the last few days. But he had had a long talk with Doreen, and he believed as she did that the ghosts had left for good. And he never wanted to talk about them again, because he knew that none of the other kids would believe his story. Except maybe Frankie.

As the children talked to Barbara, convincing her that Addison House was a great place to live, Harry-John looked around for the little deaf boy. Frankie had been keeping to himself these past few days, refusing to communicate with anyone about what had happened. It was almost as if he no longer wanted to be friends with the others.

At last Harry-John spotted Frankie standing at the window to his room. Harry-John waved, and Frankie waved back. Harry-John saw Frankie turn to his side.

But he didn't see the little boy Frankie smiled at. He didn't see Frankie take Donny Howell's hand and turn to walk from the window with his brand-new friend.